ALWAYS CRY WOLFE

Madison McGuire

PublishAmerica
Baltimore

© 2006 by Madison McGuire.
All rights reserved. No part of this book may be reproduced, stored in a retrieval system or transmitted in any form or by any means without the prior written permission of the publishers, except by a reviewer who may quote brief passages in a review to be printed in a newspaper, magazine or journal.

This is a work of fiction. Names, characters, corporations, institutions, organizations, events or locales in this novel are either the product of the author's imagination or, if real, used fictitiously. Any resemblance to actual persons (living or dead) is entirely coincidental.

First printing

At the specific preference of the author, PublishAmerica allowed this work to remain exactly as the author intended, verbatim, without editorial input.

ISBN: 1-4241-4160-5
PUBLISHED BY PUBLISHAMERICA, LLLP
www.publishamerica.com
Baltimore

Printed in the United States of America

For everyone who thought I could do this,
and especially those who didn't.

Jennifer,
Thank you for
designing my very
first Bookmark for
my very first book.

Best Always!
Madison McGuire

aka-SH

Acknowledgment

I'd like to express my gratitude to the law-enforcement agents who contributed to my research, and gave me a tremendous appreciation for the demands and restrictions they face to keep us all safe. I could not celebrate the publication of this first book without thanking the beautiful, intelligent ladies who faithfully attend our critique meetings. Sonnie (Ms. Blue Pen), Renee, Donna, Leslie, and of course, Hillary, who left us too soon but with loving memories we will forever share along with our friendship, your suggestions and corrections made this dream possible.

One

He was out there again.

Kylie could sense his presence, the imminent danger. Fear gripped her, clawing at her tensed muscles with its icy fingers. Motionless in bed, her breathing ragged, she listened, too scared to move.

Heart racing, she stared at the ceiling, praying she would hear nothing but the normal, muted sounds of the night. Her body rigid, chilled despite the comforter pulled up to her chin, she waited, uncertain as to what had awakened her. And yet positive some noise alien to the midnight hour had jarred her from the deep, dreamless sleep that claimed her soon after she crawled into bed.

Like a puppet unable to move without assistance, she remained still, aware he would not leave. Not without giving her yet another reason to fear him. Not without making sure she knew he had returned.

She heard nothing, neither the sound of footsteps on the redwood deck alerting her to his skulking presence, nor the calming noises made by nocturnal creatures marking the passage of another moonrise. The deathly silence screamed a warning, a message she heeded with a growing dread.

She knew enough about stalkers to realize what her now silent tormentor wanted: to see her rendered helpless by the fear his evil game instilled.

Unwilling to allow him that privilege, she inhaled slowly, staving off the panic seizing control of her. A measure of calm restored, she scanned the room, accommodating her still near frenzied need to identify the multitude of shadows dancing about the moonlit bedroom. Wary of every shape and movement, she studied each shady image, searched every corner of the room.

Some of the familiar, flickering shadows instantly invalidated her fear. None gave her a reason to dismiss her fright as simple, sleep-induced uncertainty.

Heart pounding, she glanced at the glass and cedar-slat wall that separated her from the outside world, aware the triple-pane windows and French doors leading onto the upper deck would prove no contest to anyone intent on gaining entry.

As suddenly as the silence had descended upon her the sounds of the night resumed, rising in a near deafening crescendo as though orchestrated by a master conductor.

Wide-eyed, Kylie listened, determined to identify every noise. The steady chirrup of crickets and the occasional croak of a bullfrog lounging in the lake below her home were familiar, as was the click and whir of the attic vent on the roof, the reassuring hum of the alarm clock on the bedside table.

Despite the natural cacophony outside, the sweet song of the insects and the bullfrog's lonely lament, she remained still and watchful, certain some sound uncommon to the night had disrupted her sleep. And alerted her slumbering brain to yet another intrusion.

Furious to realize someone was again trespassing on her terrain, and using unsubtle techniques to frighten her, she looked around the room. Doing her best to ignore the prickly feel the gooseflesh rising at her nape and down her spine, she examined every inch of the room, and each fragile pane on that vulnerable wall of glass.

Through the sheer, nubbed fabric of the drapes she could see the naked branches of the slow-budding ash scraping the rough cedar trim outside the windows, hear them softly scratch at the wood, gently tap the glass. Accustomed to those sounds, and not the least bit fearful of them, she smiled with relief. Like the soothing rustle of late spring leaves clinging to the branches of the sturdy oaks dotting her backyard, the shadow show on her bedroom wall was harmless.

A sudden breeze rattled the attic vent, shattering Kylie's momentary calm. Her heart skipped a beat, then raced, keeping pace with the twirling metal blades spun by the gentle gust.

Chastising herself for reacting like a ninny, a coward frightened by ordinary night sounds and nature's fickle whims, she managed a small, tremulous smile.

A grating scrape and metallic clatter too loud to have been caused by the wind wiped the smile off her face and sent her heartbeat beyond its uneven patter, into the hard-pounding rhythm of abject terror.

Unable to breathe, she stared at the curtained doors, her anxiety compounded by the sudden, unnatural silence outside. Something—someone—had frightened the night-dwelling creatures, caused them to cease their nightly serenade.

Expecting a forced entry added to her fear. Knowing she was still relatively safe did nothing to calm her.

Not knowing what the prowler intended—what she could do to prevent him from doing anything more—held her rigid, afraid to move and yet certain she should do something.

She swallowed hard, forced down the tension knotted at the back of her throat. No matter what he intended, no matter what he was doing this instant, her options were limited.

Time was his ally, hesitation her enemy.

Mustering her courage, she tossed the comforter aside and angled her legs over the side of the bed, cringing as her bare feet hit the cold hardwood floor. Cool air surged from the overhead vent, making her chest feel tight, weighted by the effort it took to breathe.

With fear-born stealth and cautious perseverance, she made her way to the doors. She inhaled slowly, raised her hand and pushed aside the sheer batiste drape, revealing a slit of smoky glass between the frame and her unsteady fingers. Suddenly anxious, she leaned forward, searched the moonlit shadows for anything that might confirm or deny her suspicions.

Nothing moved on the deck save the barren, lightning-struck branches of the ash towering above the portico. No sound reached her ears other than the soothing rustle of tender new leaves brushed by a gentle wind.

To the right of the double doors, one of the steel-framed lawn chairs she kept on the deck lay on its side, blocking the stairs leading to the yard below. Strategically located, she felt certain the chair had been placed so that anyone hurrying out, off of the deck and down to the backyard, would trip over the obstacle.

A shiver raced down her spine. Had she been foolish enough to rush headlong into the night, intent on escaping her stalker, she would have tumbled over the chair and down the steps. And, perhaps, into his waiting arms.

A small, halfhearted smile pushed her lips upward. She couldn't help but admire the prowler's ingenuity, his initial victory. She respected her own stubborn determination to avoid being a victim again more than his cunning ploy. She had often trusted unwisely, but she had never been accused of foolhardy behavior. Not to her face, at least, and never by those who knew her well.

She knew better than to allow emotions and her once hopeful, childish need for acceptance to control her actions and cloud her judgement.

Movement near the forested boundary of the yard captured her attention. Kylie gasped, alarmed by his boldness. Wide-eyed, she stared at the man's dark silhouette, the ominous shadow cast by his broad-brimmed cowboy hat. As still as the darkness and as real as the fear rocking her senses, he appeared to be looking directly at her, watching her with the same intensity with which she met his unseen gaze.

"No!" she rasped, cold stark foreboding paralyzing her.

Rigid, she stared, attempting to see more clearly her stalker's face. Needing to recognize something familiar about him, or to detect an uncommon trait that would help her identify him, she remained still. She wished he would step forward, into the pool of moonlight illuminating the yard. She also hoped he would turn and run, granting her the ability to again breathe.

Kylie shivered, certain he could see her, and that he was relishing the agonizing depth of her fear. She snatched her hand from the curtain, watching in silent fascination as the fabric fell into place with a subtle whisper of sound. Her focus on the wave of ripples she feared he would see as clearly as her trembling form, she backed slowly toward the bed, anticipating an immediate attempt to break the glass and violate her home, her body.

Hands stretched out behind her, she located the bedside table by feel and, finally, the telephone situated there. She dropped to her knees, grimacing as the Berber rug scraped her skin. Fumbling in her haste, she lifted the receiver, and immediately wished she hadn't. Cursing the bright green light she'd welcome at any other time, she twisted, placing the illuminated numbers between her upper body and the ruffled bed skirt. Her hands shaking so that the numbers wavered before her eyes, she punched the programmed keypad, automatically dialing the sheriff's office.

"Cherokee County Sheriff's Department. Williams speaking," the woman's calm, businesslike voice answered.

"This is Kylie Bennett. I need help!" Her garbled words scarcely audible even to her own ears, she more forcefully added, "Send someone to help me!"

"Calm down, Miss Bennett. I can barely hear you. You'll have to speak louder, and more slowly. Okay?"

"Yes."

"Good. Now, Miss Bennett, what's the problem?"

"I want to report a prowler. Someone is outside my house."

"Has the intruder attempted to gain entry?"

"No. Yes. I—I'm not sure. Something woke me. A sound...I don't know what...something odd. I can see him standing near the trees in my backyard. He's out there, and—"

"Calm down, Miss Bennett. Can you give me directions, landmarks, anything to assist the unit I'm dispatching?"

"I'm on the east side of Lake Tenkiller, about four miles from the Big Red Restaurant. Southwest of there." Kylie supplied her address and directions to the secluded property she had leased three months before.

"Joe and Tandy Oliver's house? Miss Bennett, are you leasing the Oliver property off Highway Eighty-two?"

"Yes." Pleased by the calming stability of her voice, Kylie drew a deep breath of air, relieved she had conquered the worst of her fear.

Startled by the unmistakable scrape and clang of metal grating against wood, Kylie gasped. Whimpering like a lost child, she spun to face the danger, tangling the phone cord around her waist and causing the machine to tumble into her lap. She stared at the doors, the receiver clutched in one unsteady hand, the other clamped over her mouth to forestall the scream rising in her throat.

"Kylie? Miss Bennett, are you there?"

"Yes," Kylie whispered, choking on the single word. "Yes," she repeated more firmly, "he's on the deck, near the door. Hurry, please hurry!"

"Help is on the way. Stay on the phone, Kylie. Don't talk. Listen, but don't hang up, okay?"

Kylie nodded. Smiling at the absurdity of her unseen gesture, she said, "I won't hang up. How long before someone gets here?"

"Ten minutes, fifteen at most. Hang on, and don't panic."

Kylie chuckled, amazed to realize her stark terror had ebbed into a dismal sense of humor she found vaguely consoling. "I'm not going to panic," she assured the dispatcher, "panic came and went when I saw him out there. Now I'm just plain old scared. Scared to death."

She tore her gaze from the dark glass entry, looked at the interior doorway. She wished she had closed and locked the bedroom door, though she knew having done so would help her none at all. If the intruder came in the French doors, a locked inner exit would, more than likely, hinder rather than aid her effort to escape.

Satisfied she was safe for the moment, she braced her back against the comforting softness of her bed, facing the curtained glass doors she feared might shatter any moment now. "This is insane."

"Pardon?" said the dispatcher, "I didn't hear what you said."

"My reaction is insane." Kylie cleared her throat. "I'm a psychologist. I know better than to allow fear to control me."

"Rational thought isn't predefined, Kylie. Thinking someone is about to break into your home is enough to rattle anyone. Considering the late hour and the remote location of your house, your reaction is not unreasonable." The dispatcher added, "Now do as I said, listen but don't talk. Okay?"

"Okay."

The minutes mounted slowly. Agonizingly paced sixty-second intervals during which the dispatcher described her toy poodle, Winchester, and the precocious pet's exploits in minute detail. Welcome lulls quickly gave way to a nerve-wracking silence, near quiet punctuated by the overly loud ticking of the antique grandfather clock in the hall outside her bedroom.

Huddled close to the bed, the receiver pressed to her ear, Kylie divided her attention between the outer doors and the only interior exit. *Who is he? What can he possibly want*? She shook her head, purging her thoughts of the man obviously intent on harassing her, frightening her with his nightly games. She had no time for his nonsense. No time to deal with idiots too cowardly to confront her face-to-face, to—

"Miss Bennett?"

Startled by the once again authoritative voice at the other end of the phone, Kylie jerked upright, clutched at the gaping neck of her oversized T-shirt.

The dispatcher continued, her tone soothing, "I understand that an official who lives nearby was alerted by your call and is on his way to check on you. He should —"

Kylie's startled scream echoed the pounding rhythm of the heavy fist hammering at her front door. She whipped her head around, stared at the inner doorway gaping like the sphere of terror shrouding her. Had she underestimated the prowler's ingenuity? Overreacted?

"Miss Bennett? What's wrong? Is the prowler in the house now?" Tension sharpened the dispatcher's words, sliced through Kylie like a razor.

"No." Eased by her whispered assurance, Kylie glanced at the windowed wall, toward the shadowy hallway. "Everything's fine."

"Good," Williams stated, her voice once again steady, calm. "The marshal should be there any minute now."

"He's here." Both apprehensive and hopeful, Kylie pressed her lips to the mouthpiece. "Someone is knocking at the front door. Downstairs. It's too soon, isn't it? How could a unit have arrived so quickly?"

The dispatcher chuckled softly. "We've been on the phone more than ten minutes, Miss Bennett. Go to the door, but exercise caution. Don't open it unless the person knocking can show you some form of identification proving he is a law enforcement officer."

"What if he can't? What if –"

"Don't borrow trouble, Kylie. I'm sure this visitor is legitimate. Regardless the Marshall's assistance, a county deputy is on the way. Everything is going to be fine."

"Thank you, Miss Williams. It is Miss Williams?" Kylie stood, untangling herself as she replaced the phone on the table.

"It's been Mrs. Williams for almost thirty years. Set the receiver aside and answer the door, sweetie."

"Yes. I will." Kylie did as she was told then dashed into the hall, her bare feet making hardly a sound on the hardwood floor as she took the stairs two at a time.

Arriving at the door in seconds, she pressed her eye to the peephole, peered into the shadowy depths of the covered porch. Her breath hitched as the outline of a man, a dark cowboy hat pulled low over his eyes, came into view.

"No!" Kylie clenched her hands, fought the urge to flee. "Please, Lord, don't let it be him…"

He raised his hand and Kylie leaped back, an alarmed squeak squeezing past the tension clogging her throat as he again banged on the door. One hand clamped over her hard-pounding heart, the other fisted at her side, she dragged deep gulps of air into her burning lungs, restoring a measure of calm.

"Wh—who is it?" she asked quietly, then more firmly, "who is it?"

"Deputy U.S. Marshall. Open up, Ms. Bennett." The deep, masculine drawl sent a tremor through Kylie, a frisson of foreboding that had nothing at all to do with her stalker.

Irritated, both by the audible smile in his voice and her own rising dread, she edged closer to the door, squinting as she peered through the small privacy window.

"Dear God!" she whispered, afraid to even think *his* name.

Despite her effort to prevent it, Tyler Wolfe's name and unforgettable features materialized, filling her head with the images she had escaped so many years before. Scowling, she raked her mind, searching for a viable reason to believe the familiar voice and broad shoulders barring her view of the porch belonged to any man but Tyler.

Unable to do so, she tamped down her mounting frustration, summoned her most belligerent tone and said, "Proper procedure requires that you show me some form of identification. Only a fool opens their door to a stranger."

If only he were a stranger, Kylie mused irritably, some faceless, nameless entity sent to help her—and not the one person she'd hoped never to see again. A man she'd recognize in a crowd of millions; the first of two who'd taught her the high cost of trusting too easily, loving too quickly, and expecting too much.

"Open the door, Kylie."

Tyler's curt demand disrupted her painful reverie, ignited her temper. Kylie welcomed the anger, allowed it to subdue the unwelcome joy thoughts of him still sent coursing through her system. She could allow nothing but apathy where Tyler Wolfe was concerned.

"Not until I see some identification."

As she watched, Tyler peeled back his jacket lapel with a practiced but casual flick of his wrist, revealing the shiny silver badge pinned to his light-colored shirtfront. Kylie couldn't make out the insignia or the engraved words, but instantly recognized the generic sign of authority. It wasn't enough.

"Anyone can buy a tin star, mister. I want to see additional identification. Indisputable proof you're an officer of the law, and *not* a figment of my overactive imagination."

Tyler laughed, annoying Kylie even more. She ground her teeth together, quelled the scream clawing its way up her parched throat. Still chuckling, he reached into his jacket pocket and pulled out a small, dark wallet. He flipped it open, shoved what appeared to be a picture ID toward the peephole.

"Open the door."

Groaning, Kylie braced her forehead against the door, her shoulders slumped as she attempted to regain her composure. She'd written Tyler Wolfe out of her life more than a decade ago, wanting nothing to do with him then and hoping to never again share the same air he breathed.

"Why are *you* here?" she demanded with little enthusiasm, forcing her thoughts to the present.

"I came to chase away your ghosts." Tyler's calm tone revealed none of the chaotic forces making her own voice sound unsteady, as weak and tremulous as her perfidious body. "Open the door. Please."

Save ordering him off her property—as she longed to do—Kylie had no choice but to obey. She did so with an economy of motion she hoped would relay her dismay. She threw the deadbolt free with excessive force, rattled the safety chain one time too many, twisted the knob and jerked the door wide open, making way for the tide of fury no man but Tyler Wolfe could, so quickly and with so little effort, send crashing over the shores of her control.

"Took you long enough." Tyler flashed a toothpaste-commercial-perfect smile, braced his arm on the facing. "I was beginning to think I'd have to huff and puff my way in."

"You don't *have* to come in."

"I think I do."

Tyler stepped inside, sauntered to the midway point of the wide foyer. Kylie slammed the door shut and spun to face him, eager to discover the reason for his untimely intrusion.

"What's this all about?" Hands on her hips, she met his staid look with a haughty glare. "Why are you here?"

"You tell me," he replied, a lazy, lopsided grin adding to his appeal that had diminished none at all over the years.

Kylie's overwrought nerves leaped, awakening feelings dormant so long she'd considered them gone forever. Her heart began to pound, so hard it felt as though it were bouncing off her ribs. Her blood sped through her veins, making her dizzy.

Both shocked and infuriated by her reaction, she stared at the man steadily looking back at her. Doing her best to ignore the myriad sensations diverting her attention, she gathered her wits, welcomed the rage causing her head to spin and stood rigidly in place, silently demanding that he put an end to their standoff.

"Have you got a light in here?"

"Of course there's a light!" She reached to flick the switch on the wall behind him. Soft overhead lighting flooded the foyer, bathing his impressive form with its complimentary warmth.

Reluctant admiration narrowed her gaze. Tyler had changed so little it was nothing short of amazing. His shoulders were still a yard wide, his hair the same shiny, blue-black she remembered. Classic, beautifully masculine features had improved over the years, been chiseled to perfection by time and lovingly enhanced by his Cherokee ancestry.

"It's been a while, hasn't it?" His lips twitched, forming a sexy curve that rekindled Kylie's fury as nothing else could have—and made her long to wipe that far too familiar grin off his handsome face.

"Not nearly long enough."

"Sweet talk like that could give a man a complex." His midnight blue eyes sparkling, Tyler pivoted on one booted heel and strode toward the Aztec patterned love seat located in front of the fireplace.

Seething, Kylie catalogued the athletic swagger he'd perfected in his youth, the taut play of his compact muscles beneath the snug-fitting seat of his Levi's. His broad shoulders and narrow hips formed the classic wedge men the world over sought. What other men gained by pumping iron and downing steroids, Nature and his Cherokee genes had bestowed upon Tyler generations before his conception.

She'd forgotten how his masculine beauty affected her. No, not forgotten, she grudgingly corrected, merely set aside; mentally shelved along with all the other tangible mementos she'd tried—and failed—to obliterate. She knew every lean, sinewy inch of his magnificent body by heart, how his smooth, bronze skin and the supple strength of his muscles felt beneath her trembling fingers. The giving, sensual power of his passion, the way he responded to her touch and the heady taste of his kisses were indelibly etched in her memory; so deeply ingrained forgetting was impossible.

Kylie closed her eyes, struggling to erase the unwelcome memories his presence stirred to life. She inhaled deeply and slowly opened her eyes. Striving for a measure of control, she assessed his progress across the great room, wary of the damage seeing him again had inflicted upon her. Tyler glanced back at her over his shoulder, grinning as though her narrow-eyed scrutiny were somehow complimentary.

If you knew how I felt about you now, Tyler, she thought with malice, *you'd run for cover and guard that broad back of yours.*

"Mind if I have a seat?"

Kylie shot him a disgruntled look and nodded. "Make yourself right at home, Mr. Wolfe."

Chuckling, he settled at one end of the love seat, his casual sprawl tempting Kylie to allow her appreciative gaze to tour the impressive length of his legs stretched out before her. She resisted the urge, but felt cheated rather than elated for having done so.

"Would you care for something to drink?" she asked, discouraging her unwelcome fascination and his knowing smile with a tone as rude as his intrusion.

"Maybe later. Right now I'd like to know why you called the sheriff."

Bluntly reminded of her reason for summoning assistance, Kylie pushed her annoyance aside and stamped to the chair opposite him. Once seated, she tugged the hem of her thin cotton sleep shirt lower, silently cursing her skimpy attire. Wishing she'd thought to grab a robe—or don a suit or armor— prior to answering the door, she wet her trembling lips and forced herself to meet his steady, now serious, gaze.

"There was a prowler outside."

"Did you see anyone?" Frowning, he asked, "Was someone outside?"

"Yes." Kylie longed to look away, but refused to surrender to the common sense urging her to shield herself. Staring into his eyes that had haunted her dreams since the age of sixteen ignited the chain reaction that frightened her almost as much as the thought of being stalked. Her stomach clenched. Sweat popped out on her brow, dampened her palms.

Frustrated by her withering calm, she snapped, "Why isn't a deputy here? How were you able to respond so quickly?"

Tyler removed his hat, deftly tossed the black Stetson to the cushion beside him. He raked his raven locks into sexy disarray, reminding Kylie how his long, blunt-tipped fingers felt against her own scalp—and how often he'd tumbled her fair hair.

"I live just down the road, Kylie. I was on my way home when I heard the dispatcher broadcast this address. *Your address.* I figured you would appreciate a quick response."

"I do."

Stunned to realize he lived nearby, Kylie averted her gaze, scanned the room to conceal the unwanted joy and tears blurring her vision. She truly did not want to see him again, but knowing he was near enough to protect her, and that he would respond if she needed him, was a comfort.

And reason enough for her to fear what might happen—what she might forget—if she spent time with him.

"Someone was outside." Gathering her courage, she again looked at Tyler. "I heard...something. When I woke up I knew, just knew, someone was out there.

"I looked out the door –" she pushed her numb lips into a wry smile "— eventually. There was a man standing near the trees out back."

"Did he try to get in?"

"No." Kylie shook her head. "At least I don't think he did. The alarm didn't go off, so I'm pretty sure he didn't so much as touch a window or door. The security system is ultra-sensitive."

"But he woke you up?"

"Something did. A chair was moved on the deck, placed where I'd trip over it if I ran down the stairs. He wasn't concerned about the noise when he toppled it—sent it crashing down, actually." Silently cursing the shiver racing down her spine, she continued, "I was already awake when he set that tidy little trap…"

"I'll take a look around." Tyler picked up his hat, slapped it on his head and stood. "Lock the door behind me, and don't venture out." He hastened to the door, pulled it open.

"Tyler?" Kylie's voice was a mere whisper of sound, yet he immediately turned to face her, one ebony brow arched. Forcing herself to remain where she'd moved, so close to him she could feel the reassuring heat of his big body, she added, "Be careful."

"I'm always careful, Kylie. Lock up." His grin rife with a wicked delight, he winked. "I'll be back before you have time to miss me."

"That could be a very long time," she stated, bristling. "I have no reason to miss you, Tyler. No reason to wish you anything but a hasty departure and a less than fond farewell."

"Liar."

His expression so tender she could do nothing but stare, helpless tears stinging her eyes, Tyler slipped out the door, leaving her to deal with the rampant rush of emotions turning her inside out.

Two

Shaken, Kylie locked the door and retreated to the fireplace. Seated on the hearth, she ran her hand over the cool, smooth stones, drawing comfort from the unforgiving surface as she contemplated the feelings churning inside her. Like a tornado, her thoughts twisted and turned, swirling from an almost detached acceptance of her and Tyler's tumultuous past, to a stormy determination to avoid remembering the good times.

Despite her desire to avoid thoughts of her and Tyler together, memories flooded her mind, chasing away the pain she'd dealt with so many years ago. Pain that had increased ten-fold the moment she recognized his husky, masculine voice.

Too jittery to remain still, she stood, paced the room to ease the tension coiled like a serpent poised to strike. Each step carried her closer to the memories, farther from the strength she needed to evade additional torture.

She and Tyler had shared so much, planned to share so much more. By the time she met him, he was a local legend, a football hero everyone admired. Long before she moved to Tahlequah, he'd set records in rushing yardage and points scored that stood up years after his final game for the Tigers. He had earned all-state honors in baseball and track as well, lending credence to the nickname area residents had given him.

'The Legend' was the first of many new people Kylie heard of that first year in Cherokee County. Few, other than Tyler Wolfe, made an impression on her. His familiar face and ongoing achievements, frequently featured in the local paper, encouraged her to do her best.

From the day she registered at Tahlequah High, Kylie had worshipped him from afar, as did all the girls attending his alma mater. The full athletic scholarship Tyler earned had improved upon his image, endearing him to the men who praised his success and to the league of boys eager to follow in his footsteps.

Kylie was sixteen, all gangling limbs and shy, slumbering innocence when the returning hero noticed her. As though it were occurring this instant, and not thirteen long years before, she remembered their first encounter. The feminine exhilaration and girlish fear that had rendered her speechless then kept her pacing now.

She and her best friend were walking home from a football game when Tyler's familiar rocket-red '57 Chevy pulled up beside them. Indiscreet as usual, Julie Stevens poked her elbow in Kylie's ribs and stepped around her to ogle the hometown hero. Kylie kept walking, forcing herself to breathe as she attempted to ignore The Legend's steady blue gaze.

Apparently undaunted, Tyler sped up to the next block and parked his flashy classic next to the crumbling concrete curb. He was leaning against the side of the car, his long legs crossed at the ankles, when Kylie and her starry-eyed friend reached the corner.

"Am I in luck, or what?" he drawled, his gaze riveted on Kylie's own wide-eyed look. "Are you pretty ladies touring the town or out hunting snipes?"

Julie giggled. Kylie felt her cheeks heat up, and averted her gaze. Looking at him made her feel odd, even less confident than usual. Her tongue in a knot and her chest tight, she counted the cracks in the sidewalk beneath her feet, eager to escape further distress.

She wished she had the ability to say something witty—or to do anything more appropriate than stand like a wooden doll perched on a toy store shelf. Confused and irritated by her sudden need to impress him, Kylie remained frozen, unable to move and unwilling to acknowledge either Tyler or the unwelcome emotions bubbling inside her.

"What are you doing out alone?"

"Walking home," Julie said with another frivolous giggle.

Kylie wanted to throttle her friend. And she wanted, even more, to run as fast and as far from Tyler Wolfe as she could get. She felt certain any college-aged man would consider Julie's giddy reaction childish; that he would view her own nervous silence and slender build anything but appealing.

She also hated to think he might categorize her among the many young women who wanted nothing more than one night with him—one night and the bragging rights that went with it. Kylie knew well the consequences of foolish behavior such as that. The price of reckless adventure was higher than she was willing to pay, more than she would ever risk, lest she follow her mother's disastrous example.

"Would you like a ride?" Tyler asked, so softly Kylie couldn't help but wonder if he, too, felt as unsure of himself as she did. Thinking he somehow understood her mixed feelings made her knees wobble even more, made her stomach churn.

"I have to get home." Kylie nudged Julie forward and sidestepped Tyler's booted feet.

Tyler's hand shot out, so fast Kylie had no chance to dodge his firm but gentle grip on the sleeve of her pep-club sweater. Held in place, she turned to face him, her heart pounding so hard her chest began to ache.

"Let me drive you home, Kylie." Tyler flashed the grin Kylie had so often seen pictured in the newspaper, a smile made even more appealing by his close proximity. "I'll buy you a cola...if you'll let me?"

"Come on, Kylie!" Julie yanked on Kylie's other sleeve like a persistent child. "We have time for a cherry-limeade, don't we?"

Kylie swallowed hard, nodded. His smile more relieved than triumphant, Tyler opened the passenger side door, allowing Julie to slide in. Maintaining his grip on Kylie's arm, he steered her around to the driver's side and opened the door, assuring her the seat next to him—the 'hot seat' she'd heard girls mention in awe.

As impressive as she had imagined it would be, the restored classic smelled of new leather, as crisp and clean as the handsome man behind the wheel. Reminded of the many, lurid comments made regarding the car's amenities and Tyler's romantic prowess in and out of the vehicle, Kylie scooted as far toward the center of the front seat as she could.

Obviously amused, Tyler acknowledged her move with a lopsided grin, increasing Kylie's growing discomfort—and warning her to beware.

Courteous and entertaining, Tyler made the familiar drag route seem new and exciting. As promised, he bought each of them a soft drink, tolerating Julie's endless giggles and Kylie's ongoing silence with a remarkable patience. His amusing anecdotes and occasional teasing did little to alleviate Kylie's anxiety.

Too nervous to appreciate his gentlemanly conduct, Kylie reached across Julie for the door handle the moment they pulled into her driveway. Seemingly unaware of Julie's presence and avid attention, Tyler asked Kylie out the instant he set the parking brake.

It had taken her several hours to quiet Julie enough for her giddy friend to fall asleep—and much longer for Kylie to finally drift off.

For more than a year after that memorable night, she and Tyler were inseparable. Sharing everything, dreams for their future and the myriad problems she dealt with at home, strengthened their relationship. Kylie had freely offered her heart, and gladly welcomed his attention and the unconditional support she so desperately needed.

Shortly before their second anniversary as a twosome, they quarreled. Though trivial compared to other, more serious disputes they'd had, the fight kept them apart three seemingly endless weeks, weeks during which Julie kept track of, and constantly informed Kylie of, Tyler's amorous exploits. To Kylie's immense relief, and due to Tyler's insistence that his many dates were planned and executed to make her jealous, they had, eventually, mended fences and made up—but not before events were set in motion that would separate them forever.

Now, standing before the fireplace, Kylie refused to let the bitter pain surface again. The heartache she endured due to their final break-up, like her troubled teen years, was far behind her. She would not—could not—allow Tyler to disrupt her life.

Considering what might have been was a futile energy drain, wasted time she could not afford thanks to her current, hectic schedule—and the stalker keeping her up nights.

A resounding knock put an end to Kylie's thoughts, revived her determination. She scurried to the door and opened it without hesitation, earning a scowl no man but Tyler could make appealing.

"A woman who's certain a prowler is skulking about outside should ask who's knocking before swinging the door wide open, don't you think?" Tyler's razor-sharp tone sliced through her hard-earned grit, rendering her defenseless.

Breezing past her, Tyler took no more than two steps before stopping. Scant inches beyond where she stood, he turned to face her, his narrow gaze piercing her resolve. Unable to voice the tart rejoinder stuck in her throat, Kylie looked away, dodging her sudden, unwelcome urge to beg his forgiveness for acting rashly.

"Sorry I snapped at you," he said, luring her gaze up, to the riveting blue one staring back at her.

Unable to breathe, Kylie nodded. Her heart in her throat, she watched his hand rise, felt the gentle brush of his knuckles beneath her chin, the tickle of crisp, dark hair sweeping her skin. Her flesh tingling, she remained still, spellbound as he drew the pad of his thumb across her lower lip, making it burn as hot as the indigo fire blazing in his eyes.

"How have you been, Kylie?" His deep voice sounded husky, as hypnotic as the look holding her uncertain one captive.

Tyler cupped her cheek in his warm, callused palm and stepped closer, so close his upper body nearly touched hers. Kylie felt the familiar flames ignite deep inside her. Cursing herself for a fool, she refused to move away, unwilling to deny herself the pleasure of his touch.

"F—fine," she rasped, gnawing at her lower lip as she awaited his next move. How many times had she anticipated his touch, his kiss, in moments such as this? She held her breath, afraid he would kiss her—and more afraid he wouldn't.

Tyler dropped his hand, stealing his warmth as he moved away. His nod little more than a jerk of his chin, he tucked his fingers into the palms of his hands, acting as though touching her had somehow soiled him. Hurt to think he had simply meant to comfort her, Kylie squared her shoulders.

"Glad to hear it," he said, his stony expression as cold as the disappointment making her traitorous heart feel heavy, worn. "We need to talk."

"About what?" Hating the tremor in her voice, she raised her chin. "What do we need to talk about?"

"Your prowler."

"What about him?"

"I saw no sign that anyone was near."

"I saw someone—a man!" Kylie narrowed her eyes, stepped forward. "I saw him!"

"So you said. Is this the first time you've thought someone was outside?"

"No. This is the third time."

"The third?" Tyler repeated, his tone hard, as unyielding as his expression. "When?"

"Once last week and in the previous week."

"Tell me about the other times."

"Neither incident amounted to much. I didn't see anyone either time." Kylie shrugged, unsure as to what details were important. "I was working late the first time I suspected someone was outside. I left my office long enough to look around. I didn't notice anything out of the ordinary, so I continued writing the columns due that week.

"The next morning, I found one of my flowerpots overturned. The one beneath my office window."

"Could have been a raccoon."

"That particular pot weighs at least thirty pounds!"

"Then again…" Tyler chuckled, obviously amused by her glare. "Go on."

"When I returned from Dallas the first of last week, my mail was scattered along the driveway."

"Typical teenage prank. Annoying as hell, but nothing to get uptight about."

"That didn't upset me," Kylie snapped, irritated by his nonchalant attitude. "The rosebush he'd yanked out of the ground and ripped apart did."

"Someone obviously wanted you to know they'd been here."

"Obviously."

Kylie closed the door she'd left open, brushed her hands down her shirtfront. As though compelled to do so, Tyler glanced down, seemingly fascinated. She followed the direction of his gaze to the twin mounds of her breasts visible beneath the white cotton fabric of her shirt. Knowing her feminine shape appealed to him made her flesh tingle and harden, peak along with the awareness warming her entire body.

Her cheeks burning, she dropped her hands and slumped forward, praying her response had escaped his notice. She knew better than to hope it had. Tyler missed nothing and made no excuses. Ever. Heart pounding, she looked up, confirming her suspicions the instant she met his gaze. Unwelcome desire, as hot and wild as the need smoldering in his eyes, made her tremble.

The solid rap on the door jarred Kylie to her senses. She spun toward the entry, reached for the knob.

"Hold on!" Tyler snapped, making her jump and whirl to face him. He flashed her an apologetic grin, shrugged. "Do I have to remind you of the many reasons you should ask who's there before you open it?"

"Who is it?" she inquired through clenched teeth, her tone as unforgiving as the glower with which she met Tyler's wide-eyed innocent look.

"Deputy Keets," came the reply.

"It took you long enough!" Kylie snarled in greeting as she opened the door, too irritated to consider the young officer's surprise sufficient reason to tamp down her ire. "I'm sure the prowler is long gone by now."

"Are you Kylie Bennett?" The burly officer stepped inside, seemingly unaffected by her tart welcome. A scant inch or two taller than Kylie's five-four, he narrowed his pale blue eyes, held her disapproving look with one of similar displeasure. "You reported a prowler?"

"Yes." She shoved her shoulders back, remained where she stood despite his close proximity. Feeling crowded rather than calmed by the deputy's presence, she continued. "I called the Sheriff's office at least half an hour ago. It's a good thing he didn't break in, otherwise I'd likely be injured or dead rather than merely upset by your tardy response."

"We do have other calls to answer." His cheeks flushed, making his round face appear boyish, yet only a tad less belligerent than his tone. "What can you tell me about the incident?"

Kylie repeated what she'd told Tyler. "That's about it."

"Not much to go on." Keets stepped outside. "I'll take a look around."

"You do that," Kylie said, her smile taut. "Let me know if there's anything else I can do."

"Will do." Keets tapped the brim of his hat, sauntered toward the police car lights flashing in her driveway.

Closing the door, Kylie turned toward Tyler, her expression daring him to mention her less than amicable conduct. She was in no mood to be scolded, and what she'd said was true. Had she needed immediate assistance, Deputy Keets would have arrived far too late to help her.

Silent as a mime, Tyler held her look—his unreadable one giving no clue as to how he felt about her shrewish tirade.

"I've never dealt with a stalker before." She shuffled restlessly, needing to fill the void—and ease the stifling quiet making her want to shatter it with an ear-splitting scream.

Tyler said nothing, simply continued to watch her as though doing so were somehow as vital as breathing.

Cursing the silence that stretched her nerves to the breaking point, she demanded, "Why is he doing this to me? What game is he playing?"

"You should be able to answer both questions, Doc. You're the expert when it comes to figuring out why people act the way they do."

"Other than the fact that I'm likely dealing with an unstable individual, I don't have a clue as to why I've been singled out."

"Can you think of anyone who would want to annoy you?" His expression contemplative, his tone businesslike, he said, "Have you made an enemy?"

"Almost everyone who doles out advice makes enemies. People want help, but they don't always appreciate my suggestions and what I tell them they have to do in order to overcome their problems."

"Celebrities often attract unwanted attention."

"I'm not a celebrity."

"You appear on nationally televised talk shows to discuss everything from child abuse to marital warfare. The relationship seminars you host are booked months in advance, and your columns, along with your picture, are featured in major publications." Tyler grinned. "I think that qualifies as celebrity status."

"A certain amount of exposure goes with the territory." Kylie looked away, amazed he knew so much about her career, her lifestyle. His interest shouldn't have surprised her, considering she was aware of every promotion he'd received, of the recognition he'd earned as one of Oklahoma's leading law enforcement officials.

"There are a lot of zanies out there," Tyler commented, drawing her attention once again.

"I know," she admitted with a tepid smile, "I've met a number of them."

"Any who gave you reason to think they might have more than a passing interest in you?"

"No. None." Kylie moved to the over-stuffed chair beside the fireplace, avoiding Tyler's steady gaze as she sat down. "Not knowing why he's –" she waved her hand "—hanging around, stalking me without really stalking me, is the reason I called the sheriff's office tonight."

"Have you dated anyone more serious about you than you were about him?"

"No."

"Are you dating anyone—"

"No!" Glaring, Kylie added, "I haven't dated since my divorce."

"Now that's a shame. Hasn't one of the many ne'er do wells around here asked you to paint the town or leave the state with him this time?" Tyler's snarled remark hit her with the force of an unexpected blow, irritating her as much as his narrow-eyed scrutiny.

"I don't need a date to paint this or any other town! And no one has ever asked me to leave –"

"Couldn't you get hold of Daren?" he leaned forward, aimed his finger at her heaving chest, "haven't you heard, your old beau is King of the Auto Mart in Muskogee. He's married now, got a couple of kids, too, but I'm sure he'd welcome the opportunity to renew your acquaintance."

"Stop it!" Kylie surged to her feet, furious to be reminded of her shameful past—and equally shocked by Tyler's venomous insinuation. "You have no right to suggest...to...Just stop!"

Aware of her mistake soon after she agreed to leave Oklahoma with the town's rebel, she had wasted no time bidding Daren Caldwell goodbye. Handsome and wealthy to boot, Daren's promise to show her the country from the back of his Harley had not appealed. Despite Tyler's recent marriage, she loved him too much to spend time with Daren or any other man. She'd wanted more than a spoiled rich boy and a scenic tour of the seamy side of love.

"I'm sorry." Tyler shoved back his hat, shook his head. "That was uncalled for. I had no claim on you then, and no reason to attack you now."

Kylie nodded, not trusting herself to speak. Thinking Tyler begrudged her the last vestige of pride she'd had—thought she'd had—hurt. Leaving Tahlequah before the news of his sudden marriage hit town had seemed best at the time. She hadn't wanted to hear the gossip or see the pity in her friends' eyes when they heard he had wed someone other than her.

"I'm sorry," he repeated, sounding sincere.

"Apology accepted." Kylie met his gaze, forced a smile. "Can we finish the inquisition? I'd like to get some sleep."

Tyler nodded. "You're sure you haven't met anyone who's shown an unwarranted interest in your life? In you?

"No one I'm aware of. I meet a lot of people, most seem only to want professional guidance or my assurance they are doing the right thing."

"Why aren't you dating?" he asked, his voice low, husky with an emotion Kylie refused to consider anything but compassion.

"My choice." Her gaze averted, Kylie shifted restlessly, not quite sure why she felt the need to defend her decision. Dating hadn't seemed important the past few months. Still, she hated admitting her social life had become such a dismal wasteland. Especially when the man asking about her love life was the same one who'd long ago taught her to exercise greater caution when—if—she chose to date again.

"Back to square one," Tyler stated, tempting her to again look his way. "Can you describe the man you saw? Height, weight, anything that will help to identify him?"

"He was wearing a cowboy hat," she replied, smiling as he rolled his eyes.

"Ninety percent of the men around here wear cowboy hats."

"It was too dark, and he was too far away for me to see him clearly."

"Great."

Tyler stepped closer to the fireplace, braced his hands on the mantle and leaned forward, stretching his faded denim jacket taut across his shoulders. He tilted his head, staring into the cold hearth as if the smoke-darkened stones were inscribed with the answers to the mysteries of life. His cheek flexed and bulged, yielding, she knew, to the pressure of his tongue gliding back-and-forth along his smooth, inner skin. A sure sign his thoughts were troubled, she was reminded of the many times he'd helped solve her problems.

She steeled herself against the memories, unwilling to admit how much she wanted him to tell her this trauma, too, would pass without event.

"What do we do now?" Despite the voice of reason warning her not to, she hoped he would offer a quick solution to her current dilemma. That he'd soon be out of her life again. Aware that thought should have pleased her more than it did, she repeated, "What can we do?

"We wait." Turning, Tyler tugged his hat down, peered at her from beneath the brim. Like the infamous Marlboro man whose rugged good looks graced billboards across the country, the marshal's penetrating look commanded her attention. Made her feel breathless. "And wait some more if necessary."

"Wait?" Kylie parroted, hands fisted at her sides, "Until he breaks in and steals something? Until he hurts me?"

"He won't hurt you. As you well know, stalkers seldom come near enough to harm their victims."

"And if he does?"

"He won't," Tyler stated, his tone as fierce as the scowl creasing his otherwise smooth, bronze brow.

Distressed at the thought of being alone, Kylie watched him move to the door, open it and step outside. Standing in the shadows, he motioned her forward, coaxing her to the exit with a curl of his finger. She obeyed his silent command, feeling more like a recalcitrant child than a trained professional as she neared him.

"Lock up," he said with a smile, "and don't open this door unless you know there's a Wolfe on the other side."

28

Three

Tyler skirted the perimeter of Kylie's backyard, certain his sweep of the surrounding hillside would have turned up something if a prowler had been lurking nearby the night before. He'd found nothing along the trail between his house and hers, no sign of the trespasser she was so sure she'd seen.

He glanced at the wind-swept waves of Lake Tenkiller, sparkling like blue diamonds beneath the rising sun. Weary from lack of sleep and the hours he'd spent crouched on the knoll above Kylie's home, he marched to the dumpster, frowning as he stooped to pick up the trash scattered next to the metal bin.

He opened the hinged lid and stiffened, alarmed by the swish of gray that streaked across the garbage and into the far corner. Tyler reflexively reached for protection, and just as quickly loosened his grip on the butt of his service weapon, relieved to know he had no need to use the sleek government issue safely strapped in its shoulder harness.

"Hello, there." Smiling, Tyler watched the frightened raccoon kitten staring back at him. Gathering up the litter he'd dropped, he tossed it atop the bagged heaps and pushed back the lid, leaving it open as he moved away. "Run along now, little fellow."

Chuckling at his instinctive—and blessedly unnecessary—reaction to the minor fright, he hastened to Kylie's door, glancing over his shoulder toward the dumpster to see if the kitten had escaped its trap. He rang the bell, still watching for a sign the young raccoon had accepted his offer of a reprieve. Hearing the deadbolt slide open, he turned toward the entry, not quite sure he was up to this early morning meeting.

He didn't often make an ass of himself by mentioning an old flame to anyone, still couldn't believe he'd foolishly tossed Caldwell's name in Kylie's face. He also knew that dealing with his current demon—the desire seeing her again had fanned to a raging inferno—would require more rest than he'd gotten while watching over her last night.

"Good morning," Kylie said, her smile as bright as the sunlight streaming over his shoulders.

"Morning." Tyler swallowed hard, amazed to think anyone who'd slept so little could look so fresh, so vibrant. Her tawny hair in a ponytail, the denim shorts and tank top Kylie now wore made her look more like a teenager than a renowned psychologist. And far more appealing than anyone should look at seven in the morning.

Tyler glanced at the dumpster, silently cursing the tension that had been his companion since he'd knocked on her door the night before. The evasive action helped none at all. Looking anywhere but into her wide, green eyes alerted his other senses, allowed him to more clearly hear the soft sound of her breathing; smell the clean herbal scent of her shampoo. The sensual combination made his body tighten, quake with a need Tyler recognized for what it was: the primal reaction to feminine appeal no woman but Kylie seemed able to unleash in him.

"Come with me." Ignoring the clench in his stomach, he headed toward the dumpster. Appeased to hear the sound of her footsteps echoing his own, he stopped next to the metal bin, turned as Kylie reached his side. "There's your prowler."

Frowning, she stood on her tiptoes, attempting to peer into the corner Tyler indicated with a jab of his finger. Being too petite to see over the rim didn't stop her from trying. Nor did her efforts to succeed without his assistance prevent him from wanting to help her. Lifting her high enough to improve her view would require little strength, aid them both. And also satisfy the untimely desire tempting him to act upon his impulse.

The need to touch her stormed his defenses, urged him to do so with or without her approval. Impatience snapped at him, slapping his restraint like the sharp sting of a whip.

"I don't see anything." Leaning forward, she craned her neck, then shot him a disgruntled look. "I can't see *anyone*."

Amused by her glower, Tyler put his hands on her narrow waist, lifted her until her tawny head rose above the steel rim. Amazed by how little she weighed, and how good it felt to hold her, he boosted her higher, silently urging her to stop squirming and allow him this small pleasure.

"What do you think you're doing?" She covered his hands with hers, apparently prepared to push him away and risk a fall rather than accept his touch.

Unwilling to let go, Tyler tightened his hold, lifted her higher. "Look in the corner, behind that cardboard box."

Scowling, Kylie did as she was told, and then glanced down at him, her smile so sweet Tyler felt as though he'd swallowed a cupful of sugar. "It's a raccoon!" she said with a chuckle, "A baby raccoon!"

"It's young, but not exactly a baby."

"He's so small and cute!" She gave him a hard look. "He's big enough to make a lot of noise, but if you're thinking this little guy woke me up last night you're wrong, Tyler."

"There was trash scattered around the bin. My guess is he's been trapped for several hours, definitely long enough to have made a little racket."

"There wasn't anything near the bin when I looked out earlier."

"Are you sure?" Tyler knew he sounded skeptical, but needed to confirm her certainty.

"Positive."

"Raccoons are curious. He probably pilfered around the house for a while before he found the trash."

"He's too short for me to mistake him for a man, and I doubt he's the type to wear a ten-gallon hat."

That said, she turned to watch the masked creature still huddled in the corner, seemingly unmindful of Tyler's hold on her. His hands tingling from the contact, Tyler ground his teeth together, aware he should have considered the consequences before he dared to touch her.

"Do you think we can catch him?" She tugged her lower lip between her teeth, nipped at the lush, pink flesh Tyler had often dreamed of kissing, tasting. "Raccoons make wonderful pets. I'm sure I could tame him."

"Wild animals are best left in their own habitat. Besides, you don't need a pet." Tyler lowered her to the ground, removed his hands from the temptation of her slender curves. "You travel too much, and finding good care for a pet when you're out of town can be a hassle."

"Sounds like the voice of experience speaking."

"It is." Tyler stepped back, pressed his unsteady fingers against his palms. Her expression, an appealing blend of childlike innocence and saucy inquiry, made him want to wrap his arms around her and never let go. Thinking he might actually act upon his urge also made him want to reach out and shake her, make her realize how much her long ago desertion had hurt.

He'd wanted to explain the circumstances surrounding his sudden marriage, to ask her forgiveness before he let her go forever. Instead, he returned from his hasty shotgun wedding in Arkansas to find her gone, and had no alternative but to accept her cranky stepfather's advice to leave Kylie and her new boyfriend, Daren Caldwell, alone. He'd finally done that, but not before attempting every means available to contact her. As though she'd vanished without a trace, he heard nothing of her for nearly two years. By then it was too late for him to lessen the damage.

"I take it you have a pet." She tilted her head, sunlight making her hair gleam like polished amber. "Don't tell me you still have Chief."

"According to my folks, Chief still has me."

"He was just a puppy the last time I saw him." Kylie shook her head, smiling as she pictured the fuzzy brown mutt Tyler had taken when her stepfather refused to allow her to keep the pet. Refusing to dwell on Carl Bennett's hateful, controlling ways, she asked, "How are your parents?"

"Fine."

"I've missed them." Kylie started toward the house, glancing sideways at Tyler as she spoke. "I didn't realize how much until I ran into Julie Stevens last week."

"It's Julie Wilkins now."

"I know." Kylie chuckled. "I still can't believe she's married to a minister and the mother of three children."

"Soon to be four, if rumor proves true."

"It's true. We bumped into each other at the gas station Thursday and spent an hour at the café catching up on old times."

Tyler peered over his shoulder, put one hand on Kylie's back and turned her around. "Look, there." He pointed toward the dumpster, smiling as the raccoon slid down the side and ran for the nearest tree.

"Thank goodness. I was afraid he wouldn't find his way out." Frowning, she continued toward the house. "Julie told me your father had a stroke. Is he okay?"

"You know dad." Tyler flashed a dazzling grin. "Nothing short of death will ever hold Amos Wolfe down."

"I'm glad to hear it." Kylie stepped through her front door, held it open until Tyler joined her inside. "And your mother?"

"Still volunteering to work at everything from the tribal powwow to Mothers Against Drunk Drivers."

"Because of Wyatt?" she asked softly, hesitant to mention Tyler's brother. Injured in a car accident involving a drunk driver, his younger brother had been confined to a wheel chair since high school.

"Because Mom…is Mom." He shrugged, apparently satisfied Kylie did not intend to open old wounds. "Wyatt's injuries served as motivation for her to take action. With or without the personal involvement, she wouldn't be happy being a stay-at-home wife."

"Marti isn't the stay-at-home type." Kylie couldn't imagine the redheaded powerhouse bustling about the house all day, every day. Marti needed more than daily chores to occupy her busy hands and active nature. "Would you care for some coffee?"

"Definitely," Tyler replied, his smile warm. "I didn't take time to make any before I left the house."

Kylie led the way to her kitchen, oddly at ease as she reached for the coffee canister and busied herself with the chore. Certain the safe topic of family and friends would keep her on an even keel, she asked, "Does your mother still make quilts?"

"About a dozen a year, one for her and dad and each of her children."

"And the other six?"

"She donates the rest to charity or families in need." Tyler pulled a chair away from the round oak table and sat down, removing his hat to hang it on the back of another. "Mom would love to see you. She's been asking about you ever since she heard you had moved back home."

"How long is that?" Kylie dumped a measure of coffee into the filtered basket, cursing her unsteady hands as she refilled the small tin cup with the aromatic grounds. "How long have you known I was living here?"

"I've been keeping an eye on the place since the Olivers moved to Arizona. Joe mentioned you had leased it, and asked me to lend a hand if you needed help."

"So you knew I was here from the beginning." Kylie poured water into the basin of the coffeemaker, splashing it over the side. She pushed the ON button and mopped up the spill, hating the way her hands were shaking. And hating even more the way her body had begun to tremble.

"Yes."

Tyler's simple admission hung in the air like a lead balloon, as heavy as the tension adding to her growing unease. Knowing he'd been so close all along, and that he hadn't so much as called to welcome her home, told her more than words could have as to how he felt about her. Aware he'd put their past behind him, and that she had no choice but to do the same, she turned to face him, careful to keep her smile bright and the rioting emotions swirling inside her hidden.

"It's good to know you have my landlord's blessing should I need help." Her forced smiled felt tight, as false as the bogus courage behind it. "When you have time, there's a loose hinge on the patio gate I've been planning to have fixed."

"I'll take a look at it before I leave."

"Good." Kylie reached for the over-sized mugs hanging beneath the cabinet, careful to avoid another spill as she filled one for each of them. "Sugar or cream?"

"Not for me." Tyler shook his head, chuckling as she added both to her cup before joining him at the table. "I see you still like a little coffee with your condiments."

"It's an acquired taste." She set the spoon aside, not quite sure she hadn't doubled the amount of sweetener she usually preferred. "Matt thinks I should give it up entirely."

"Your husband?"

"Ex-husband," Kylie corrected, her gaze averted. "Our divorce became final the month after I moved."

"You don't sound pleased by that fact."

"No one likes to admit they failed."

"Failure is little more than an opportunity to improve," Tyler said, his tone cool, "unless you use it as a reason to stop trying."

"Your logic doesn't apply."

"Why not?"

"I'm supposed to be an expert, Tyler. I teach couples how to work through their problems, how to make their relationships stronger." Kylie chuckled mirthlessly, raised her gaze to his hard blue one. "I can't imagine why my career hasn't taken a nosedive since the divorce. I certainly wouldn't take advice from a woman whose marriage crumbled due to the same unforeseeable forces I caution seminar participants to beware of."

"The media claimed the divorce was mutual. Friendly."

"The media reported many aspects of our divorce. Some were true…most were embellished with the slightly slanderous half-truths necessary to keep the public clambering for more." Her mood as sour as her tone, Kylie stared at her coffee mug. "Friendly is about the only descriptive tag the horde of reporters eager to unearth every dirty detail got right."

"How so?" Tyler asked, tempting her to again meet his gaze.

"Losing one's husband to her best friend is about as friendly as you can get, don't you think?" Kylie chuckled, amused to realize she had no hard feelings toward her former associate. Despite their recent travails, she still respected the skilled psychiatrist Matt married the week after the divorce was granted. "Liza and Matt are far better suited than he and I were. I'm surprised I didn't see just how well until one rather brassy reporter confronted me with the obvious."

"They were having an affair?"

"Right under my nose." Kylie shook her head. "In my own house, so they say."

"That must have been tough." Tyler held her steady look, unsure as to what he should say. He'd read the papers, heard the nightly entertainment telecasts headlining her separation and the affair that had triggered it. Losing his wife to cancer had been difficult, and would have been much harder had his private life been made public. Considering Kylie's quiet demeanor, he figured she'd had more than she could handle at times. "It's behind you now. Time to move on."

"It will never be totally behind me."

"Sure it will." Tyler managed a meager smile, unwilling to admit the knot in his stomach had anything to do with her somber tone and bleak expression. "Time heals all wounds, even those love rips wide open when you least expect it."

"Love had little to do with the wounds this time," Kylie admitted, "and much to do with my current attitude." She raised her chin, gave him a weary smile. "Now, what did you find out about my prowler?"

"Nada." Glad for the change of subject, Tyler braced his elbows on the table, prepared to brave the storm gathering force in her eyes. "I saw nothing to indicate anyone had been near."

"Wonderful!" Kylie rolled her eyes. "I suppose you're going to tell me I didn't see someone standing in my backyard, or that I'm making the whole thing up."

"Are you?"

"If that's what you think, Tyler Wolfe, you can go straight to –"

"The other side of your property?" Tyler grinned, amused by her verbal assault—and by the fury narrowing her glorious green eyes. His sudden untimely desire to see passion blazing in those twin emerald orbs made his stomach clench. "I haven't completed my search. I'll take another route home and see if I can locate something out there to prove you aren't seeing things."

"I'm not. I didn't."

Tyler finished the last of his coffee, reached for his hat. "Call me if you suspect anyone is prowling around tonight."

"I'd just as soon call the sheriff," Kylie stated, aware she sounded like a stubborn child. "They'll send a patrol car, and–"

"Take long enough to get here that your prowler will be gone again."

"Okay, okay. I'll call you if I hear anything." She shoved the neon orange notepad she'd set on the table earlier his way. "Jot down your number."

Tyler did as he was told, pushed it back to her. He rose, smiling as he set the black Stetson atop his head, angling the brim until it suited him. "No matter what time, call. Alecia won't be home until next week, so I'll be able to head right over if you need me."

"Your daughter?" Kylie swallowed the lump of emotion lodged in her throat. Had she and Tyler married as they had planned, the child he wouldn't leave unattended would be theirs.

"Yes." Pride making his blue eyes gleam, he said, "She's in Tennessee this week, playing in a softball tournament. She's quite an athlete."

"Like her father." Kylie stood and moved toward the foyer. "You must be very proud of her."

"I am. She's a doll, lively but considerate if I do say so myself."

"I'm sure she is." Kylie opened the door, held it open as Tyler stepped outside. "I'm sorry about your wife. Losing one's mate so young is never easy."

"It wasn't." Tyler glanced toward the sun-brightened horizon, his expression somber. "Despite our occasional tiffs, I would never have wished for my daughter to grow up without her mother."

"Growing up with a mother doesn't always make life easier." Puzzled by the rigid jut of his chin, the unyielding clench of his jaw, Kylie added, "People make mistakes, Tyler. Marriage doesn't –"

"My marriage wasn't a mistake," Tyler stated, his tone as harsh as his expression. "Don't ever think it was."

* * *

Tyler squatted next to the small pile of ashes he'd nearly stepped on, frowning as he scanned the hard, rocky ground surrounding it. His mood dark, he scattered the gray litter with his fingertip, uncovering unburned shreds of tobacco beneath the tiny mound. Scooping a portion into the palm of his hand, he smelled the debris, certain the ashes had been discarded by a careless pipe smoker. The scent was vaguely familiar, common.

He stood, allowing the meager evidence to float to the ground as he mentally measured the distance between his hillside position and Kylie's house. Close enough to clearly see the smoked glass wall of her bedroom, he knew whoever emptied the pipe had also had a bird's-eye view of the impressive structure. Hoping the individual responsible had been nothing more than a hunter or someone taking a shortcut to the lake, Tyler again searched the ground, aware he would likely find nothing to prove that true.

Frustrated to think someone had been close enough to spy on Kylie, he turned to continue—and nearly missed the shallow impression next to his feet. He stooped to examine the footprint, the shallow dip where the deep tread of a boot had left its mark in the rocky soil.

Scowling, he again looked at the sprawling split-level house, positive Kylie had indeed seen someone the night before.

And equally certain he had left her feeling confused, hurt due to his blunt remark and hasty departure.

Tyler knew he should have explained, told Kylie the reason he would never consider his marriage a mistake. Aware he couldn't do that without jeopardizing his daughter's security, he resumed his search, his thoughts as dark as his growing fear for Kylie's safety.

He followed the narrow trail running along the ridge above the lake, the haunting image of the pain he'd put in her wide green eyes fouling his mood even more.

He could deal with the knowledge that he'd acted like a jerk and unintentionally hurt Kylie. He couldn't bear the thought of hurting Alecia.

Knowing his daughter would be the one most affected by the devastating news her mother shared with him the day she died, Tyler intended to keep Connie's deathbed revelation to himself.

Four

"I'm not sure." Kylie turned her car onto the graveled driveway, the cell phone pressed to her ear. "I'll be in Dallas the first of the week, then off to Philadelphia on Wednesday. Check my calendar and see if they'll consider the next available date."

She guided the mid-size car to a stop in front of her house. "And Grace, don't forget to call Matt and ask him if the Phoenix interview is still on." Amused by her assistant's acidic remark, Kylie smiled. "I agree, but there is no way to avoid it. The Arizona seminar and five others were booked long before Matt and I separated. As luck would have it, Liza will be speaking at two of those."

Kylie rubbed her temples as she listened to Grace's tirade, too weary to wage an argument as to the many reasons Grace felt she should not take part in the seminars that included Matt. She knew the spunky assistant had her best interest at heart, but also felt she owed her ex-husband. If not for her former professor's suggestion that she co-author their now famous *We Do, We Don't, We Will* series of relationship improvement books, Kylie figured she would be little more than an entry-level psychologist struggling to make ends meet.

Contractual obligations aside, she still considered Matt a friend and a valued associate. Fifteen years her senior, he had offered guidance and much needed moral support, as well as unfettered advice, long before their romantic attraction caught them both off-guard.

"I've got to go now, Grace. My ice cream is melting and I still have to proof my column and fax it to Harvey by noon. Check my calendar and schedule the Oprah appearance accordingly. If my availability coincides with theirs, make the necessary arrangements and send me an email so I can update my daily planner." Her mood improving, she turned off the engine, and added, "Don't worry, Grace. I'm a big girl. I can handle seeing my ex-husband and his new wife together. Bye, now."

Kylie slipped her purse beneath her arm, smiling as she popped the trunk to retrieve the grocery sacks stored there. A bag on each hip, she pushed the lid down, made her way to the house. She reached the porch and froze, her wide-eyed gaze locked on the rope dangling from the overhead light fixture.

Fashioned in a hangman's noose, the eerie message sent a shiver down her spine, as did her sudden certainty that someone was nearby, watching her, observing her reaction to his handiwork.

Trembling, she stepped around the noose and jammed her key into the lock, twisting it so hard she feared it would break before the latch clicked open. Juggling the cumbersome sacks, she glanced over her shoulder, scanned the tree line along the front of the property. A gleam of silver high atop the hill struck her eyes with the force of a lightning bolt, blinding her as she shoved open the door, scattering her purchases in her haste.

Canned food landed on the concrete porch with a resounding thud, rolled along the level surface in a noisy procession. Eggs bounced out of the carton, breaking the fragile shells. A jar of pickles shattered on the tiled entry, hindering her effort to close the door.

Too nervous to consider the danger, Kylie knelt to scrape the smelly green heap and broken glass over the threshold. Grimacing as a shard sliced her finger, she slammed the door shut, slid the deadbolt into place and doubled over, nausea making her stomach churn and her head spin.

Heart racing, she slowly raised her head, braced her back against the wall. Seeing her purse amidst the mess next to her feet, she reached for the sticky leather bag, removed her cell phone. Unable to remember Tyler's number, she dialed 9-1-1.

"Cherokee County Sheriff's Department."

"This is Kylie Bennett, I need help!"

"Kylie?" the familiar male voice inquired, "What's wrong? What's going on?"

"Someone is outside. Send someone out here, please!"

"Calm down, Kylie. Where are you?"

"Home…in the house." Kylie rolled her shoulders, easing the tension stiffening her neck. "I'm inside."

"Is the door locked?"

"Yes."

"Do you think someone's in the house with you?"

"No—Oh no!" Kylie jerked upright, alarmed to realize her keys were nowhere in sight.

"What's wrong? Kylie?"

"I think I left my keys outside, in the lock!"

"Can you hear anything? Do you think someone's outside now?"

"No." Kylie listened, but could hear nothing other than the ragged sound of her own breathing. "I don't hear anything."

"Good. Open the door and get the keys, Kylie. Let me know as soon as you've done that, okay?"

"Okay." Hands shaking, Kylie released the deadbolt and eased open the door. She yanked the keys from the lock, causing her injured finger to throb as the car alarm control raked her bleeding flesh. Uncaring as to the blood stains soiling her coral silk blouse, she pushed the door shut, slid the deadbolt into place. Aware she had not entered her pass-code to disarm the alarm, she jabbed at the keypad, smearing the ivory casing with the crimson stain of her own blood. "It's done. I have the keys and the door is locked again."

"Good. I called Tyler, he's –"

"Who is this?" Scowling, she surveyed the odorous muck littering the earth-toned ceramic squares.

"This is your old bud, Wyatt."

"Oh my goodness! I can't believe I didn't recognize your voice."

"That's understandable. You've just had bit of a shock. And we haven't seen each other in years."

"Not since Mom's funeral." Kylie swallowed hard. "I really appreciated you coming to the memorial service. It meant a lot to me."

"Friends don't let friends down, Kye. Mom and I attended because we love you."

"I love you too, Wyatt. You're the best."

"Second best," he said with a chuckle, "You like my bro—"

"Don't go there, Wyatt." Kylie massaged her forehead, afraid he would continue. Tension throbbed at her temples. She closed her eyes, praying the pain would ease.

"You're right. That old comedy routine is as ancient as I am," he said, "and we have more serious business to contend with. Are you sure no one else is in the house?"

Alarmed to realize she hadn't thought to check, Kylie looked deeper into the entry, up the stairs, toward the living area to her right. Satisfied no one had entered ahead of her, she said, "Yes. I don't see anything out of the ordinary."

"Did you see someone outside?"

"No. Nothing more than a bright flash of light...and my stalker's calling card."

"What calling card?"

"He left a noose hanging on my front porch."

"Holy—" Wyatt bit back the colorful invective. "Stay calm, Kylie. Tyler should be there any minute now."

Alerted by the doorbell, Kylie whirled to face the entry, kicking a can against the wall in her nervousness. "He's here. Someone's here."

"Make sure it's Tyler before you open –"

"I know the routine, Wyatt." That said, she stepped forward, peered through the peephole. Grateful to see Tyler's familiar face, she advised Wyatt of his brother's arrival, set the phone aside and opened the door.

"Are you okay?" Tyler clasped her shoulders, drew her forward until her head rested against his solid chest. Kylie nodded, too emotional to reply as he gently guided her into the house. "What happened?"

"I'm not sure." Eased by the comforting haven of his arms, she wanted to remain where she stood forever. Aware she could not allow herself that pleasure, she pushed back, met his probing gaze. "I saw the noose, then a blinding gleam on the knoll and...and..."

"Easy, now," he soothed, "calm down and tell me what happened."

"Nothing more than I've already told you." Kylie chaffed her arms, chilled despite the warm spring sunshine streaming through the open door. Her damp, sticky palms did nothing to ease her discomfort.

Scowling, Tyler reached for her injured hand, gently turned her bloody palm up to better examine her wound. "You're hurt."

"I—it's nothing. J—just a little cut." Breathless, Kylie pulled her hand free, less affected by her throbbing finger than his tender grip.

"Do you have a first-aid kit?"

"I'll take care of it later." She stepped back, distancing herself from the temptation urging her to allow him to tend her injury. "Right now, I'd like to find out who did this."

"Tell me exactly what happened."

Kylie recounted her story, shrugged. "I felt uneasy…scared because I thought he might still be nearby, watching me."

"Nothing more?"

Kylie shook her head. "I panicked at that point. As you can see, I made a mess of things." She indicated with a wave of her hand the groceries littering the porch, the broken eggs and pungent pickles strewn across the colorful Spanish tile.

"Your reaction was justified." Moving onto the porch, Tyler lifted the thick rope, dropped it as though the rough hemp burned like molten lava. Kylie watched it sway, wishing it would disappear and take the trepidation tightening her chest along with it. "Whoever did this is definitely no expert."

"Why do you think he isn't?"

"The knot's loose, amateurish at best. He's also a fool." His expression contemplative, Tyler glanced toward the pine-covered hillside. "Anyone experienced at committing terror wouldn't hang around after the fact…or give you a reason to think he's still here."

"Are you saying he wanted me to know he was still nearby?" Kylie swallowed hard, tamped down the fear rising inside her. Thinking her stalker intended to take his evil game to a more frightening level scared her more than discovering the noose had earlier.

"I don't know. Maybe." Slanting her a narrow look, Tyler clasped her uninjured hand and tugged her further inside, closed the door. "I'm sure he's long gone now, but I need to make sure."

"What are you doing?" Kylie followed Tyler through the downstairs rooms, up to the second floor landing outside her bedroom. Frowning, she watched as he searched every nook and cranny—closets and bathrooms included—before descending the stairs, her at his heels. "Satisfied?" she asked, head tilted as she held his gaze.

"Not quite." He spun around, headed toward the back of the house.

"Where are you going now?" Hands on her hips, she remained in the foyer.

"To the kitchen to make you a cup of tea." Pausing, he looked over his shoulder, one dark brow arched as he cast her a teasing grin. "Unless you'd prefer something stronger?"

"Tea is fine." Glad she would not be alone for at least a little while, she smiled. "Thanks."

Suddenly somber, Tyler moved closer, tucked an errant lock of hair behind her ear. Her heart pounding, Kylie remained still, unwelcome need warming her from head to toe. He leaned forward, kissed her forehead, each sizzling cheek, the tip of her nose. Feeling cherished and safe, she released a shaky breath, inhaled slowly. He smelled of soap and sunshine, as clean and fresh as the wondrous sensations causing her knees to shake.

Tyler eased back, searching her wide gaze with his intense one. Apparently satisfied by what he saw there, the gratitude she felt—the untimely desire she dared not voice—he brushed her lips with his. Feather light, little more than a whisper of a touch, his kiss made her head spin.

It also made her yearn for more—a true lover's kiss and all the joy that precious treasure promised.

The peal of the doorbell startled them both, caused them to leap apart like children caught pilfering through their teacher's desk. Guilt burning her skin, Kylie reached for the doorknob, and then hesitated. Apparently sensing her distress, Tyler gently pushed her hand aside, stepped in front of her and opened the door.

The fresh-faced deputy standing there looked from Tyler to Kylie, then back at the taller man. "I'm here to investigate an attempted break-in." He again glanced at Kylie. "Did you report the incident?"

Kylie nodded. "There was no attempt to break in, just that –" she indicated with a wave of her hand the noose "—hanging from the porch when I came home."

"That's why you called the sheriff?" His youthful smile indulgent, he shook his head as though unable to comprehend her reasoning.

"I doubt it will do any good, but you should probably dust for prints." Tyler's commanding tone brought the deputy's head around, drilled home the purpose of his visit. "The light cover is smooth enough to hold a print, as is the door."

"Who are you?" the younger man demanded, sounding offended by Tyler's suggestion.

"Tyler Wolfe –"

"Marshal Wolfe?" Rosy color flooded his face. "I'm sorry...I had no idea...I..."

"Can you manage the task without my assistance?" Tyler spared Kylie a quick glance, and a shadow of a smile she sensed might erupt into laughter if he dared to give in to the humor making his eyes sparkle.

Kylie pitied the deputy if that happened. Already embarrassed, the officer would likely faint if he realized his awkward behavior was the source of Tyler's amusement.

43

"Can do." The deputy extended his hand. "I'm Joel Denton. I work with your brother."

"Nice to meet you...despite the circumstances." Tyler accepted the handshake, no longer attempting to subdue his laughter. Warm and rich, the sound of it brought an answering smile to Kylie's lips. "Now, if you'll get started, I'll see to the lady's comfort."

"Oh. Sure." Clumsy in his haste yet eager to impress the marshal, Deputy Denton dashed toward the idling police cruiser parked in the drive.

"Does that happen often?" Kylie asked, admiring the way Tyler had handled the deputy's obvious hero-worship.

"Often enough to keep me honest." Acting as though he expected her to accept his teasing reply as enough said, he aimed a finger over her head. "Time to patch you up."

Putting word to action, Tyler hustled her into the kitchen. As efficient as a skilled nurse, he washed her hands, carefully patted her skin dry with a towel as soft as his expression when he gingerly examined her wound.

"You don't need stitches."

"I didn't think I would." She drew her lower lip between her teeth, nipping back the smile threatening to break free. He looked so serious—focused and sexy at once—she almost wished her wound did require further attention.

A hand on her elbow, he steered her toward the table, insisting she sit in the chair he pulled out despite her grumbled protest. "Treating the injury will be easier if you're sitting down," he admonished, his tone both firm and tender. "Where's your first-aid kit?"

"In the cabinet under the sink, on the right."

Tyler retrieved the small metal box, quickly removed the supplies needed to protect her injured digit. Cradling her hand as though it were fragile China, he dabbed the cut with antiseptic that burned far less than her skin beneath his fingers.

Unnerved, she wanted to yank her hand away. She also longed to turn her palm up, to more fully experience his disturbing touch.

Silently cursing her lack of willpower for even considering the latter, she said, "You don't have to do this."

Kylie inhaled sharply, surprised more than pained by the sudden sting of the medicine. The sound of her shock snapped Tyler's head up, widened his eyes. Unable to look away, she stared back at him, her heart tumbling like a leaf in a whirlwind.

"Did I hurt you?"

She shook her head, afraid to speak for fear her voice would betray the feelings zigzagging through her: the hot rush of desire, the cold blast of panic it triggered. Kylie knew she'd never again consider blue a cool color—not after seeing the Indigo fire blazing in his eyes. She squeezed her eyelids together, shielding herself from further temptation.

"Are you sure?"

"Positive." She raised her lashes, forced a smile. "The antiseptic burned a bit."

He smiled as though her admission relieved him of a great burden, as if the thought of causing her pain had somehow hurt him. Puzzled yet pleased to think her well being mattered, she raised her hand, inspected the small, narrow cut.

"Good as new." She reached for the first-aid kit, intending to put it away.

"I'll do it." He covered her hand with his, gently pushed it aside. True to his word, he quickly packed the box, started to close the lid. Reaching inside, he fished a Band-Aid from the store of supplies, ripped it open.

Kylie snatched the adhesive strip from him, careful to prevent her fingers from touching his. Responding to his curious look, she shrugged and said, "I'll put it on after I shower."

"That makes sense." He snapped the box shut, stashed it where he'd found it. "I'll take a look around while you're showering, and then see what I can do about the mess in your hall."

"I'll take care of it." She stood, eager to complete the unpleasant chore. "You've already done more than enough."

"It's no trouble." He bracketed her shoulders with his warm palms, turned her toward the stairway. "Now, go clean up while I get started."

"That's silly," she protested, "why should I clean up when I'll just get messy –"

"Go!" He pointed toward the gleaming oak steps leading upstairs. "Your shoes are going to sport yellow polka-dots unless you get the egg yolk off soon."

Kylie glanced down, frowning as she surveyed the spots making her new tennis shoes look worn and ugly. The blood stains on her shirt and jeans did nothing to improve her appearance.

She met his determined look with one of feigned severity. "I don't particularly enjoy having to say it, but you're right, Mr. Wolfe."

She mounted the stairs, the joyful sound of Tyler's laughter making her feet feel as light as her spirit. She hated to think his amusement could affect her mood so dramatically. She also hated to think she could become addicted to his company, but knew she easily could.

* * *

"Did you find anything?" Kylie met Tyler at the front yard gate, too anxious to remain inside once she had seen him approaching the house.

"Not much." He pushed his hat up, swiped his sweaty brow with the back of his hand. "It looks like a vehicle has recently been parked beside the highway. Probably a motorist having car trouble."

"Or a stalker watching this house...watching me."

"Or someone spying on you."

Kylie shrank back, cringing at the thought of anyone having such easy access.

"Don't worry." Tyler settled his hat in place, gave her an encouraging smile. "At that distance, he didn't see much."

"There wasn't much to see," she stated, unable to keep her rising bitterness out of her voice, "other than my cowardly reaction to his prank."

"Kylie, you're blowing this out of proportion. We have no proof anyone was nearby."

"You don't believe me, do you? You think I'm imagining –"

"I didn't say that!"

"You didn't have to." Fury boosting her courage, she stepped forward, jabbed her bandaged finger in the center of his broad chest. "You saw the rope, Tyler. Do you think I strung it up before I called the sheriff?"

"No."

"If you don't mind me asking, what do you think?"

"I'm not sure –"

"Yes, you are!" Glaring her opinion, she tamped down the urge to stamp her foot. "I've never known you to *not* have an opinion. Tell me what's going on, what you found!"

"Right now all I know is that you didn't actually see anyone. What you did see could have been nothing more than sunlight reflecting off of a mirror. A harmless flash triggered by a motorist stepping out of his car to change a flat tire...or someone taking a break during a long drive."

"I know." Her temper overshadowed by disappointment, she shrugged and moved back. "Not knowing whether or not that blinding light was aimed at me is the reason I'm still upset. I have to know what's going on, Tyler. I need to know what he wants, what he's planning to do next."

"I know you do," he said, his tone hard. "Believe me, I do too."

"Perhaps the deputy found something." Frowning, she added, "prints or other evidence that will help us identify the stalker."

"He didn't." Apparently unwilling to acknowledge the irritation narrowing her eyes, he said, "I talked to him before he left for Cookson. He's going to ask a few questions and see if anyone from that direction has noticed anything unusual."

"Considering his star-struck reaction to you, I'm surprised he didn't ask you to ride along with him."

"He did. I squirmed out of it by claiming I had another commitment." Tyler flashed her a broad grin. "And by promising to lend a hand if he discovers anything suspicious."

"I'm sure that boosted his ego." Her tart rejoinder garnered an unexpected response—his hearty laughter. And a sizzling burst of her temper she'd just managed to control.

Rather than bash him over the head, she brushed past him, intent on putting this episode behind her. And equally determined to learn who had chosen her as his victim—with or without *his* professional assistance.

"Have dinner with me."

Kylie stopped so fast she nearly lost her balance. She turned to face Tyler, not quite sure she'd heard him correctly. "Tonight?"

"There's a great barbeque place not far from here."

"Why should I go anywhere with you?" Kylie asked, hoping he would give her a reason to believe they could share an evening free of the discomfort she felt in his presence. She'd wanted to cling to him, kiss him, and punch his lights out—all within the last forty-five minutes! She narrowed her eyes, not quite sure she should risk further torture. "Why?"

"To see if we can find out who dropped this?" He held up a clear plastic bag containing a battered matchbook. Dangling from his long fingers, the gold-trimmed square looked small and unimportant, yet still managed to make her skin dimple with gooseflesh.

Unwilling to allow herself to fear an inanimate object, she snatched the baggie from him, turned it over. "Mackey's Bar & Grill," she read aloud, then glanced at Tyler. "Do you know where this place is?"

"As I said, it's a great barbeque joint."

Five

Nestled high above Lake Tenkiller at the end of a narrow blacktop road, Mackey's appeared little more than an unassuming log-frame structure. A stone paved dogtrot separated two large, square buildings reminiscent of the pioneer homes Kylie had seen in history books. Save for the crowded parking lot and customers streaming in and out, she would not have guessed anyone would drive so far off the main road to visit the secluded restaurant.

Tyler parked his Jeep on a steep incline at the edge of the graveled lot and switched off the engine, casting his profile in shadow. "I hope you're hungry."

"I am." Kylie's stomach rumbled indelicately. Her smile sheepish, she added, "Famished, in fact."

"Good. You're in for a treat." Tyler stepped out, hastened to the passenger side of the red four-wheel drive vehicle to open her door. He assisted her out, then guided her toward the entrance, his hand resting at the small of her back as though years hadn't passed since their last night out. "Watch your step, the gravel is a little loose and those sandals don't look any too sturdy."

Her skin tingling beneath his touch, Kylie glanced down, eyeing the slender white straps of her shoes with concern. Thin and flexible, the soft soles did little to protect her mostly bare feet from the gray stones crunching with each step. Unlike Tyler's boots and jeans, her casual but dressy attire seemed out of place, as uncomfortable as she felt walking so close to him.

"You could have warned me we'd be traipsing across rocks rather than sidewalks," she stated, her frown intended to prick his conscience. "I'd have worn sneakers and jeans if I'd known we'd be dining in the boonies."

"There's nothing wrong with the way you're dressed." He scanned her from head to painted pink toenails, his expression approving her simple white-eyelet sundress. Her tanned skin bared by the scooped neckline and spaghetti straps blushed beneath his look. "Not a thing."

"I wasn't fishing for a compliment."

"You deserve one," he said with a disarming smile. "That dress will make us—you—the center of attention…and me the most envied man in the place."

Her cheeks warm, Kylie stepped through the wide screen door he held open, squinting as her eyes adjusted to the interior lighting. Rustic yet contemporary, the vast dining hall featured rough-hewn tables and ladder-backed chairs, native-stone floors and red-checkered linens. Carriage style lights along each wall complimented the wagon-wheel chandeliers hanging overhead. Bustling with activity, the room seemed to absorb the din of chatter emanating from the diners clustered around rectangular tables, making it appear both expansive and cozy.

"Tyler!" a feminine voice called out. "Where have you been hiding?"

Kylie turned, smiling as the petite brunette who'd greeted Tyler wrapped her arms around him and plastered her full red lips to his. Her smile drooping, Kylie looked away, unable to bear the sight of his long arms snaking around the attractive woman's slender waist.

Her heart sinking, Kylie again faced the embracing duo, aware she was not the only one eager to observe the happy reunion. At least half the patrons at nearby tables seemed fascinated by their public display. She felt like a fish in a bowl, exposed to all who cared to look.

"Easy, Jodi Marie," Tyler said with a chuckle, "you're going to break my ribs."

"I'll break more than your ribs if you don't call the next time you have a free night. You promised me a real date when I turned twenty-one, remember?"

"That was a bribe, honey. I never—"

"It worked," Jodi Marie stated, her smile forgiving. "I haven't seen Homer since the night you sent him packing." Blinking back tears, she added, "I never told you how much I appreciated your help. I don't know what I would have done if you hadn't made him leave me alone."

"You would have done fine." Tyler eased back, raised the hem of the white apron covering her jeans and dabbed at the moisture trickling down her smooth olive cheeks. Obviously of Native American ancestry, Jodi Marie possessed the clear skin and impressive cheekbones that allow models to earn vast fortunes.

"Maybe." The brunette flashed him a smile Kylie knew would have made her rich had she captured the attention of New York fashion photographers. Jodi Marie glanced at Kylie, her wide brown eyes speculative—and more than a tad envious. "Who's this?"

"My neighbor, Kylie Bennett." Tyler met Kylie's inquisitive gaze. "Kylie, this is Jodi Marie Knight, the reigning Miss Cherokee."

"Hello." Kylie extended her hand, not quite sure the younger woman would appreciate the traditional gesture.

The beauty queen latched onto Kylie's outstretched hand with her two, leaned forward and in a stage voice whispered, "Rope and tie him before I have a chance to…or this will be your last night out with the handsomest man this side of Texas."

"She's also a champion calf roper." Tyler laughed, apparently amused by the playful fist his adoring conquest poked in his lean stomach.

"You make me sound like a raving success." The young woman turned to Kylie, her expression amicable. "I'd rather be known for my grade point average than for that danged crown and this buckle." She brushed the apron aside and indicated with a jerk of her thumb the wide silver buckle making her waist look even narrower.

"I was getting around to that." Tyler glanced around the packed room, then at Jodi Marie. "What's the chance of us getting a table any time soon?"

"Excellent, if you don't mind a patio table."

"The patio is fine."

"Follow me." Jodi Marie winked at Kylie, grabbed two menus and headed toward the open doorway on the opposite side of the room. Once they were seated, she handed each of them a menu. "This isn't my area, but I'll take your drink orders and send Valerie right out."

"I'll have my usual." Tyler glanced at Kylie, raised an inquisitive brow.

"I'll have his usual, too." Kylie smiled at the waitress. "Whatever that is."

"Beer." Jodi Marie wrinkled her nose and rolled her eyes. "Mackey makes a mean margarita."

"That sounds better."

Kylie watched Jodi Marie dash toward the bar, then met Tyler's steady gaze. "She's beautiful."

"Yes, she is."

"An old friend?" she asked, wishing he would elaborate so she wouldn't have to pry.

"A fairly new friend." Tyler waved at an older couple crossing the broad stone patio, then looked at Kylie. "She's a good kid."

"I'm sure she is."

Tamping down the curiosity urging her to learn more about the calf-roping beauty queen, Kylie watched another waitress approach their table, a frosty mug of beer and a sizeable margarita balanced on a tray. The plump redhead set the drinks down, introducing herself as their server as she completed the task.

"I'll give you a few minutes to look over the menu," she said, "unless you already know what you want."

"Give the lady a little time." Tyler removed his hat, set it on the chair seat between them. "This is her first visit."

"I love first-timers." Smiling, the waitress turned to go. "Yell if you need anything."

Chuckling, Kylie opened her menu. "What's good?"

"Everything."

"You're a big help."

"I could be," he responded, his smile mischievous. "If you trust me enough to allow me to order for you."

"I'm game." Kylie folded the half-scanned menu, raised the salted glass to her lips. "That is fantastic!" She took another sip, reluctantly set the frosty glass down.

"Jodi Marie would never steer you wrong."

Irritated to be reminded of his attractive friend, Kylie surveyed the crowded patio. Long and wide, the exterior gallery ran the length of the building, its native stone floor and beamed ceiling complementing the weathered log wall. Though filled with tables, the area appeared unobstructed, largely due to the lake view beyond the split-rail perimeter. Artful landscaping and a garden teaming with brilliant spring flowers and neatly trimmed shrubs added to the natural beauty of the board walkway leading down to the lakefront.

"It's beautiful out here." Kylie glanced at Tyler and smiled.

"So are you."

"Tyler, don't..." She averted her gaze, unsettled by his sudden intensity.

"Don't what, Kylie?" His soft tone commanded her attention, and made her even more uncomfortable. "Don't tell you that you look beautiful?"

51

"Just…" she shook her head, at a loss for words. She couldn't deny she enjoyed his praise, not without lying. Knowing he still found her attractive, that he was courteous enough to tell her so, made her feel beautiful. And too content to risk ruining the evening by asking him to not pay her an occasional complement.

"Hello again," their server said, "have you made a decision?"

"We'll have the ribs for two." Tyler quickly completed the order, making Kylie wonder if he expected someone to join them. The vast array of food he'd told the waitress to bring would feed the guests attending one of her larger seminars. Once the waitress had disappeared, he said, "don't worry, Kylie. They have to-go boxes."

"And antacid, I hope."

Tyler tossed back his head, laughing as though her grumbling remark had somehow surprised him. Smiling in response, she said, "I wasn't joking."

"I know." He gave her a wink. "You never did have much of a sense of humor."

"I didn't always have a reason to laugh."

Annoyed at how quickly thoughts of her younger years could alter her mood, Kylie again looked at the lake. The calm water shimmered like a dark mirror, its surface glittering beneath the blanket of stars above. Suited for romance, the silver sphere of moon rising in the night sky served only to remind her of all the evenings she'd watched it climb to the heavens alone; of how often she'd wished she had someone beside her to share the beauty.

"Have you seen him?"

Kylie shook her head, aware he could only mean one person—her stepfather. "No. I haven't."

"Are you going to visit him?"

"I don't know. Maybe."

"Kylie—"

"Maybe." Kylie met his steady blue gaze with her narrow one. "When I'm ready. When I know I won't tear into him and stand up to him the way mother and I should have done long ago."

"He's an old man, Kylie. A sick old man."

"I know." She lowered her head, shrugged. "I occasionally run into his home health nurse."

Truth be known, she'd only met the woman once, yet the health-care professional seemed to think Kylie appreciated the weekly updates she had provided since that chance encounter. She hated to admit it, but Carl's declining health did concern her.

"I'm sure Carl regrets many of the things he did. Losing your mother couldn't have been easy for him. Considering his declining health—"

"He's eighty-years-old, Tyler." Kylie shook her head, frowning as she held his steady look. "Most men his age tend to experience ill health."

Tyler opened his mouth, then closed it, afraid he would breach the trust Carl Bennett had recently placed in him if he said anything more. Mostly confined to his home—the small frame house where Kylie once lived— Bennett now spent his days watching game shows and awaiting his nurse's visits. And dwelling on the past, as men approaching their final months often do.

Tyler felt certain Kylie did not know the full extent of Carl's medical problems. Though they had discussed many things the two times Tyler had recently visited Bennett, the older man had insisted he not mention his illness to anyone. Weakened by emphysema and the ravages of a hard life, Bennett was still a proud man. But not too proud to admit he had made mistakes, most of which involved his stepdaughter according to the ailing man.

Tyler hoped Kylie would allow Carl the opportunity to bridge the gulf separating them still; that her stepfather would have a chance to tell her that she had unwittingly become the sole source of his pride.

"Here you are." Their waitress arrived with a flourish and quickly filled their table with a mountain of food.

"My goodness!" Wide-eyed, Kylie looked from one heaping platter to the next.

"Enjoy," the server said as she dashed to another table, leaving them alone once again.

"I really think you should talk to him." Tyler waited for Kylie to respond, barely concealing his irritation when she merely gave him an owl-eyed look. "What have you got to lose?"

"Besides my appetite?"

"Kylie—"

"Do you plan to beat this issue to death, or enjoy what you claimed to be the best barbeque in the state?" She reached for the platter of ribs, apparently satisfied he would not press her further. "We also have some investigating to do. You haven't asked one person about that book of matches."

If not for the taut press of her lips Tyler might have believed her act of indifference. The tension radiating from the corners of her mouth and the stubborn jut of her chin gave her away, told him she had yet to resolve the anger she'd focused on Carl Bennett since her teen years. Though he knew she had reason to hold the once bitter man in contempt, he could not justify the lingering effects that rocky relationship had on her. As a professional counselor, he knew Kylie was aware of the damage that could result from refusing to confront such an emotional force.

Tyler knew the consequences well. He'd done much the same, refused to consider Kylie's abrupt departure as anything but an excuse to avoid hearing his reason for jilting her. He hadn't deserved her loyalty, but he had expected it. Not being able to at least offer her an explanation had left him angry and bitter.

He didn't realize his late wife had absorbed the brunt of his frustration until long after Kylie left town. Connie had finally told him to snap out of it or hit the road. With a baby on the way—and his first love nowhere to be found—Tyler realigned his priorities and put forth the effort he felt Connie deserved.

If he'd known the truth then, he would have searched until he found Kylie, begged her forgiveness and, hopefully, had at least a little influence as to how she now viewed Carl Bennett.

Then again, he mused, reclaiming Kylie's love all those years ago would have denied him the daughter he adored. Despite the circumstances surrounding her birth, he would never forgo his time with Alecia. Nor would he consider cheating Kylie again.

Kylie deserved better than a single father whose work often claimed as much time as parenthood.

* * *

"Do you intend to question the wait staff?" Kylie laid her napkin aside, smiling as she watched Tyler polish off the last of the ribs. "That book of matches is the only clue we have."

"I doubt it will do any good." Tyler patted his stomach, glanced at the few remaining bits of food. "So much for the to-go box."

"I'll have to watch my diet for a week," she stated dramatically, "but I'll probably be back out here at the first available opportunity." She inclined her head. "Thank you for bringing me. I enjoyed every bite."

"Good. You deserved it, considering how much time you spend alone."

"How do you know how much time I spend alone or—"

"Wolfe."

"Hello," Tyler greeted the man who'd just stepped up to their table.

Kylie glanced up, into Deputy Orvil Keets' pale blue eyes. She forced a smile, hoping the young officer had forgiven her for taking him to task for his tardy response to her emergency call. His unblinking gaze and the grim press of his lips made her wonder if she should apologize. It also made her feel inexplicably uncomfortable.

"Hello," she said, attempting to ease her unsteady nerves. "It's good to see you again, and under different circumstances."

Acting as though equally disturbed by her presence, Keets gave her a jerky nod and quickly returned his attention to Tyler. "Did you run across anything that might help us identify the trespasser?"

"No. Did you?"

Kylie looked from one man to the other, miffed by Keets' question and curious as to why Tyler sounded disinterested. She had no idea why he wouldn't want to know what, if anything, the deputy had found. Aware he had not yet asked anyone about the matchbook, she couldn't help but wonder if he planned to pursue that or any other evidence they discovered. Thinking he might have mislead her as to the reason they'd visited Mackey's irritated her almost as much as the deputy's public discussion of her recent ordeal.

"Not a thing." Keets cast Kylie a reproachful look. "I'm beginning to think we're chasing a ghost."

"Ghost's don't cast shadows or uproot rose bushes," Kylie responded tartly, no longer caring who overheard them.

"Men leave footprints," he stated, "and at least a trace of evidence they've been around."

Kylie stiffened, annoyed both by the deputy's unreadable expression and his accusing tone. She'd never seen eyes quite so light, so dull they appeared as blank as those of a marauding shark. Nor had she heard an officer of the law say anything so inflammatory.

"I have no explanation for the lack of proof, Deputy, but I can assure you someone was prowling around my home."

"There is only one explanation, Ms. Bennett."

"And that would be?"

"You didn't—"

"I'll drop by the office tomorrow morning," Tyler interrupted, his blunt tone leaving no doubt as to who had just gained control of the conversation. "We'll continue this discussion then."

"Fine." Keets puffed out his chest, making his pudgy build appear even more top heavy. He glanced at Kylie, gave her a tepid smile. "Take care, Ma'am."

Her teeth clenched, Kylie watched the deputy stride toward the cash register, toss a guest check and money onto the counter. Frowning, the tall, dark-haired man tending the till rang up the sale, handed Keets his change. Keets reached into the basket beside the register, and said something that made the employee scowl even more as he stared after the officer who'd just slammed the door on his way out.

"He's young," Tyler stated, reclaiming Kylie's thoughts. "He has a lot to learn."

"Good manners are usually learned much earlier."

"So is common courtesy."

"Meaning?"

"You should visit Carl this week."

"And you should ask the staff about those matches."

"I don't have to." Tyler set his hat atop his head, tugged the brim down so far she could barely see his eyes.

"Isn't that the reason we came here?"

"Did I say I intended to ask anyone about the matchbook?"

"No, but—"

"Give me a little credit, Kylie." He pocketed the credit card and receipt the waitress had left on the table. "I've learned a thing or two in the years I've worked in law enforcement."

"Such as?"

"The power of observation." He stood, stepped around the table and eased her chair back. "And the fact that questions often raise suspicion and don't always reap usable information."

"I'm not following you." Kylie headed toward the exit, her irritation mounting. "How can you learn anything if you don't ask questions, especially—"

"I learned quite a lot."

"Do you mind sharing a bit of what you learned?" She cast him a look over her shoulder, not even attempting to conceal her annoyance.

"Ten people took a mint from the candy jar next to the register. Two of them nabbed a handful." He gave her a grin. "Four men and one lady picked up a book of matches from the basket beside it. None of them are suspects," he stated, smiling as though her wide-eyed look amused him.

"What makes you so sure they shouldn't be considered suspects?" she asked, amazed he could have noticed so much while seemingly focused on her. Irked to think she had noticed little other than him, she said, "don't you think it's a bit early to rule anyone out?"

"Nope." Tyler unlocked the Jeep, waited until she had climbed inside, and

56

then leaned in, so close he could feel her warm breath fanning his cheek. "What I think, is that you should stop worrying and leave the investigating to me. When I have reason to believe someone deserves further observation or a word of caution, I'll let you know."

Though he wished that were entirely true, he didn't want to frighten her. One of the men who'd taken a matchbook had a lengthy record, and a fondness for hassling the women in his life. He hated to think that derelict might have chosen Kylie as a possible conquest—or that she had far more reason than he'd suspected to fear the man she'd seen outside her house. Will Conrad was not a man to be trusted.

He stared into the wide green eyes looking back at him, aware Conrad was not the only man he needed to watch, and closely.

Tyler knew he'd have to keep a safe distance between himself and the woman making him want to cast hesitation aside and kiss her. Just looking at her petal pink lips parted as though she, too, would like nothing more than for him to give in to his desire, made him lightheaded.

Scowling, he eased back, ignoring her questioning look as he shut the door and hastened to the opposite side of the vehicle. Yielding to his urge, no matter how much he longed to, was not an option.

Neither of them needed a reminder of the passion that had made their relationship a source of torture as well as delight. Nor did he want to remember that the sweet pleasure he'd savored only once had also been freely—and quickly—offered to Daren Caldwell.

Kylie had, apparently, had no trouble forgetting all they shared that one long ago night. Tyler wished he could as easily put thoughts of that memorable evening behind him.

Six

A few miles from Mackey's, and shortly after they'd passed the neon lights of a new mini-mart, Tyler steered the Jeep onto a rutted dirt road that seemed vaguely familiar to Kylie. Lined with huge oak trees and small pines that had escaped the scraping blade of county maintenance crews, the narrow graveled lane soon widened, revealing a grassy clearing and a picturesque view of Lake Tenkiller.

Swamped by a sobering sense of deja vu, Kylie remained silent, as she had since leaving Mackey's, until Tyler guided the vehicle to a stop near the lakeside edge of the deserted clearing. She turned to face him then, an unsettling disquiet stretching her nerves taut.

"Was there something on our agenda I missed?" She gave him a fleeting smile, sure his easy-going demeanor would return if she offered him an outlet. Though she hadn't felt like talking, his responsive silence during the short drive had made her growing unease almost intolerable. She appreciated the reprieve, but hated to think she had triggered his stony calm.

Certain he had intended to kiss her moments before, his sudden withdrawal and the grim press of his lips had alerted her to his determination to maintain a professional distance. Had he known how much she'd wanted him to kiss her, that the thought of his mouth on hers had dominated her focus, she felt sure both of them would have yielded to the temptation. And that she would have quickly regretted her desire to again taste his passion.

She could not allow herself to consider him anything but a law enforcement officer, lest she open the door to the pain losing him made nearly unbearable.

"I have to check Charlie Goodson's trotline." He gave her a somber look. "He broke his ankle this afternoon, soon after baiting the line. I told him I'd run it tonight and give him time to find someone else to take care of it tomorrow."

"I haven't baited a trotline in years," Kylie commented, more to herself than to him, amused to think the chore appealed.

"It shouldn't take more than a half hour or so." His expression neutral, he shrugged and said, "I'll take you home first, or you can stay up here if you don't mind the wait."

"Not on your life." Kylie opened the door and slid out, smiling as the dome light reflected his surprise. "I'm not going to pass up the chance to watch you take a midnight swim…boots and all."

Tyler grinned, obviously not offended by her reminder of the time they'd run his father's trotline. He had been standing in the bow of Amos's bass boat, attempting to fish a minnow out of the Styrofoam bait bucket, when a wave caused the small craft to bob, knocking him off-balance. Arms waving, he'd toppled over the side, into the cold dark water. Unable to help due to her uncontrolled laughter, Kylie had teased him long after his ungraceful tumble ruined his new boots and dented his reputation as a skilled fisherman.

"You would remember that," he stated, a seemingly forced lightness making his remark sound somewhat condemning.

Irritated by his unpredictable moodiness, Kylie spun around, scanned the clearing with a critical eye. Except for the concrete picnic table and brick barbeque pit, the level grassy plane looked exactly like the secluded hideaway she and Tyler once considered 'their place'. She stiffened at the thought, unwilling to believe he would be so cruel as to taunt her by taking her *there*.

Heart pounding, she stared at the stately oaks shading the neatly mowed grass, toward the graveled lane leading into the sheltered area. Certain this was, indeed, the special place where they spent so many nights together, she squared her shoulders, slid a covert glance in Tyler's direction. Busy slipping his hat into the overhead carrier designed to protect it, nothing about his countenance indicated he had anything but fishing on his mind.

"Are you about ready?" Kylie asked, resolved to act as unaffected by their location as he seemed to be. And equally determined to not demand an explanation as to why Charlie Goodson had chosen this particular spot to fish.

Tyler cast her an odd look, one of equal parts curiosity and irritation. "Do you have a curfew?"

"Just a deadline." She pivoted, clutching at her skirt as she headed toward the lone path leading toward the lake. Tears stung her eyes, no doubt due to the brisk breeze lifting her hem. She refused to even think Tyler's failure to mention their destination had anything to do with her foul temperament. That he hadn't apologized—or at least acknowledged by word or action the significance of this place—did not merit the wail of agony swelling inside her.

"Watch your step!" he called after her.

"I intend to," she snapped, "believe me, I intend to."

* * *

Moments after locking the Jeep, they were speeding over the moonlit waves aboard Charlie's new pontoon boat, an amicable silence keeping them both still and watchful. A blanket of stars and a full, silver moon lighting their way, they searched for the plastic milk jugs with which Goodson and other fishermen commonly marked their lines.

"There it is!" Kylie pointed toward the first of a dozen bobbing floats.

"Good job." Tyler's even white teeth gleamed in the moonlight. "I'll recommend you to Charlie."

"I don't think I'm ready to give up my day job." Laughing, she added, "besides, if memory serves me correctly, this chore gets messy and smelly about now."

Chuckling, Tyler slowed the craft, slipping the gear into neutral as they neared the jug she had indicated. He dropped the anchor over the low rail and stepped out from behind the wheel, his fluid motions as smooth as the sweet strains of the fiddle coming from the stereo speakers. Instantly recognizable, the country music standard made Kylie feel both comforted and melancholy. An occasional fan of the Nashville sound, she had not listened to the popular genre much since leaving Tahlequah.

Doing so reminded her too much of Tyler, of the warm, summer nights they'd listened to it while talking of the many things they wanted for their future. Hearing it now brought to mind another evening that had begun similar to this, with dinner and a short drive to the isolated lakeside clearing they considered their own private paradise. Unlike those before, country music played a small part in that idyllic evening.

They had spent nearly no time at Kylie's senior prom before dashing to his car, eager to make the occasion more memorable than the chaperons would allow in public. Soon after arriving at their destination, Tyler ejected his favorite country music tape, and then escorted her to the handmade quilt spread out and awaiting their arrival. Surprised to see a picnic basket and ice chest placed next to the colorful quilt, she laughed in delight. Smiling in response, he quickly banked a red-orange blaze atop the fire he'd built in the center of the clearing.

Thrilled by his romantic preparation, Kylie slipped off her high-heeled pumps and stepped onto the patchwork pattern. Pulling the lacey shawl she'd worn over her satin sheath more snugly around her bare shoulders, she said, "Dare I ask what you're up to?"

"Nope," he'd replied, bussing the tip of her nose with his warm lips before returning to the car.

Amused by his determination to keep her in suspense, she watched him forage in the trunk, retrieve a small duffel bag, and then jog around to the driver's side. He fiddled with the stereo, and the soft, poignant notes of a flute and the rhythmic beat of drums accompanied by the chants of a Native American song filled the night air. Touched by the primal lure of the ancient tune, Kylie sank to her knees, entranced both by Tyler's forethought and the mysterious task keeping him on the opposite side of the car so long. He emerged from his shadowy concealment and her breath hitched, arrested by the sight of him.

Clad in a breechclout, bold red, blue and white paint artfully streaking his broad chest, accentuating his high cheekbones and the straight slope of his nose, he met her gaze and her heart fluttered. Wide-eyed, she watched him move toward her, his lean, nearly naked body so beautiful, thoughts of anything other than the physical perfection revealed to her were impossible. Barefoot and bronze, he paused before her, searching her expression with an intensity that made him appear much older than his twenty-two years.

"My ancestors marked achievements with grand celebrations. Successful raids, times of peace, marriages and births, were merry occasions, a reason to thank the Great One for all He provided." He knelt beside her and cupped her cheek in his palm, his touch so tender tears misted her eyes. His expression somber, he said, "They danced to show their appreciation. As my forefathers did, I hope to show you how precious you are, how much I treasure all you have given me."

That said, he stood, strode toward the fire burning as brightly as the love filling Kylie's heart. Tears blurring her vision, she leaned forward, awed by the emotion making her tremble as she watched him approach the blaze. Hands uplifted, he circled the flames, arching his body as he embraced the four corners of the earth. Homage paid, he began to sway, moving with an unconsciously provocative rhythm that made her own body thrum with excitement. Pausing only long enough to pick up the feathered lance he'd placed next to the fire, he raised the spear and began to sing, softly at first and then with a growing determination. He shifted his weight from one foot to the other as the intensity of the dance claimed him, his athletic grace making each step appear effortless, timeless.

Spellbound, both by the formal honor of his dance and the immeasurable gift of this age-old ritual, she swallowed hard, blinked away the moisture obscuring her vision. No one had ever made her feel so special. So cherished. Her heart lodged in her throat, hampering her ability to breathe. Tears streamed down her cheeks, dappling her blue satin gown. Joy bubbled inside her, igniting a love as powerful and all consuming as Tyler's solitary dance.

Minutes or hours later, Kylie could not have said which, the tempo of the chant increased, as did the agile bounce and erotic sway of Tyler's sweat-glistened body. He raised the lance one final time, arched his lean torso as the loud beat of the drums drowned out the flute. As the haunting melody faded into the night, he straightened slowly, holding her gaze from across the dimming fire. His expression steady, intense, he skirted the blaze, moving closer to her with each deliberate step.

"I love you, Kylie Bennett," he stopped near the edge of the quilt, shoulders squared, "too much to hand you a trinket and expect you to treasure it as a reminder of all I wish for you." He gave her a lopsided grin that made her heart swell. "Despite the scholarship, college expenses often demand more money than I can scrape together.

"I hope you aren't disappointed." He tossed the lance aside and eased down in front of her, his blue eyes as bright as the embers glowing behind him. He looked away and quietly said, "I couldn't think of anything else to give you…at least nothing I could afford that would show you how much I care."

Kylie bracketed his shoulders with her two hands, gently gripping his sweat-slick flesh and the firm muscles that had so fascinated her. "You never disappoint me, Tyler. I'm the one who doesn't—"

He pressed his finger against her lips, halting the apology she intended to offer him. As though intent on avoiding the argument she knew he'd memorized by now, he said, "It doesn't matter, Kylie. Tonight isn't the time to disagree. I want you to look back on this evening with no regrets."

"There will be no regrets." She shrugged free of the confining shawl and eased forward, rising to her knees before him. "I want this night to be a true beginning, Tyler. All the delays and arguments over whether or not we should do it are behind us. Tonight is—"

"Kylie—"

"Hush, love!" Her smile as seductive as the desire making her bold, she entreated, "Make love to me, Tyler. Show me why you danced for me."

"You don't have to do this." He leaned back, searching her lash-veiled gaze with his heated one. "I danced to honor you, not to tempt you to –"

Empowered by her need to get closer, she raised her mouth to his, silencing his whispered protest and the small voice inside her warning her to beware. Greedy for his kiss and reckless because of it, she embraced her growing need, tempting each of them beyond the limits of their youthful endurance. She moaned when his arms slid around her waist; smiled as his nimble fingers found the top of the zipper and eased it down. The thin straps glided along her upper arms, pushed aside in his growing haste. She gasped as the cool spring air bathed her exposed breasts, caressing them with the same loving attention with which Tyler now viewed her feminine form.

"Is this what you want, Kylie?" Tyler asked in a low, gruff voice. He eased back, gently braced her face with his trembling hands. "Are you sure?"

"More sure than I've ever been." She kissed him softly, then with a growing passion that demanded ease. Her smile filled with the knowledge of a woman eager to claim all her new station in life promised, she pulled away, pushed her satin dress into an untidy pool at her waist. "Absolutely positive."

Needing no further prompting, Tyler made quick work of removing her wrinkled gown, and reached for the thin leather tie at his own waist. Kylie covered his hand with hers, her smile confident as she whispered, "let me…"

"Kylie? Kylie!"

Kylie jerked upright, startled by the sound of her name. She looked up, into the frowning face so close to her own. She swallowed hard, unsure as to whether or not she should risk a response. She felt certain her voice would betray her, that the emotions making her heart pound and her breathing harsh would alert him to her upsetting arousal.

"Are you okay?" Tyler peered at her, his expression an odd mix of irritation and concern. As he had that long ago night, he seemed torn between clinging to the control he'd exercised until then and seizing the unexpected pleasure awaiting him—and not quite sure either was a sound option. "You look like you've seen a ghost."

"Nothing quite so dramatic," she managed, her cheeks warm despite the chilly night air tossing her hair into disarray. She glanced toward the distant shore, then pulled her gaze back to his. "I was just daydreaming."

"Do you think you can postpone another excursion until we're finished here?" Scowling he indicated with a wave of his hand the string of milk jugs bobbing atop the moon-brightened water. "I could use a little help."

"What do you want me to do?" She stood, gingerly stepped around him as she made her way to the rail. Calmer now, she said, "how many hooks have you baited?"

"About half of them." He joined her at the open gate, head tilted as his narrow gaze searched her too-wide one. "Are you sure you're okay?"

"Absolutely." She gave him a reassuring smile. "What can I do to help?"

"Move the boat ahead, but not too fast. The wind is kicking up a little, and I'm afraid the line will tangle around the propeller if I'm not careful."

Kylie moved behind the wheel, squinting as she stared at the dim lights of the control panel. Tyler reached around her, brushing her breast with his forearm as he pointed toward the lever to her right. She sucked in a sharp breath and closed her eyes, praying he would step away before she yielded to the temptation urging her to turn into his embrace.

"Pull that gear down and you'll engage the trolling motor," he said next to her ear. So close she could feel his warm breath fanning her temple, his low tone gave no indication he intended to do anything but help her guide the boat. "Steer straight ahead a few feet, then disengage the throttle."

Teeth clenched, she pulled the gear into the first slot, hoping the speed would not cause the boat to rush forward—and that she would quickly regain control of her ragged nerves. Pleased when the pontoon moved slowly toward the bobbing line, she gave him a somewhat arrogant thumbs-up.

"Piece of cake, Wolfe."

Shaking his head, Tyler hastened to the open gate. Crouched next to the narrow space, he tugged the line closer and quickly completed his promised chore. The many hooks baited, he again joined Kylie at the helm.

"Would you like to drive back to the cove?" he asked, wind whipping his raven hair. He looked like a pirate with his shirt open at the neck and moonlight bathing his dark features in a silvery glow—wildly sexy with a hint of savage appeal that rocked her senses.

"I don't think so." She moved away from the wheel. "No."

He cocked his head at an inquisitive angle, but remained silent as he stepped behind the controls. Kylie made her way to the padded bench, her mood somber as they sped across the water and quickly to the narrow lagoon where Charlie docked his boat. Tyler soon had the anchor in place and the boat secure. He helped her climb onto the weathered dock and joined her there, hands in his pockets as they followed the rocky path to the parking area.

The strange, overpowering sense of familiarity again assaulted Kylie as she neared the Jeep, Tyler at her side. Shaken, she paused to look around, remembering another time, another night, when the circular clearing did not look like any of the countless other public campsites around the lake.

"It's changed a bit." Tyler unlocked her door, met her startled gaze with his mildly disappointed one as she turned to climb in. "The table and fire pit were built about ten years ago…the litter barrels added last summer, courtesy of our newly elected congressman."

"It seems familiar," she commented more to herself than to him, hoping he would not elaborate and force her to admit she'd recognized their hideaway. Anxious to be gone, she stepped into the Jeep.

"I should hope so." His smile too sad to be described as anything but melancholy, Tyler curled his finger beneath her chin and tipped her head up. Searching her gaze as though waiting for her to suddenly say or recall something of great importance, he said, "Most women tend to consider the time and location where they lost their virginity as somewhat of a sacred place."

Kylie inhaled sharply, aware her shock was evident. That he'd known, and said nothing, defied reason—and made her feel guilty for pretending she hadn't recognized it. She closed her gaping mouth, unable to think of anything to say. Silent as a sinner during alter call, she watched Tyler withdraw, his expression unreadable as he closed her door and hastened to his side of the vehicle. Once behind the wheel, he slid the key into place and started the engine, then just as quickly shut it off. Hands gripping the wheel, he turned to face her.

"You have no reason to be embarrassed, Kylie. What happened that night could have occurred any of a hundred other nights." He shook his head, held her wide-eyed gaze with his narrow blue one. "Fact is, it's no small wonder we didn't make love much sooner. We were destined."

"I'm not ashamed of what happened!" she said, more harshly than she intended. "I wouldn't change a thing about that night!"

"Nothing?"

"Not a thing." Kylie stared through the windshield, her chin as firm as her resolve to keep the events of that night in a proper perspective. She hadn't *lost* her innocence. She'd freely shared it with the man she loved! That he didn't love her as well no longer mattered. She had long ago accepted the fact she would have altered nothing—not one tender kiss or gentle touch!—to reclaim that precious price no man but Tyler could have made so sweet. So special.

"I'm glad at least one of us feels that way." He again started the engine, his profile as stony as the cliffs rising toward the trees across the cove.

"What would you change about it?" Kylie asked, her heart knotted so tightly it felt as though it were clenched in the taut grip of his fingers curled around the wheel.

"I'd make damn sure it marked the beginning rather than the end." He snapped his head around, piercing her with a look so hostile her skin prickled with gooseflesh. "I'd have it be the first of thousands, not the last of the many good times we shared. And I would much rather it have occurred after I'd put a ring on your finger and had at least a half measure of certainty you'd remain a part of my life."

"I didn't do anything to discourage you, Tyler." She swallowed hard, blinked back the mist of emotion stinging her eyes. "You controlled our destiny, yours and mine."

"No," he shook his head, "Fate and youthful stupidity had a hand in it…as did the deceitful nature of a—"

"I never deceived you!"

"I didn't mean…" He slumped as though defeated, shook his head. "You did nothing wrong. I did. If only I'd known—"

"Known what?" she said, her tone accusing. "That I wouldn't wait around for whatever time you could spare after pleasing your new wife?"

"That isn't—"

"Isn't it?" she finished for him, glaring as he slammed his fist atop the wheel. "How do you think I felt when you called to tell me you had just gotten married? Happy? Elated to think you were so proud of your accomplishment you couldn't wait to share the good news?"

"That isn't the reason I called you!"

"You know, that's one thing that has remained a mystery to me," she stated snidely. "Why did you call me?"

"I wanted to be the one to tell you…I needed to explain," he admitted, "I wanted you to understand…to forgive me for what I'd done."

"I did understand." She forced a smile. "Someone else mattered more to you than I did."

"That isn't true. Not entirely."

"Isn't it? No one held a gun to your head, Tyler. No one forced you to hightail it to Arkansas and marry Connie."

"Now there's where you're wrong," he said, his expression fierce, resolute. "One person more important than you or me or Connie mattered a hell of a lot. More than even I could have imagined at the time."

"And that person would be...?"

He clamped his mouth shut, making Kylie wonder if she should have kept her venomous-toned comment to herself. Placing blame or revealing her feelings at this late date would serve no purpose—except to make the drive home seem more like a journey to the moon and back than a few short miles.

Apparently thinking much the same, he backed the Jeep around, scattering gravel as they sped out of the clearing. If his driving was an indication, he couldn't wait to be rid of her once again. Wishing she didn't feel so glum because of it, Kylie rested her head against the plush leather seat, prepared to weather the storm of emotion raging inside her.

"It wasn't intentional," he said some miles later. Looking straight ahead at the highway, he added, "I didn't plan it."

"Baiting Charlie's trotline?" she quipped, purposely misinterpreting his blunt remark, "or my prom night finale?"

His short bark of laughter eased her still antsy nerves. "I planned every small detail to celebrate your prom." He glanced her way. "Almost every detail."

"And tonight?" She held his steady gaze, her cheeks as warm as the midnight blue fire in his eyes.

"Definitely not." He flashed her an uncertain grin that quickly became one of an almost cocky assurance. "I'd much rather it had turned out like the last one."

Seven

The phone calls began shortly after midnight three days later. By the time Kylie answered the one that woke her at three a.m., she'd had more than enough of the childish prankster. More annoyed than scared, she snatched up the receiver, determined to put an end to the caller's fun and games.

"Hello." Scowling as dead air again hummed in her ear, she glanced at the lighted alarm clock dial. "Is anyone there?"

Still prone, she reached to disconnect the call. Her finger was a scant inch from the cradle when she heard the sudden racket coming from the earpiece. The hushed crackle of paper and what sounded like the click of a lighter were clear and distinct, but not nearly as frightening as the sharp rapport of the gunshot that followed.

Her blood stalled in her veins, then surged, filling her with a surreal fear so intense every cell in her body reacted. Shaken, she sat up, gooseflesh prickling her skin. The stilted rasp of her breathing sounded as loud as thunder, so loud the noise seemed to echo throughout the dark bedroom.

The deadly message was unmistakable—and far too intimidating for her to consider it anything but the threat it was intended to be.

Heart pounding, she listened, but could hear nothing more. Trembling, she wet her lips, pressed the phone closer to her mouth. "Who is this? Why are you harassing me?"

No one answered her, not that she expected him to. Revealing his identity or advising a victim of his intent was not something prank callers typically did.

"Hello?" Kylie ground her teeth in irritation, certain the caller was following her lead: listening and awaiting a response. "This isn't amusing! I don't have time for your nonsense!"

Frightened and furious because of it, she slammed the receiver in place, and immediately lifted it. She set it aside, but soon realized that fix would not work. The rapid buzzing beeps followed by the recorded operator's message to hang up and try the call again annoyed her almost as much as her reason for leaving the receiver off the hook.

Frustrated, she pulled the plug from the base unit, putting an end to the irritating noise—and the caller's access. The hall phone downstairs rang an instant later and Kylie cringed, certain she would again hear nothing if she dared to answer the call.

Resolved to end all potential harassment, she yanked on her robe and descended the stairs. Anger spurring her on, she flew through the house like a winged avenger, the hem of her peach silk wrap flapping as she marched from room to room, pulling the plugs from each jangling phone.

Satisfied she would hear no more from the prankster this night, she mounted the stairs, determined to return to bed and sleep despite the trickle of fear her rash act had lessened none at all.

She was halfway up the stairs when the security alarm went off. Gasping, she spun around, gripping the rail for support. Heart pounding, she stared at the dark lower floor, the shadowy alcove and vacant foyer she'd just crossed. Paralyzed by her rising fear, she looked toward the den, peered through the dense foliage of the greenery lining the stairway into the small section of the kitchen visible from her position.

Loud and repetitive, the alarm continued to wail, reminding her she might not be alone, that someone could be lurking below her—or behind her!

Alarmed at the thought, she whirled around, afraid she would discover the source of her terror. Wide-eyed, she searched the upper level within her view. Relieved to see no one above her, she slowly moved up, toward the least likely avenue of entry. She felt certain she would have heard the glass shatter had someone entered through the locked French doors.

Unsure as to how long it would take the monitoring service to respond to the alarm, she continued upstairs, to the room she favored most. No longer the haven it once was, she closed the bedroom door, snapped the lock in place and hastened to the phone. Quickly reconnected, she pressed the programmed button.

"Wolfe," Tyler answered the second ring, his voice groggy from sleep.

"T—Tyler?" she whispered, the single word sounding as shaky as her trembling body felt. "I need you here...Now!"

"Kylie? Kylie, is that you?"

"Yes! Help me, Tyler. Please help me!"

"What's wrong? Where are you? Kylie?" Obviously wide-awake now, his tone was both concerned and authoritative, calming.

"I think someone's in the house. The alarm—"

"Where are you?"

"My bedroom…the door is locked, and—"

"I'll be there in five minutes. Lock yourself in the bathroom as soon as you hang up, and don't budge until you hear me tell you it's safe to come out."

"I won't," Kylie promised, relief eddying through her. "Hurry…please, hurry!"

She dropped the receiver into place and dashed into the master bath, the ear-splitting peel of the alarm urging her to haste. Fingers shaking, she locked the door and backed to the far side of the luxurious space, unable to appreciate the usually comforting atmosphere. Neither the tranquil oriental print wallpaper nor the scented candles soothed her. She doubted anything could ease her jittery nerves. Fearing her home had been invaded made her feel violated, afraid and angry at once.

Grappling with her convoluted emotions, she eased down onto the edge of the oversized ivory tub, fury overcoming her fright as she waited for Tyler.

"I will find out who you are!" she said with conviction. Bolstered by the thought, she searched her memory for a clue, any reason for which someone would want to stalk her—or harm her. Unable to recall anything she'd done to warrant such treatment, or anyone malicious enough to resort to such drastic measures, she heaved a weary sigh.

Someway, somehow, she silently vowed, she would learn who was behind the annoying pranks. "You won't get away with this!"

Determined to discover her tormentor's identity and stop the harassment, Kylie welcomed her growing anger, and the tense calm that made the agonizingly slow minutes spent alone pass less quickly than she would have liked.

Anxious eons after secluding herself, the alarm suddenly stopped. Puzzled by the silence, she stiffened, every sense alert. She heard a stair creak, and a moment later the unmistakable sound of footsteps crossing her bedroom. Her heart lodged in her throat, Kylie stared at the bathroom door, at the levered knob jiggling from the unknown force testing it from the other side. Her breath hitched, stalled in her lungs.

She didn't doubt that Tyler would hasten to her aid, but felt certain not even he could have arrived so soon—or gain entry with so little sound. She shrank back, searched the limited space around her for a weapon with which to defend herself should the lock give way. Frustrated to realize perfumed soap and dusting powder would offer scant protection, she stood, hands fisted at her sides as she watched the door handle rise and fall yet again.

"Kylie?" The hinges rattled, no doubt due to the fist now pounding the door from the opposite side.

"Tyler?" Kylie stepped forward, then halted, her pulse surging as wildly as the relief making her dizzy. Indecision mounted, as did her trepidation. Had she given herself away too soon? Alerted someone other than Tyler to her hiding place?

"Lord, help me!" she whispered, afraid not even He could help her now. Unwilling to face the unknown without a fight, she once again searched the room for something—anything—that would allow her a prayer of a chance to surprise her suspected foe.

She snatched up a can of hairspray and the nail file she kept tucked in a basket atop the shelf. Wielding the aerosol container like a can of mace in one hand, she concealed the file in her other palm and approached the door. "Tyler?"

"You can come out now," Tyler responded, his deep, familiar voice a salve to her rising fear.

No longer hesitant, Kylie set aside her meager weapons and crossed the cool marble tile, unlatched the gold-plated handle. She swung open the door, met Tyler's searching gaze and felt her knees wobble. Shaken, she swayed like a drunkard, trembling as she stepped into his waiting arms.

"It's okay, Kylie. You're safe." Tyler tucked her head beneath his chin, pulled her more snugly into his welcome embrace. "Easy now, honey. Everything's okay."

"Th—the alarm…it…" She leaned back, putting as much space between them as he would allow so she could more clearly see his face. "It went off and I panicked." Scowling, she added, "It was screeching and –"

"Hush, babe." Tyler rocked her gently from side to side, chaffed her silk-draped spine with his warm palms, encouraging her to accept his comfort. "I turned it off when I came in."

"Oh…good." Kylie pressed her forehead against his chest, savored the crisp, clean scent of fresh night air clinging to his denim jacket. She idly fingered the button placket, slid her hand between the layers of fabric, along

71

the soft cotton fabric of his shirt. Soothed by the firm strength of his chest beneath, she caressed the broad muscular plane, wishing she could touch his skin and not the downy cloth restricting her from acting upon her impulse. "I was so scared, so certain—"

"Don't think about it now, Kylie." His voice sounded strained, as uneven as the gentle gusts of his warm breath tickling her ear. "You're safe, and that's all that matters."

"Did you see anyone? Any sign that someone had broken in?" She felt the negative motion of Tyler's chin brush the top of her head. "Nothing?"

"Nothing," he confirmed. "None of the doors were open and all the windows appear untouched. I checked every possible point of entry once I'd searched the house. I saw nothing to indicate –"

"But the alarm!" she protested, "and the phone calls—"

"What calls?" Tyler set her away from him, drilled her with an intense look that would have scared her senseless had she been the source of his upset. "Did someone threaten you?" he asked softly, the simple question far more daunting due to his ominously quiet tone.

Kylie shook her head. "He didn't say a word. He didn't have to. The gun shot—"

"Whoa, there." Scowling, Tyler clasped her shoulders in a firm grip, and guided her to the foot of the bed rumpled from her futile attempt to sleep. He urged her down with a gentle nudge, and then joined her atop the plump sage comforter. "Back up a bit, and tell me everything that happened."

"I turned in early…around eleven or so, and read for short time. I hadn't been asleep long when the first call jarred me awake a few minutes after twelve." She met his steady gaze, aware he must surely see the fear in her own eyes as she recalled the irritation and initial terror with which she'd reacted to that and each successive call. "He didn't say anything, just held the connection long enough for me to know he was there.

"The last call was the same, nothing but dead air until…until…" She swallowed hard, quickly recounted the noises she'd heard, including that of a gun fired close to the phone.

"Are you sure?" His expression a sobering mix of fury and a somber determination, he asked, "Are you positive it was a gunshot?"

"I was raised in Oklahoma and my stepfather enjoyed hunting, Tyler. I know what a gun sounds like." She looked away, closed her eyes as a shiver raced along her backbone. "It sounded more like a rifle than a pistol, too loud for it to have been a handgun."

"Come here." Tyler lifted her onto his lap, cradling her as though she were a frightened child. "You're trembling."

Kylie was shaken, but not because of the annoying calls, the frightening gunshot nor the resounding alarm that had forced her to summon help. With Tyler's arms around her, his warm palms and strong fingers skimming the length of her spine, she had something other than a stalker to fear: her reaction to the man making her feel anything but childish.

Aware her apprehension stemmed from the doubts any woman about to make her wishes known might suffer, she snuggled closer. She needed to be held.

"We'll take care of the prankster tomorrow. I'm sure the phone company will install a trace, considering all that's happened in the last few weeks."

"They should," she said with little enthusiasm. Sitting on his lap made thinking difficult. The firm press of his thighs beneath her scantily clad bottom seemed far more important than idle chatter.

"I'll call first thing and get the ball rolling." He shifted slightly, settling her weight more evenly as he hugged her close. "I promise we'll put a stop to this nonsense."

Though she hated to admit it, Kylie wanted *this* nonsense to continue forever. So thinking, she burrowed her nose beneath the sheepskin collar of his coat. She inhaled deeply, breathing in the subtle, spicy scent of his cologne lingering in the fabric, the crisp, clean freshness of the soap he'd recently used on his skin.

"You always smell so good." She raised her head slightly, brushed her cheek along the warm column of his throat as she drew another breath rife with the unique masculine fragrance that smelled of no man but Tyler. He swallowed hard, and she smiled. Empowered by her ability to move him, she asked, "Have I embarrassed you?"

"No." He chuckled, filling the room with a deep, rich sound as heady as the scents making her feel wanton, reckless. "Just surprised me."

"How so?" Half dazed, Kylie moved her mouth along the path her cheek had abandoned. His skin felt incredibly warm beneath her questing lips. Touching the supple flesh at his nape, where her hands now lingered, made her fingertips sizzle.

"I didn't expect you to, that is I didn't—" Tyler drew a shaky breath, acting as though her fingers tangled in his hair were hindering his ability to breathe. "Do you know what you're doing, Kylie? Is this what you want?"

"Uh-huh," she whispered, more certain than she'd ever been as to what she wanted. What she needed. "Kiss me, Tyler."

"Are you sure?"

"Positive," she replied, her voice a mere purr that somehow confirmed the absolute certainty humming through her.

"You've just had a scare. You're probably reacting to—"

"I'm not afraid now, Tyler." Kylie leaned back, peered up at him through the veil of her lashes. "Kiss me…please…"

Tyler gave her a look that made her toes curl—one of total pleasure tempered by an endearing hesitancy that told her he, too, wanted this time together. And that his fondest wish was to surpass her wildest dreams.

His smile tender, he lowered his head, brushed her lips with his. Feather light, he kissed her once, twice, so softly Kylie thought she might die if he didn't kiss her the way she wanted him to: as though his life depended upon her kiss, her passion for him.

As if privy to her thoughts, he deepened the kiss, granting her no time to think of anything but his mouth—his wild, wonderful mouth making sweet love to hers!

Tyler's hat fell onto the bed, toppled to the floor and landed with a gentle thud. He kicked out of his boots, sent them to the hardwood with slightly more force. Dizzy from the taste of her passion, he flipped Kylie onto her back, covering her slim body with his. Veiled by sheer, peach silk, her pliant curves fit the rigid planes of his own, so perfectly he felt as though she was a part of him. A precious piece of his life misplaced and suddenly, miraculously found.

Awed by the thought, he braced his weight on his elbows, stared down at her, his chest so tight he could scarcely breathe. Her lovely features were drawn by the same sizzling need tightening his muscles. Her lashes lowered, her porcelain skin flushed to a soft pink hue, she'd never looked more beautiful, more appealing.

He'd dreamed of this moment so long, wanted to be with her like this so many times.

"Kylie—"

"Don't talk," she implored, reaching to pull him down. "Don't talk!"

"I don't want any regrets…any—"

"There will be no regrets." She wound her arms around his neck, gently urged him down. Her sultry smile that of a seductress, a woman sure of herself, she said, "I want you, Tyler. I need you. Only you."

Both humbled and pleased by the need making her green eyes blaze, Tyler heeded her plea. They could talk later. Much, much later.

Hot and sweet, Tyler kissed her as though there would be no tomorrow, granting her every wish before her desire-fogged brain had time to form the request. Kylie responded with an eagerness she'd never before experienced, touching the love of her life as she'd fanaticized so often.

Clothes were discarded in a heartbeat, skin bared by a haste that increased the urgency lending their fingers a nimble dexterity neither of them would have imagined possible.

Their eager hands stroked and fondled, renewing the need that had made their first time together so sweet, so special. Lips and teeth and tongues became welcome weapons of sensual warfare, gentle tools that allowed them to learn the feel, the texture, the taste of passion.

Tyler trailed warm kisses along her collarbone, making her gasp with each soft touch. Kylie dragged her hands down his spine, cupped the firm, rounded globes of his buttocks in her palms, making him groan.

He explored the valley between her breasts with his lips, searing a hot path to the first of the twin peaks made rigid by his attention. He circled the dark nub with the tip of his tongue, and she moaned. His mouth closed over her tender flesh greedy for his touch and she arched her back, silently urging him to continue the blissful torture.

She discovered the velvety strength of his manhood, wrapped her fingers around the proof of his desire. Tyler threw his head back, approving her touch with a pleased, guttural sound that encouraged her to continue touching him, teasing him as he'd so lovingly enticed her.

"Enough!" His smile both tender and feral, Tyler clasped her hands and raised them above her head. Holding her gaze with the midnight blue fire blazing in his, he trailed his fingers along the inside of her arm, to her cheeks he cupped with the fierce yet gentle force of his palms. "You're killing me, babe." He followed his hoarse admission with a gentle but insistent move, a subtle shift of his hips that brought his body closer to hers.

His features taut, he reached for the foil packet he'd placed nearby, ripped it open. Sheathed to protect them both, he eased forward, fitting his body to hers, inside hers. Kylie moaned, raised her hips. Succumbing to the blissful need vibrating within her, she wrapped her arms around him, drew him closer with the slight pressure of her knees against his thighs.

"I never...knew...didn't think—" she gasped, "Tyler!"

He stole the sound of his name from her lips with a kiss, robbed her of all thought with the steady, rocking rhythm of his desire. Near the brink of ecstasy, Kylie matched his every move, keeping pace with the need rising inside her. Limbs entwined, shared breaths carrying unspoken words from one heart to the other, satisfaction claimed them in the same instant. Tyler acknowledged his contentment with a groan. Kylie welcomed her own with a scream.

Like the lingering sweetness of a moment captured forever in a memory, the pleasure slowly faded. Her breathing near normal, Kylie laid her head on Tyler's chest, draped her arm across his damp flat waist. He pulled her closer, stroked her bare hip as though his need to touch her remained unfulfilled.

Sated and elated, she snuggled deeper into his embrace. "Thank you."

Tyler stiffened. "For what?"

"For...everything," she replied, only mildly perplexed by his reaction. "For proving that life goes on...in the most delightful way, if I do say so myself."

"My pleasure," he said with a chuckle, "and yours if that primal scream was an indication as to how—"

"It was." Kylie lowered her chin, concealing the warmth she knew would be a visible blush on her cheeks. Why she felt suddenly shy, she couldn't comprehend. Considering the volume of said scream...

His hand resumed its idle play, coasting along the curve of her waist to the underside of her breast, back down to the slope of her hip. He continued, seemingly unaware of the effect his caress had on her. Unable to think of anything else but his hand warming her skin, Kylie mustered her thoughts, searching for the words she wanted to say, needed to say.

"Do you have to go home tonight?"

"Do you want me to?" he asked, his hand once again still.

"No," she responded, "unless, of course, you need to. If you do—"

"I don't." Tyler toyed with a strand of her hair, wrapped it around his finger and then released it with a deliberate slowness she found as distracting as his touch. "We need to talk."

"About...this?" Kylie waved her hand over the rumpled linens, not quite sure she wanted to discuss the last hour or so. She wanted to treasure their time together, not discuss the pros and cons of what they'd just experienced—what she'd enjoyed so much.

"Only if you need to talk about it."

"I don't," she said stiffly, miffed to think he'd make light of her half-hearted suggestion. That she didn't care to debate the merits of their intimacies accounted for a small portion of her mental pout. "If not *that*, then what?"

"The calls. Your suspicions. All you believe has happened these past few weeks."

"Such as?"

"Who could be responsible. Why you've been singled out. What—"

"You wouldn't be here if I knew who was responsible," she stated, a bitter edge to her tone. "If I knew who was behind this…this madness, I'd have had him—or her—arrested long before now!"

"Is that so?" he asked quietly. Like the quiet before a storm, she sensed the tempest brewing—a squall brought on by her insensitive remark.

"I didn't mean…that is I didn't intend to…" She levered herself up, glared down at him. "I wouldn't have had to call you if I knew who was harassing me!"

"Are you glad you did?" His smile revealed a wealth of masculine pride, a hint of the pleasure to be had if she admitted such.

Keeping her own smile hidden, she once again lay down beside him. "I'd say yes, but that ego of yours seems big enough already and—Owe!" She rubbed her hand over the flesh of her hip tingling from his slightly ungentle pat. "Brute."

"Back to the topic that landed me here." He held her close when she would have scooted away to show her annoyance. "Tell me everything that happened, from the beginning."

Irritated by his insistence and her own hesitation to discuss the latest incident, Kylie tersely repeated all she'd told him earlier. "That's it in a nutshell," she concluded. "Satisfied?"

"Very." His smile once again bordering cocky, he added, "Completely."

"Good," she said with mock sourness. "Now that we've retired that *topic*, is there anything else you'd like to talk about?"

"Your alarm." ·

"What about it?"

"It's motion sensitive."

"Meaning?

"You might have set it off yourself."

"But the calls, the—"

"I didn't say you did, merely that you could have." He gently tapped the upturned tip of her nose, trailed his finger down the stubborn line of her jaw. "The security patrol arrived when I was outside checking the doors and windows. The guard said the sensor midway up the stairs triggered the alarm. My guess is that the plants along the stairway were stirred by your movement, or possibly set in motion by the air from the overhead vent."

"What if that isn't what set the alarm off? What if I didn't trigger it?"

"Then we're back to square one, both of us afraid someone is up to no good but still unable to prove it." He shrugged his broad shoulders, causing a delightful rippling sensation in her upper body where it lay nestled so close to his. "I'm stumped as to what we should do now. Set a trap and hope he's foolish enough to expose himself, or keep a low profile and prepare to pounce when he screws up. And he will, eventually, leave a clue as to who he is."

"How did you turn the alarm off?" She pushed back again, frowning as she held his steady blue gaze. "And how did you get in?"

"I used the same code you'd enter to shut if off," he replied with another shrug, "and I used the key Joe Oliver gave me before he and Tandy left for Arizona."

Kylie narrowed her eyes, not quite sure she appreciated Tyler having such easy access to her home—no matter that she had asked him to come to her aid *and* welcomed him into her bed.

"That's good to know." She tilted her head, gave him a sour look. "You could have told me you had a key."

"So you could demand that I turn it over?" Tyler flashed a smug grin. "Mama didn't raise no fool."

"I couldn't agree more," she snapped, only half joking. "She raised an arrogant ass who—"

His soft, slow kiss put an end to her tirade. And made her wish she had falsely accused him much sooner.

Eight

Smiling, Kylie stretched like a lazy, sun-warmed cat. She rolled toward the middle of the queen-sized bed, expecting to find the source of her good mood lying next to her. Rumpled sheets and a pillow dented from where Tyler's head had rested only a small portion of the night were all that remained of him.

It didn't require the IQ of a rocket scientist to determine his whereabouts. The smell of coffee and bacon that filled the air, and the occasional clang of pans coming from the kitchen, could mean only one thing: Tyler had found her meager store of breakfast supplies.

She wished he'd stayed in bed with her and, perhaps, resumed where they'd left off sometime near dawn. Cursing her warm cheeks, Kylie realized she was also glad he hadn't. She probably looked a fright. And, truth be told, she needed a few minutes of solitude to make herself presentable.

Too happy to consider his exodus impolite, she climbed out of bed, dashed into the bathroom for a quick check of her appearance. She peered at her reflection in the mirror, only slightly surprised to see little evidence of the damage she'd expected. Her eyes looked bright and clear, her lips only slightly swollen from Tyler's many, wonderful kisses. Bright patches of pink bloomed on her cheeks, a visual reminder of the countless times she'd felt them warm up throughout the long, sweet night due to his occasional teasing.

Feeling foolish for acting like a giddy teenager, Kylie tamed her tangles with a few strokes of the brush, and completed a mini-version of her morning routine in record time. Knotting the sash on her white terrycloth robe, she descended the stairs, her stomach rumbling as she neared the kitchen.

* * *

"I'm not sure, Wyatt. Everything about it is puzzling. Kylie has no apparent enemies, and she has no idea who's harassing her." Tyler lowered his head, pinning the cordless phone between his chin and shoulder. He flipped the last slice of bacon, scowling as hot grease popped onto his wrist. "Ow!"

"What's wrong?" Wyatt asked, sounding concerned.

"It's nothing. The bacon popped on me, and—"

"Bacon? You're cooking?" Wyatt's hearty laughter reverberated inside the ear Tyler had pressed to the receiver. "Must have been some night. Do I know her?"

"What do you have for me?" Tyler lifted the perfectly crisp slice of meat onto the platter he'd set next to the range. Now was not the time to reveal where he'd slept or with whom, not even to the brother he seldom kept anything from. His time with Kylie meant too much, and was far too personal a milestone for him to discuss with anyone—even Wyatt.

"So that's the way the wind blows..." Wyatt chuckled knowingly. "Congratulations, Bro."

"For what?"

"Never mind," Wyatt replied, obviously not offended by his brother's blunt tone. "I'm afraid I don't have much. As you guessed, the ashes are from pipe tobacco, a common variety sold at most convenience stores."

"Figures." Tyler set the hot skillet onto a back burner. He'd hoped the minute amount of evidence he'd sent to the lab would prove to be a special blend, more easily traced. "What about the phone records?"

"Nothing registered during the time you asked me to check. The caller is either using some kind of sophisticated blocking system, or no calls were made to Kylie's home."

"She was scared, Wyatt. She wouldn't pretend someone called if no one had."

"I didn't say she did, merely that there's no record of calls any time after midnight. She has caller ID, doesn't she? Have you—"

"I checked it last night. One private and two unavailable calls had registered."

"Then he's obviously blocking the calls. Did you try auto-redial?"

"Of course."

"Don't sound so all-fired put-out. I'm trying to help."

"Sorry." Tyler ran a hand through his hair. "You are helping. It's just so damned frustrating. Knowing someone is pestering Kylie, possibly stalking her, and not being able to find a single clue to identify the bum is driving me nuts."

"I'm sure it is. How does Kylie feel about all this?"

"She's scared. She's furious." Tyler lifted the receiver off his shoulder, held it to his ear. He stared out the window, his mind racing as he watched a squirrel scamper across the yard. "She has no idea who could be behind it."

"Do you think anyone is?"

"What do you mean?"

"She could be imagining it, at least some of what she claims has happened. Her career is stressful. Her divorce wasn't pretty. She's traipsed a rocky road for as long as we've known her. Perhaps she's—"

"Imagining it?" Tyler scowled. "I don't think so. Kylie isn't the type to vandalize her own property. She wouldn't make up the kind of details she's revealed about the times she's heard or seen someone outside…or pretend she's received prank calls."

"Pressure can make the sanest person behave irrationally…even Kylie."

Tyler heaved a weary sigh. "I suppose she could be making more of it than I'd thought. Or possibly be letting her fear take control, so she isn't entirely sure where reality ends."

"Terror would make each episode seem worse than they actually were," Wyatt agreed, "it usually does. You're probably right, though. Kylie really isn't the type to make up something of this magnitude. She's a trained professional. My bet is she'd play down both the scope of each incident and her own fear until she knows what's going on and who is responsible."

"Definitely. That's what has me worried most of all."

Alerted by a slight sound, Tyler turned to find Kylie standing in the doorway. He motioned her forward, but could tell she was in no mood to greet him as he'd hoped she would: with a kiss and her usual sunny smile. She looked as though she wanted to smash something—possibly his face.

"I've got to go," he said to his brother. "I'll call you later."

Tyler set the phone on the counter, his gaze on the stormy green one telegraphing a wealth of unkind thoughts. "Good morning."

"Morning," Kylie replied stiffly, her spine arrow straight. "Sorry if I intruded."

"You didn't interrupt anything." Tyler moved toward her, hoping she would forgive him. The thought of offending her, even unintentionally, made his chest ache. "Wyatt and I were—"

"Discussing my mental state?"

"No." Close enough to reach out and touch her now, he stopped, aware she'd heard too much to accept anything but the truth. "We were debating the possibility some or all of what you've told me was blown out of proportion. That your fear may have—"

"My *fear* is the direct result of what's happened!" She squared her shoulders. "I have more than enough to occupy my time without adding unnecessary worry, Tyler. I have no reason to pretend someone is calling me in the middle of the night! I'd never dial 9-1-1 and falsely report a prowler!"

"I never said you did." Tyler stepped forward, ignoring the stubborn jut of her chin as he neared her. He wanted to hold her, but knew she would not allow him that pleasure. Not yet. "We're baffled, Kylie. With no evidence to support your claims, we're stumped as to what we should do. What you've seen and heard is all we have to go on."

"Don't you think I know that?" Kylie shook her head, waved her hands in a helpless gesture. "Everything about this is insane. I don't treat patients in a clinical setting. That pretty much eliminates the possibility I've counseled someone ill enough to harbor a grudge that would trigger behavior of this nature. The few friends and acquaintances I've run into since moving back seem truly glad I'm living here again. Even if they weren't, no one I know is vicious enough to resort to such tactics."

"Someone obviously is."

Her eyes widened as though she truly hadn't considered the likelihood, then narrowed accusingly. "Unless I'm making it all up. Unless I'm—"

"You aren't." Tyler bracketed her shoulders with his palms, pulled her close despite the resistance holding her rigid. "You're scared. And as clueless as I am, which is more than likely the reason you were so quick to judge my end of a fruitless conversation."

"You think I'm nuts!"

"What I think," he said, "is that we need to put our heads together and come up with a list of people who, for any reason, might want to see you uncomfortable."

"A list?"

"A list." He hugged her tight, rubbed his chin against the tawny silk of her hair. The soft tresses smelled like wildflowers, fresh and sweet. "We'll sort this out, Kylie."

Kylie slid her arms around his waist, leaned into him. Tyler felt his body tighten, respond to her slender curves pressed so trustingly close. Wise enough to realize she needed comfort, he held her tight, and tamped down the physical yearning making his own knees weak.

"Did you believe me last night?" she asked softly.

"I wouldn't have stayed if I hadn't." Tyler eased back, cupped her chin in his palm and raised her head, forcing her to meet his gaze. "I believe you, Kylie."

"I'd hate to think you…" her lip quivered "…that you stayed because you thought I wasn't capable of dealing with this. That I—"

"I stayed because you asked me to." He kissed her once to silence her doubts, and a second time to satisfy the need urging him to kiss her as he wanted to: deeply, thoroughly. "And because I wanted to."

"And the other?" she whispered, a sheen of tears making her eyes a misty emerald.

"The *other*?" Tyler flashed a grin. "What other?"

"You know very well—" Hot pink color bloomed on her cheeks. She threw back her shoulders, shot him a haughty glower. "Tyler Wolfe—"

"The *other* is the real reason I stayed," he stated, albeit insincerely. Protecting her had been his sole motivation, and the source of his own gut-wrenching fear as he drove the short distance to her house.

The thought he'd be spending the night in her bed, making love to her as he'd so often wanted to, hadn't once crossed his mind. At least not until after she stepped into his arms.

Now that he had again tasted her sweetness, he couldn't imagine sleeping anywhere else—or with any woman other than the one whose close proximity had his heart pounding like a jackhammer.

Her cheeks darkened, pleasing him almost as much as the fiery desire blazing in her eyes.

"I didn't make the bed," she said, her smile both shy and seductive. She put her arms around his neck, stepped into his arms. "I thought we might spend a little more time there."

"A little?" Tyler scooped her up, enjoying her mildly protesting scream as he cradled her close, and quickly headed for the stairs. "A week wouldn't be long enough for me."

* * *

Hours later, Kylie stared at the blank sheet of paper lying on the kitchen table between her and Tyler. They had warmed the bacon he'd cooked earlier, devoured the omelet she whipped up, and emptied a second pot of coffee. Despite a valiant effort, they had made no progress on the list of potential suspects he'd insisted they compile before he headed home to feed Chief.

"Everyone," Tyler said for the second time, his tone indicating the same waning patience making her wish they were finished. "Friends, coworkers, everyone you know and have come in contact with the last couple of months."

"No one I know would do this, Tyler." She tossed the ink pen she hadn't used onto the table. "This is a waste of time."

"I have time to waste," he stated, his expression determined. "Start writing."

"Tyler—"

"Everyone."

Kylie snatched up the pen, pulled the paper in front of her. "Fine. I talk to my assistant at least once a day." She scribbled Grace's name on the first line. "She's a middle-aged mother of three who wouldn't harm an annoying fly."

"She'll soon be eliminated if that proves true."

"I speak to my agent at least once a week. He's a workaholic, all business and not an option."

"Put his name down."

"Fine." Kylie jotted Harvey Lawrence's name beneath that of her assistant's. "I doubt he's ever even had a parking ticket. He wouldn't do anything to hurt me or my career."

"We'll see." Frowning, Tyler tapped the growing list with his index finger. "Add the names of individuals and service oriented companies you deal with—your hair stylist, lawn maintenance contact, mechanics, anyone you've employed recently."

"I get my hair cut in Dallas when I'm there on business. I moved in last fall, so I have yet to hire a lawn service, and I haven't needed a mechanic."

"You get the oil changed in your car, don't you?"

"Of course, but—"

"Where?"

Kylie supplied the name and location of the franchise she'd last used for that purpose, and added it to the list when Tyler insisted no one could be ignored at this point.

"Carl's home health nurse calls once a week or so, and I talk to Matt or Liza every few days."

"Your ex and his wife?"

"Yes." Kylie nodded, not quite sure she liked his incredulous tone. She definitely didn't care for what appeared to be angry speculation narrowing his eyes. Her relationship with Matt and Liza was somewhat unorthodox, and an ongoing source of curiosity and occasional gossip. It was, however, no reason for Tyler to act as though speaking to them was a major faux pas.

"Why?"

"We're a team, Tyler. Like it or not, we will share center stage at most of the seminars booked this year."

"Do you like it?"

"Not particularly," she replied honestly. She held his slightly skeptical look, forced a smile. "We get along well enough, but I'd prefer not having to associate with either of them just now if that were an option."

"Why do you?"

"As I said, we're booked together for the next few months. The seminars were scheduled long before Matt and I separated, much as they have been since we began holding the relationship marathons two years ago. Liza was and still is a vital part of those dual sessions."

"How do they feel about it?"

"Fine, I suppose. Neither of them has complained, at least not to me." She chuckled. "Harvey may hear a few disparaging remarks from time to time since he negotiates our contracts, but if that's occurred, he's said nothing to me."

"That has to be an uncomfortable situation." Tyler shook his head, slanted her a curious look. "How do you deal with it?"

"Seeing my ex-husband and my former best friend together?" Kylie shrugged, gave him a grin. "It really doesn't bother me, not like you'd think anyway."

"Not at all?"

"They're better suited than Matt and I ever were." She ignored his dubious tone, held his level gaze. "I'm surprised I didn't realize that long before I did. Both are career-driven, and as motivated by the financial boons of what has become a lucrative profession as they are by our accomplishments."

"Meaning?"

"They enjoy their work, but the celebrity and big bucks appeal, too." She glanced out the window, then once again met his inquisitive gaze. "I can't say I don't appreciate the money, I do. Having grown up without a lot to spare, it's nice to know I can take care of myself and not have to budget every dime I earn. Despite the monetary rewards, I'd prefer a lower profile and more time to devote to counseling."

"Have you thought about opening a private practice?"

"Yes," she answered, "often. In fact, that's probably what I'll do once I complete the schedule currently booked. Harvey has assured me he'll continue to represent me if I opt to continue my column and lower the number of seminars…or forego them entirely."

"How do Matt and Liza feel about that?" Tyler gave her an odd look. "They can't be too happy, considering you're part of the team keeping them in high cotton."

"Matt is behind me, totally. He knows I don't always enjoy the limelight."

"And Liza?"

"If she isn't okay with my plans, I'm not aware of it." Kylie reached for her coffee cup, took a sip of the lukewarm brew. "We haven't really talked about it. There usually isn't time. Between the hectic pace and back-to-back sessions held at each location, we barely manage a few minutes to catch up on the other things going on in our lives when we do have a chance to talk."

"Do you really want to know what's going on in her life?"

"Sometimes." Kylie laughed at his wide-eyed incredulity. "For years Liza was my best friend, Tyler. She's a gifted psychiatrist. I respect her skill despite our personal differences. She adds a lot to the seminars, a sound perspective neither I nor Matt can dispute."

"She's also married to your ex."

"She's married to a man I never should have wed, Tyler." Kylie shifted in her seat, feeling oddly uncomfortable due to her admission. She searched for the words to relay her thoughts, the realization that had come after many sleepless nights some months ago. "Matt and I were destined to be friends, not a couple. We had a lot in common, and shared goals that made our union seem natural, sound. Marriage seemed the perfect solution to the long hours we spent together, working to write and proof our books.

"I think both of us knew, soon after we eloped, that marriage didn't enhance our relationship as we'd expected it to. We were, and still are, good friends, which is probably why we've been able to continue working together without the animosity one would expect."

"And Liza?"

"She always adored Matt, but never once, by word or action, indicated she felt more than a friend's respect and kinship for my husband." Kylie looked away, not quite sure why she felt compelled to reveal the shortcomings that led to her divorce. And equally certain Tyler would understand why she held no grudges. "Matt and I shared a house and little else for the last several months we were together. Though neither of us had broached the subject, both of us knew our marriage was over. I'm sure most would consider what happened between them unforgivable. I believe it was inevitable."

Tyler expelled a long, slow gust of air. "That's big of you."

"Admitting I made mistakes?"

"That, and remaining friends."

"Our friendship ultimately made it easier."

"How so?"

"I knew that neither of them intended to hurt me, and that what occurred was both natural and the end result of my absence and waning commitment. They were together a lot—more than Matt and I were in those last few months—planning the upcoming sessions while I was touring solo to promote my column. Liza was willing and able to meet his needs, emotional and physical. She was also eager to be the kind of wife I wasn't. I can't fault either of them for that."

"But the publicity, the—"

"I definitely could have done without the scandal," Kylie confessed with a chuckle. "I'm not entirely sure I've forgiven either of them for making a public spectacle of their affair and my life, however inadvertently."

"I'm not sure I could." Tyler shook his head, looking as though her logic escaped reason. "God knows Connie and I had our troubles, but I don't think I would have been generous enough to accept her relationship with another man so well."

"Generosity has nothing to do with how I feel."

"If you don't mind my asking, what does?"

"Acceptance. Hope." She gave him a bright smile. "Matt and I failed. I don't want them to suffer the same fate."

"Still…" Tyler's voice trailed off, granting her a moment to consider what he had just admitted. He obviously loved Connie, enough to acknowledge doubts as to whether or not he would have been able to deal with her loving anyone other than him.

Kylie couldn't help but feel cheated, and more than a little jealous of his deceased wife. She wondered if he would have felt the same about her if they had married, if he would have harbored the same devotion to her, even after death, as he did for Connie.

Feeling foolish for envying his late wife, she forced a smile and said, "Are we finished?"

Tyler shook his head. "Add Matt and Liza to the list."

"What?" Kylie stiffened. "They wouldn't do anything to harm me!"

"We'll soon know, won't we?"

"What do you mean?"

"Everyone on that list—" he tapped the sheet of paper "will be checked out. If they're innocent of any wrongdoing, we'll soon know."

"Tyler—"

"Add their names." He held her narrow look with one of stubborn determination. "Or I will."

"Fine." Kylie put both Matt and Liza's name on the paper, then shoved it toward Tyler. "This is a waste of time."

"Maybe." He flashed a sexy grin that warmed her far more than the irritation making her temper sizzle. "If it is, we'll just have to put our heads together again, real soon, and come up with another list."

He stood, smiling as he transferred his Stetson from the chair where it had been to his dark head. He gave her a kiss that curled her toes, then winked and said, "Real soon."

Her cheeks burning, Kylie watched him go, too pleased to chastise him for voicing her fondest wish: that she would enjoy his company—his kisses—again. And also confident he would quickly realize she had been right, that none of the people on the short list he'd tucked into his shirt pocket would be a suspect once he'd completed a little background search.

Had she not cared for all of those mentioned, she might have hoped one would prove worthy of a thorough investigation. She truly wanted the individual responsible for harassing her caught.

More importantly just now, she wanted to spend time with Tyler—many hours during which they would not have to discuss suspects.

Nine

Kylie paid for the gas she'd just pumped and hastened to her rental car. Safe inside the vehicle, she surveyed the convenience store parking lot, not quite sure why she'd felt like a germ under a microscope the entire time she'd been filling the tank. No one was nearby, and she could see nothing untoward about those few customers attending to the same necessary chore for which she'd stopped.

Anxious to be home, she shook off the uneasy feeling adding to her weariness. Once on the highway leading out of town, she glanced in the rearview mirror, and immediately felt much calmer. The police cruiser following her maintained a comfortable distance, yet allowed her to know that whatever—or whomever—had triggered the antsy tingle up and down her spine would do her no harm.

Kylie pulled into her drive a short time later, eager to call the rental agency and rid herself of the uncomfortable compact. She hoped her own car battery had been replaced, as the local mechanic had promised it would be. She hated car trouble, and the inconvenience of having to depend upon others.

If she hadn't been pressed for time, and frustrated to learn there were no other flights available, she would have rescheduled her departure and delayed her arrival in Dallas long enough to have her car repaired. Having done so would have eliminated the hassle of returning the rental, and—

"Shrug it off!" she chastened irritably. Scowling, she parked the car and headed toward the house. She'd had no other option. The North Texas seminar had been fully booked, her timely attendance mandatory.

Except for one uncomfortable tête-à-tête with Liza, Kylie had enjoyed the chaotic atmosphere. Unlike before, Liza's occasionally saccharine attitude had gotten to her, as did the psychiatrist's constant reliance upon Matt. The petite brunette had acted as though Matt's input were vital to her every decision. And as if Kylie should also defer to his judgment when minor problems occurred, as they sometimes did at such large gatherings.

Liza's uncharacteristic chattiness and meddling remarks had caused all three of them unnecessary tension. At least Kylie hoped both Matt and Liza had experienced the same discomfort she'd felt much of the time in their presence.

She hated admitting it, but she was suddenly looking forward to the end of the seminars that included both her ex and his new wife. Matt she could tolerate. Liza and her uncharacteristic probing inquisitions, she could do without—permanently.

Kylie felt like a hypocrite, having assured Tyler she and Liza and Matt worked well together. Until this seminar, they had, each aware of the importance of participating in the team effort, and to honor their contractual obligations. This trip had been different, Liza seemed different. Kylie did not care for the new, simpering Liza. Kylie much preferred the saucy, analytical friend she'd been before and after her and Matt's marriage.

"Enough!" Rolling her eyes heavenward, Kylie pushed thoughts of work aside. She had a few short hours to herself before she had to begin work on her column—hours she did not want to share with Liza or Matt, no matter how remotely.

Tossing her purse onto the hall table, Kylie marched toward the garage, ready to test the mechanic's word—and ease at least one of her current concerns. She flicked on the light as she descended the steps, thoughts of a hot bubble bath lifting her from the doldrums threatening to steal the pleasure from her homecoming.

She rounded the front bumper of her car and skidded to a halt, alarmed by the havoc visited upon her. "Oh, my God!"

Incredulous, she stared at the mess that was her car—the broken windows and shredded upholstery that no longer resembled seats. The scratches crisscrossing the once shiny red paint were deep, a haphazard collection of lines and scrolls that left no surface untouched.

Stunned by the scope of the damage, she moved closer, attempting to determine what, if anything, had escaped the vandal's attack.

"Why?" She shook her head, unable to comprehend the mind-set of the person capable of such destruction. "Better yet, *who*?"

Bluntly reminded that whoever had destroyed her car might very well still be nearby, watching her view his handiwork, Kylie stiffened. Her heart slamming against her ribs, she backed toward the door. Wide-eyed, she scanned the few hiding places in which the vandal could be lurking. The storage closet door remained closed; the stack of boxes in the corner labeled for a charitable donation untouched. She looked up, at the attic entrance that appeared shut and secure.

Though relieved to find no one inside the once tidy garage, she could not tamp down the fear rising inside her—terror so deeply personal she felt both intimately violated and somehow detached.

Her breathing labored, she spun around and dashed up the stairs, into the home likely also sullied by the sick individual who'd demolished her car.

Trembling, Kylie snatched her purse up and ran out the front door, to the relative safety of the small rental car. She locked the doors, jammed the key into the ignition and sped away, tears of fright and a growing rage blurring her vision.

"How dare you!" she hissed, angrier than she had ever before been—so mad her waning fear seemed little more than a nuisance. "How dare you do this to me!"

Hands shaking, she pulled the cell phone from her purse, poked at the numbers barely visible through the haze of her fury. Frustrated by her uncooperative fingers, she slammed the brake pedal down, causing the car to skid. Tossing the phone aside, she clutched the wheel with both hands, gaining control of the sedan seconds before it would have crashed into Tyler's rural mailbox.

She dropped her head, defeated by her anger and calmed by her relief to have avoided wrecking. She inhaled slowly, quelled the urge to give in to the sea of tears threatening to flood her eyes. More in control, she looked up, toward the two-story redbrick structure at the end of the winding drive. Stately yet welcoming, the rows of windows and wide front door beckoned her.

Calmer now, Kylie picked up the phone and dialed Tyler's number. She disconnected after five rings, frowning as she parked beside his Jeep. She hastened to the front door, but soon realized he did not intend to answer her knock.

In the distance, somewhere near the lake, she could hear a dog barking. Following the sound of the eager yelps, she soon discovered the source: Chief. Pacing back and forth along the shoreline, the huge Shepard-chow mix seemed determined to oversee whatever activity it was that had piqued his playful nature.

Cautious as she picked her way over the rocky path, Kylie looked beyond the prancing brown mutt, to the sleek bronze physique of the man swimming across the cove—and nearly lost her footing. She stood frozen, glad Tyler appeared not to have noticed his captive audience.

He sped through the turquoise water, his muscular arms and long legs propelling him with the strength and grace of an Olympic champion. As though both freed by the elements and eager to conquer nature's wet wonderland, his powerful strokes and thrusting kicks made his pace look leisurely and competitive at once. Mesmerizing.

Unashamed at the thought of watching what he surely considered a solitary joy, Kylie moved along the private dock, to the end of the peer. Breathless, she stared as he slowed, dived down and came back up, granting her a fleeting glimpse of his lean, tanned form. Her cheeks warmed by the notion he'd doffed his trunks in favor of Nature's suit, she followed his swim back across the lagoon.

Too intent upon her own pleasure to turn away, she jumped when she felt the insistent poke of a wet nose against her bare leg. Startled, she glanced down, at the large dog now sitting beside her. Chief, his fringed tail wagging like a pendulum, met her gaze with the wide-eyed curiosity of an animal intrigued by its new companion.

"Hey, big guy." She knelt to pat Chief's head, not quite sure she should. The dog whined, nudged her hand with his muzzle as though welcoming her attention. "You remember me, don't you? Good boy, Chief. Good boy."

She looked across the lake, pleased to see Tyler still seemed not to have noticed her. Anxious to continue enjoying his swim, she raised her finger to her lips, hushing the sizeable pet as though it were an intelligent child. Acting as if he understood her near silent command, Chief immediately stopped whining—and started barking!

"Hush, please!" she pleaded gently, eager to return to the visual feast awaiting her. "Please be quiet."

Chief cocked his head, studying her with a decidedly curious look, then yelped. Kylie reached to stroke his broad back. The mutt instantly quieted, alerting her to the action necessary to keep him from warning Tyler of her presence.

"Easy, big boy." Shaking her head, she moved her hand along the dog's broad back, scratching his ears as she again turned toward the lake. "So much for remaining unnoticed."

Unable to see Tyler, she abandoned the friendly pet. Anxious, she scanned the narrow inlet, concern furrowing her brow as she searched for the man no longer visible. She stepped to the end of the dock, trepidation tightening her chest.

She scanned the entire cove, the gently rippling waves where she'd last seen him.

Her heart thudding with the slow, steady thump of impending doom, Kylie whirled to face the open waters of the lake, praying he'd simply chosen the longer route back. Frightened by the seemingly endless waves rising and falling in an ominous rush, she turned toward the calmer shoreline, but could see no sign of Tyler.

Panic gripped her, made her tremble.

"Tyler?" Stiffened by her fear, she cupped her hands around her mouth and yelled, "Tyler!"

"You shouted?"

Kylie spun around, so quickly she teetered like a drunken sailor. Regaining her balance, she shot the source of her worry a disgruntled look. "That wasn't amusing!"

"Answering your call?"

"Disappearing so far from the shore." She raised her chin, unwilling to admit she was more relieved than irritated by his arrival. "I thought you'd drowned."

Smiling, Tyler rolled his shoulders in a careless shrug, annoying her even more. He grasped the ladder hanging from the side of the peer, hoisted himself up and out of the water. Kylie closed her eyes, not quite sure she should look until he'd reached the folded towel lying next to the aluminum apparatus.

His resonant chuckle tempted her to again look at him. She did so, and immediately wished she hadn't.

Fit and vital, he was far too appealing. Sexier than any man should be with rivulets of water trickling down his broad chest, along his ribs and the muscular ridges delineating his lean torso. The bronze colored trunks hugging his hips and thighs matched his skin tone so well it was difficult to tell where the cloth ended and his tanned flesh began. And easy to see why she'd thought he was nude.

"Penny for your thoughts."

Her cheeks blazing, Kylie raised her gaze to the amused blue one staring back at her.

"Were you worried?" he asked, his teeth a gleaming white in the growing dusk.

"Not the least little bit." She gave him a sugary smile she knew he'd see right through.

"You're a terrible liar."

He draped the towel around his neck, seemingly oblivious to the water streaming from his dark hair. Wet and mussed by his swim, just looking at those raven locks made her fingers itch at the thought of pushing them into even greater disarray. She fisted her hands, unwilling to risk the temptation urging her to act upon the impulse.

He moved toward her, his expression both curious and anxious. "To what do I owe this visit?"

Standing in front of her now, his height forced her to look up, into the midnight blue eyes watching her with an intensity that rendered her witless. And also made her even more aware of the tension gathering force inside her.

Kylie opened her mouth, snapped it shut. Her tongue felt dry and heavy, too weak to manage a reply.

"Did you finally decide it's time to call on your nearest neighbor," he said with a smile, "or has boredom driven you to spying?"

"I wasn't spying!" she retorted, a defensive edge to her voice. Guilty as charged, she refused to acknowledge either his accusation or her own chagrin to have been caught in the act. She knew she'd do it again if given the opportunity.

"Why are you here?"

"I needed—need—your help."

"What happened?" Scowling, he stepped closer, so near she could feel the heat of his body. Already uncomfortably warm, she wished he would move away—at least far enough to grant her the space she needed to reclaim her senses. "Are you okay?"

"I'm fine," she said, "now." She told him about her car, her anxiety building once again as she related the destruction. "It's a mess."

"What about the rest of your house? Did you see any signs of further damage?"

Kylie shook her head, licked her lips to ease the dryness still making her mouth feel cottony. "I didn't take time to look. I was too afraid he might still be there…hiding somewhere to gauge my reaction."

"I'll check it out." Tyler cupped her shoulders in his palms, drew her forward. Strong and comforting, his embrace allowed her to relax. His touch also made her tremble. "You're shaking. Come here, babe." He pulled her closer, tucked her head beneath his chin. "Easy now, honey. It's over now…all over."

Not quite, she mentally contradicted. She wondered if her attraction to Tyler would ever diminish. She'd been a quivering mass due to her fear when she found her car vandalized. Standing within the protective circle of his strong arms, she was humming inside, shaken by a powerful need more compelling than the terror she'd fled.

"It will never be over." She leaned back, met his questioning gaze through the veil of her lashes. "We were together a week ago, but it seems more like a year since I've seen you, touched you...So long..."

She raised her mouth to his, silently urging him to make the next move.

Tyler did so with a hesitant brush of his lips across hers, a kiss so gentle she felt as though she'd been touched by sunlight. Warm and insistent, his mouth settled on hers, leaving no doubt as to who now controlled the contact. Her lips parted on a sigh, granting him the freedom to explore their soft inner side and the recesses beyond to his content.

Obviously pleased by her welcome, Tyler groaned his approval. He cradled her face between his warm, callused palms, angled her head with a gentle persistence that allowed him even greater access. Acting as though the taste of her might somehow elude him, he kissed her with a thorough zest, a growing sensual fury so tender she felt both treasured and intrigued.

Not to be denied, Kylie kissed him with the same zeal, meeting the thrust and retreat of his talented tongue with a daring demand that increased her pleasure—excitement that seemed to also bolster him.

Encouraged by his approving rumble, she snuggled closer, eager to feel the muscular strength of him against her. Melded to his solid wall of flesh, she twined her limbs with his much longer ones, fitting her body to his with a perfection that made her breathless—and even more anxious to savor that most private part of him she knew would complete her.

Tyler tore his mouth from Kylie's, feeling both lucky and troubled by the thought of taking what she so freely offered—gifted because she still wanted him and afraid it would not prove a lasting bond. Quaking inside, he feared the passion urging him to seize the pleasure would weaken his resolve, limit his ability to make her realize they were meant to be together.

He wanted to show her what they had was not a fleeting thing, but a vital link that would either make their futures better or destroy any chance of happiness for both of them. Fear had brought her back into his life. The desire making her kisses sweeter, and causing him to crave more of her heat, was elemental, possibly the key to keeping her by his side long enough for his wishes to also become hers.

Unwilling to deny himself the joy filling him to overflowing, Tyler lifted her in his arms, watching her reaction as he carried her the few short steps to the storage shed next to the boat slip. Her tousled hair and flushed cheeks made her look young and innocent, the flames of desire shimmering like emerald fire in her eyes anything but. Beautiful. Sexy. Perfect.

"Beautiful. So beautiful," he rasped, awe and honor edging his whispered praise. He gently pinned her back against the sun-warmed metal wall and loosened his hold, caressing her body with his as she regained her footing.

"Please…" Clinging to him as though she might fall, she rolled her head from side-to-side, writhed against him. "I want you, Tyler…need you…please…"

A raging need, all-consuming and increasingly demanding, blazed inside him. The fiery spirals of desire tempted him to hurry, urged him to proceed with care. He wanted to ravish her, leave her as breathless as he felt. He also wanted to spend an eternity savoring the sensations making his head spin, tightening his body.

"God, Kylie! What you do to me…"

Achingly aware restraint was nearly beyond him, he kissed her again, slowly, deeply. While he would have preferred her to have the soft comfort of his bed, neither time nor the desire coursing through him would allow the amenity.

"I want you, here…now! Too much to wait one second more." He also needed to know she wanted the same sweet satisfaction wracking his body with a pleasure/pain so intense he ached.

Teeth clenched, he eased back, stared into her green eyes, and felt his hesitation slip away. Hazy and heavy with her growing desire, those sultry emerald orbs telegraphed a welcome invitation, all he needed to know.

"Don't stop! Tyler…"

Strengthened by her insistent plea, he slipped the buttons of her blouse free, pushed back the silken barrier. Pristine white lace cupped her breasts, revealing a seductive glimpse of her heavenly shape. Entranced, he trailed his finger along the scalloped edge, palmed the feminine weight. Alarmed by her gasp, he again searched her gaze for a hint of resistance. Seeing none, he freed the delicate mounds, lowered his head to the first peachy crest awaiting his attention.

What he feared to voice out loud he articulated with his touch, expressing a fierce tenderness Kylie answered in kind.

Kylie's back arched like a bow, drawn by the heat of his mouth and her own desire. Taut and tingling, her nipples hardened, swelled to receive more of his dizzying kisses. Hot and demanding, his lips and teeth and tongue ignited a sensual fury, made her tremble.

She clung to him, writhed against him, needing more. Wanton and wanting, she trailed her unsteady fingers along the breadth of his shoulders, kneaded his warm pliant flesh yielding beneath her touch. Dazzled by the feel of him, a heady rush of emotion ricocheted inside her, making her want still more.

"Give me your mouth!" Unwilling to await his compliance, Kylie clasped his head, raised it despite his slight resistance. She thrust her fingers beneath the damp cap of his raven hair, pulled him closer. Shaken by the need coursing through her, she kissed him as if her life depended upon it, unleashing an urgency too great to deny another moment.

His nimble fingers making her skin burn with each bold touch quickly removed her shorts, sent her silk panties shimmying down her legs. Braced against the wall and blanketed by his big, warm body, she savored each caress, relished the subdued power making his hands shake as they skated over her bare skin.

Her senses heightened to a state of near madness, she thrust her hips forward, seeking the rigid proof of his desire. Tyler groaned. Kylie smiled, thrilled by her power to also move him closer to the threshold enticing her to embrace the passionate storm overtaking her.

She ran her hands along his ribcage, slid her fingers beneath the waistband of the wet fabric separating them. Gone in a heartbeat, thanks to her determination and his swift assistance, she moved to embrace him more completely. Bold and unencumbered, she wrapped her fingers around his velvety hardness, testing his strength with a brazen delight that heightened the pleasure soaring inside her.

"Yes!" he growled through bared teeth. The approving sound that rippled through his chest pleased her, encouraged her.

He pushed her more firmly against the wall, met her gaze and eased forward, pressing for entry with a sure, steady thrust that left her breathless. Sheathed inside her, he threw back his head, clenched his teeth. Responding to the urgent fervor spurring her on, Kylie wrapped her legs around his narrow hips, arched her back as the myriad sensations threatened to consume her. Heeding her silent plea, he began to move, slowly at first and then with a torrid pace she welcomed, treasured.

Swept to the shores of unbridled joy, they moved in unison, seeking a synchronized harmony; finding a pleasure so intense it rocketed inside them. Tyler tensed, groaning as he scaled the pinnacle peaking inside her. Kylie's release followed his, so quickly her scream echoed his guttural acknowledgment.

Replete, Tyler slumped forward, hugging her languid form so close she felt as though they were one. Content, she rested her head atop his shoulder, more at peace than she could remember ever having been.

Though Kylie knew the regrets would soon come, she refused to allow herself to dwell upon those demons now.

Ten

Kylie watched as the forensic specialists completed their assignment. Seated on the top step leading into her garage, she marveled at the speed with which the crime scene investigators worked, the expertise apparent in their every move. Having already dusted every available surface for fingerprints, the duo was now busy searching for and meticulously bagging what they'd referred to as 'trace' evidence left by the intruder.

Considering their casual dress—sweat pants and a baggy t-shirt for one, jeans and a much-washed University of Oklahoma sweatshirt for the other— Kylie doubted either of them had planned on working this Sunday afternoon. She did not doubt they'd both probably volunteered to help once Tyler advised them of the situation. Obviously old friends, they'd greeted him as men often do—with hearty claps on the back and the teasing remarks reserved for those comrades they respect.

"Aha!" exclaimed the robust redheaded FBI agent in charge. Using the long-handled tweezers he wielded with a somewhat arrogant flourish, he picked up, and promptly exhibited, a dark button. "Guess he didn't notice this."

"He was probably too busy covering his tracks to care," quipped the younger agent. The slender man, whose wire-rimmed glasses made him look more like an accountant than a respected crime scene investigator, frowned at his partner. "That little button isn't a whole lot to go on."

"Maybe not," said his superior, "but it's a start." He glanced at Kylie, his blue eyes bright beneath the heavy shelf of his rusty brows. "Do you recognize it?"

"Not from here," she replied dryly, smiling when he immediately moved toward her. Two feet away, he lowered his arm, extended the tweezer-held button to improve her view.

Unable to breathe, Kylie studied the small black disk, both hoping she would recognize it and that it would be unfamiliar. Heart pounding, she raised her gaze to that of the steely blue one observing her with a sobering intensity. She mustered a smile, aware his penetrating look would have rendered her witless had she not been so glad the State's premier agent was here to help her.

"I've never seen it before." She swallowed hard, glanced at Tyler. Standing next to her, his back braced against the garage wall, he appeared not to notice her mild upset. He gave her an encouraging nod, a small but gratifying boost she sorely needed. Grateful for his presence, she again looked at the agent. "It isn't mine."

"Good." The burley redhead dropped the button into a small plastic bag he quickly labeled, and then returned to the spot where he'd found it. He resumed his search, only occasionally stopping to examine or pick up another object he apparently considered worthy of further study.

Intrigued by the agents' thoroughness, Kylie startled when Tyler gently tapped her shoulder. He motioned her inside, holding her hand as she stood and preceded him into the house. Once in the kitchen, he gave her a quick hug, and then eased back.

"I need to talk to your mechanic. You're welcome to ride into town with me, if you want to," he said, hoping she would agree to accompany him. Though he knew she'd be safe as long as the agents remained on site, the thought of leaving her here chilled him to the bone.

"I do."

Kylie raised her chin, attempting a bravado that fooled him none at all. She'd been on edge since they entered her house, so distracted he wondered if she realized how many times she'd lost track of a conversation in midstream. Or if she truly thought her wide-eyed apprehension had escaped his notice.

Even Eric Henson, the tough-as nails expert still combing her garage for clues, had commented on her quiet demeanor. Unlike his younger companion, the seasoned agent obviously recognized the signs of her trauma: sudden spans of silence, the intense yet sometimes vacant look in her eyes, the jerky movements that made her willowy form appear both rigid and clumsy.

The urgency with which she'd made love to him earlier, Tyler knew, had also likely been triggered by her ordeal. Though he wouldn't change one thing about their heated lakeside tryst, he wished she'd come to him because she wanted him. And not because she'd escaped the visual nightmare that was her garage.

She'd needed a safe haven. Rather than give her the simple comfort she deserved, he'd shown her the compassion of a randy teen. Tyler hated to think how she must have felt, her home ravaged by the vandal and him wanting her too badly to grant her at least a modicum of real solace.

His behavior and the terror responsible for her ending up at his mercy were enough to rock the strongest soul's foundation—certainly sufficient to shatter the composure of a woman as gentle and unassuming as Kylie.

Aware of the emotional damage such turmoil could wreak upon a victim, Tyler vowed to exercise more control, to do everything within his power to find the person stalking her. If he could manage that, he felt certain he'd be able to help Kylie overcome the invasive fear keeping her quiet as a church mouse on Sunday. He was prepared to keep her within sight until he knew she had conquered the worst of it—forever if need be.

So thinking, he said, "Good. I'll warn you up front, it may take a while. Interrogations aren't always cut-and-dried. One series of questions often leads to another and, sometimes, require that I locate and interrogate another witness."

"That's fine. I don't have anything pressing to do this evening." She flashed him an elfin grin that reminded him of the one with which she'd gifted him earlier that evening—while adjusting her disheveled clothes. His stomach tightened, as did that part of him most affected by the memory of all that had occurred prior to her first unintentionally sexy smile.

He doubted his wish for control would weather many of those looks. He knew his resolve couldn't withstand her touch, not when the mere thought of her soft hands on his body made him feel light-headed.

"Why don't you pack an overnight bag, and plan on staying at my house tonight." He held her wide-eyed look, silently willing her to agree. They'd been apart only one week, but he couldn't bear the thought of her sleeping anywhere other than in his bed. He'd been out of town a good portion of those seven long days, yet not one minute had passed without a thought of her crossing his mind. He'd missed her, wanted her, more than he could have imagined possible.

He couldn't remember a time when he'd missed anyone—other than his lively young daughter—quite so much. Not altogether pleased by the realization, he said, "I'd prefer you stay with me until we find out what—if anything—Eric and Josh learn once the lab examines the evidence."

"Okay," she acquiesced, her smile he adored now mischievous. "Promise you won't complain if I snore?"

"Cross my heart." Chuckling, Tyler charted the familiar X on his chest, hoping his unsteady finger would escape her notice. His hands were shaking, as were his knees.

"I won't be long." She backed toward the door. "Just a few minutes."

"Take your time."

Smiling, he watched her turn and sprint up the stairs, acting as if she couldn't wait to gather a few essentials and rejoin him. He hoped that was the reason she seemed eager, that she longed to be with him as much as he needed her near him.

Tyler wanted to think this night would mark a new beginning, that the joy bubbling inside him might allow him to make the right choices this time.

Connie had often told him he made a lousy husband, more times than he cared to recall. Perhaps he had, considering the way their marriage crumbled in the latter years of her short life. A sane man probably would have heeded Connie's advice that he hole up in a cave and not subject the fair gender to his occasional pensive silence—or to his tendency to take charge when she and others of her sex were perfectly capable of dealing with most situations.

Tyler wasn't entirely sure he had a choice this time. Not seizing control had caused him to lose Kylie once.

He'd be damned and dead before he allowed anything—or anyone—to give Kylie a reason to doubt him this time.

* * *

"Like I said," the mechanic repeated for at least the third time, "I changed-out the car battery and left inside of thirty minutes. I didn't see a soul before or after I left Ms. Bennett's house."

"Did you hear the phone ring while you were there?"

Tyler's question, like the many before it, sounded matter-of-fact. So unobtrusive Kylie figured he felt as she now did, that Artie Simpson had neither seen nor heard anything that would help them learn who had vandalized her car. She wondered why Tyler didn't just politely thank Artie for his time and consider this interrogation over.

"Nope." His patience obviously wearing thin, the lean middle-aged man stepped away from the small foreign car on which he was now working, shook his head. "I doubt I would have heard it...since I was working in the garage and nowhere near a phone.

"Besides, listening to engines all day affects a man's hearing." Artie flashed a teasing grin, revealing the vacant space where his two lower front teeth had once been. "At least that's what I tell the old lady when she nags me about not getting to her honey-do list."

"I understand," Tyler remarked with a chuckle. "Did you give the key Kylie left with you to anyone, or leave it where someone else had access to it?"

The mechanic again shook his head. "No one touched it. I hung it on the ring next to the office door long enough to grab a bite to eat, then dropped it in my pocket so I could head on over to her house first thing the next morning." He gave Kylie a level look that revealed the warmth and honesty Julie said he possessed. "I knew you'd want the car fixed pronto, and I wasn't keen on keepin' that key any longer than I had to. These days a man can't be too careful with other people's property. Unnecessary liability and lawsuits are something I try to avoid."

"What did you do with it after you'd replaced the battery?" Tyler tucked his thumbs in his jeans pocket. To the casual observer he appeared relaxed, totally at ease.

Kylie knew better. The rigid set of his shoulders and the hard line of his jaw indicated the marshal was attuned to every word, both spoken and stated by the other man's body language. Tyler reminded her of a lion ready to pounce on its unsuspecting prey—perhaps a little too eager to read into the much smaller man's words what he wanted to hear.

She also knew the mechanic was innocent of any wrongdoing, that Artie Simpson had done all he'd been asked to do and nothing more. Kylie wouldn't have left her house key with him if she'd feared he would do otherwise, and he'd come highly recommended. Julie said she wouldn't find a better, more reasonable mechanic this side of the Red River.

"Did anyone have access to the key while you were eating?"

Tyler glanced her way, and Kylie realized her assessment had hit the target—dead-on. The predatory look in his eyes made her feel like squirming; as though she, too, were fair game.

"My wife...if she'd had reason to come in here. Or the punks who'd rip me off if they had half a chance." Artie waved his hand toward the small cluttered office visible through the open doorway. Like the garage and its owner, Kylie sensed the untidy room would smell of gasoline and sweat, the by-products of this workingman's labor. "As you can see, there isn't much to tempt a burglar...except my tools, of course."

"Did you lock the door when you left?"

"I set the alarm," Artie scoffed, "and it didn't go off. Besides, I had supper with one of the County's finest. Anyone who saw the cruiser parked out front would've been a fool to risk slipping in to snatch Ms. Bennett's key." He gave Kylie a cursory look, then returned his attention to Tyler. "I'm sorry her car was trashed, but I can't tell you anything more than I have. It was purring like a sassy kitten and in mint condition when I left."

"I appreciate your honesty." Nodding, Tyler glanced at Kylie, and then back at the mechanic. "I was hoping you'd seen something, anything that might help identify the perp." He fished a business card from his shirt pocket, handed it to the shorter man. "Call me if you recall anything."

"I'll do that." Artie tucked the card into his grease-stained pocket and turned back to the engine awaiting his expertise, dismissing his guests with a murmured, "see you 'round."

Once in Tyler's vehicle, Kylie fastened her seatbelt. "What now?"

"We wait for the lab report." Tyler backed the Jeep around, guided it onto the highway.

"And if that reveals nothing more than we learned from our best prospect?" Kylie knew she sounded disappointed. She couldn't help but feel cheated, at a loss as to what, if anything, they could do now that would prove more fruitful.

She also recognized the fear knotted in her stomach and scrabbling for purchase. She hated to admit it, but the thought of returning home made her feel like running, as far and as fast as her feet would carry her, to any place other than the peaceful lakeside house she loved.

No longer the quiet, safe retreat she'd rented three months before, it now seemed to harbor fear and foster the doubts she'd long ago escaped. She didn't want to go there—ever.

"We search until we find at least one clue your stalker failed to eliminate." Tyler flashed a toothy grin, snapping her thoughts to the present. To the sexy marshal who seemed blithely unaware of the angst churning inside her. "You can be sure he overlooked something. Few criminals are clever enough to cover their tracks completely."

"He has so far."

"Oh, ye of little faith." He gave her an exaggerated wink, tsked as though she'd broken a rule of major consequence. "I've just begun the search, my dear."

Kylie laughed at his light-hearted arrogance. And because he no longer resembled a prowling lion eager to claim its next meal.

The sparkle in his midnight blue eyes and the teasing, sensual smile lifting the corners of his mouth, told her he had things other than questioning suspects on his mind.

Aware of all the delightful things that sexy look entailed, she found it difficult to think of anything but the evening ahead.

Eleven

"Are you sure you're up to this?"

"I'm sure."

"We don't have to make an appearance. My parents will understand if we don't." Tyler guided the SUV along the narrow graveled lane, beneath the canopy of elms and towering pines that lined the driveway leading to his childhood home.

"They'll be disappointed if we back out now," Kylie said. Entranced by the simple two-story frame house visible now, she swallowed hard, tamped down the anxiety building inside her. She treasured every visit she'd made to Amos and Marti's happy home, the acceptance with which they'd always welcomed her. "I heard your mother hooting in the background when Wyatt told her he was bringing you along."

"Us." Grinning, Tyler glanced her way, then back at the driveway. "I told you she'd be glad to see you again."

Kylie slanted Tyler a look, gave him a smile she hoped would mask her nervousness. She'd been on pins and needles since they'd run into Wyatt at the Sheriff's office and accepted his impromptu invitation to accompany him to the Wolfe clan's barbeque.

Though Wyatt assured them a hearty welcome and more food than they could eat, the thought of seeing Tyler's family after so many years made her feel both anxious and uncertain. Kylie had always admired his mother, respected his father and adored his brother and three sisters. Not one of the

106

many close kin who frequently surrounded the Wolfes had given her reason to believe they considered her anything other than one of the numerous friends also often in their midst.

Still, Kylie couldn't quell her growing concern as to how they'd view her return to the community—or her sudden reappearance in Tyler's life. No matter how short or long the duration of their newly discovered and increasingly wondrous relationship, she couldn't convince herself their attending together would not spawn overt speculation. Or that she wouldn't feel like an outsider, no matter how warm their welcome.

Tyler parked next to Wyatt's specially equipped van, turned off the ignition. He reached across the console, clasped Kylie's cold, unsteady hand in his warm one and raised it to his lips. Soft and gentle, his kiss made her skin tingle. The serious expression making his eyes seem much larger, so dark his pupils were nearly lost in the Indigo depths, awakened the butterflies inhabiting her stomach.

"We don't have to go in." He held her hand against his lips, his grip undemanding, reassuring. The warm rush of his breath across her flesh comforted her and excited her at once. Tender and sexy, his smile caused her heart to race, pushed all hope of calming down out of her head.

"Yes, we do," she said on a shaky sigh. She inhaled slowly, aware how uneven that much needed breath of air also sounded. "We accepted Wyatt's invitation. It would be rude to show up and disappear without a word." Kylie flashed him a grin. "Besides, your mother is standing at the door."

Tyler glanced toward the house, eased his hand holding Kylie's own out of view. Not offended, Kylie knew he intended only to protect her from the curiosity for which Marti Wolfe was well known. His mother's interest in those near and dear to her triggered many a conversation, and spawned much good-natured teasing. What some would consider common gossip, Marti viewed as the knowledge necessary to make and keep a friendship strong and honest.

To her credit, Marti never repeated an unkind rumor or spoke of anything harmful to friend or foe. Kylie doubted his mother had an enemy, and knew Marti's host of friends would form a human chain from Texas to Arkansas if called upon to do so for Mrs. Wolfe's benefit.

"So she is." Tyler waved, and was rewarded with his mother's warm smile. Marti pointed to the concrete porch steps below her, leaving no doubt as to where she wanted her son—and quickly. "I believe we've been summoned."

Kylie chuckled, relieved to realize she no longer felt quite so uneasy. Allowing herself to get so worked up over a simple backyard family gathering seemed silly. A frivolous waste of time she could have applied to a better use.

Other than Wyatt's occupation, his parent's health and their general interests, she knew little as to what Tyler's other siblings and close kin were now doing. While she wished she'd asked, or that Tyler might have shared some news of their current lives, Kylie knew she would soon learn all the pertinent details. And that Marti would relish the task of updating her unexpected guest.

The walk from Tyler's vehicle to the wide, wrap-around porch where his mother and a growing throng now stood took less than a minute, yet seemed a mile long. Aware she and her escort were the center of attention, Kylie's feet felt leaden, as heavy as the anxiety rising inside her once again.

She scarcely noticed the rows of white-clothed tables bearing food enough to feed a regiment of soldiers, the dozens of folding chairs stacked nearby. The unseasonably warm air trapped in her lungs and the sudden quiet that accompanied their arrival, however, she couldn't have missed if she'd wanted to. Breathing required a major effort, and Kylie felt certain a feather landing on the lawn would have made a racket loud enough to wake the deaf.

The lingering doubts Kylie had as to her welcome were greatly diminished by Marti's rib-crushing embrace—and discarded completely when she noticed the sheen of tears glistening in the shorter woman's sky blue eyes.

"It's so good to see you!" Marti exclaimed, her voice thickened by emotion. A redheaded pixie, Tyler's mother looked much too young to have a thirty-four year old son. And far too trim to have given birth to five children.

"And you." Kylie's throat felt tight. Grateful for Tyler's hand firmly wrapped around her own, she glanced from one familiar face to another. Smiles alight with anticipatory delight greeted her, calmed her. "It's good to see all of you."

As though released from invisible bonds, Tyler's relatives rushed forward, some to shake her hand, most to offer a warm hug and words of welcome as his mother had a moment before. Shuffled from one small cluster of his kin to another, Kylie was kept busy, answering questions and posing a number of inquiries of her own as she reacquainted herself with Tyler's large, loving family.

Always within her sight, Tyler seemed amused by the attention Kylie received. His reassuring smiles and occasional winks told her he was aware of the sometimes personal nature of the conversations to which she and all those in attendance were subjected. Contrary to what she had anticipated, it was his sister, Laurel, and not his mother who filled Kylie in on all of their recent activities.

"I can't believe he kept *that* news to himself!" Laurel snapped with exaggerated asperity. Tyler fielded her haughty glower with a broad grin, annoying his legal-minded sister even more. Not the least bit dissuaded, the newly appointed assistant district attorney turned back to Kylie and, with succinct verbal dexterity, continued as though briefing a client. "The baby is due in August. Aubrey and Dale are excited," she stated, her Indigo eyes sparkling. "I can't believe our little sister is about to have her third child. And well on her way to becoming a famous artist. Aubrey's still life won first place at the Southwest Native American art show in Phoenix, and she snagged second prize for a sculpture she almost didn't enter."

Kylie looked toward the canopied swing where Aubrey and her handsome husband were sitting. Petite and swollen with child, Tyler's youngest sister looked both content and slightly uncomfortable. Tall and lean with the proud, bold features of his Cherokee ancestors, Dale Whitehorse wore a constant smile, and seemed ever eager to see to his lovely wife's comfort. From fetching her plate to refilling her tea glass, Dale responded to Aubrey's needs—often before she had a chance to voice them.

The two small boys playing hide and seek around and about the swing and honeysuckle vines growing on each side of it were adorable replicas of their father. Trim and dark-eyed, they needed only the matching black braids Dale sported to complete their miniature bookend appearance that announced to the world they were Dale Whitehorse's sons.

A pang of envy stabbed Kylie. While her biological clock was still ticking strongly, she couldn't help but wish she were the one sitting in that wide canvas swing, the fruit of her womb giving her the same sweet glow enhancing Aubrey's natural beauty.

"I passed the bar last fall and started working for Muskogee County in January," Laurel said, reclaiming Kylie's attention. "*Most* of the family is proud I only had to sit for the exam once. Unlike that rogue." Laurel cast her brother a mockingly venomous look. "You owe me a hundred bucks!" she yelled, pausing only long enough to roll her eyes when Tyler pulled the inside of his jeans pockets out to indicate their empty state before continuing.

"Now, where were we?" Laurel said, more to herself than to Kylie. The talkative attorney drew her long legs up, tucked them beneath her on the cushioned rattan chair as she faced her captive audience. Tall and slim like her brother, Laurel's raven hair, dark blue eyes and chiseled cheekbones were a feminine version of Tyler's—a breathtaking combination made even more so by her lissome build and feline grace Kylie envied.

Kylie imagined Laurel's courtroom adversaries were often distracted by her beauty—that and the intelligence evident in her expressive Cherokee blue eyes now focused on Kylie.

"Selena is living in Tulsa, still bent on saving the world. She works for a private adoption agency that specializes in hard-to-place older children...when she isn't campaigning to raise public awareness of one unheard of cause or another."

"She's a social worker?" Kylie knew she looked puzzled. Quiet and unassuming, Tyler and Laurel's middle sister had never mentioned interest in social work. Come to think of it, Selena seldom said much at all.

Kylie glanced at the auburn-haired young woman standing next to Marti. Unlike the memories Kylie had of the quietest Wolfe sibling near her own height and build, Selena's mouth was moving non-stop as she and Marti shared a private mother-daughter moment. Their spontaneous hug caused a short lapse in the conversation, and sent another splinter of envy shooting through Kylie's heart.

She couldn't remember her own mother ever having hugged her—nor a time when they'd talked of anything of more consequence than the grocery list. Watching Selena and Marti, Kylie felt cheated. Happy for them and saddened to realize she should have worked harder to achieve at least a semblance of the closeness making Tyler's sister and mother appear seemingly unaware of the people around them.

"Yes," Laurel said, smiling as she, too, watched her parent and sister. "I envy her sometimes."

"Why?" Kylie asked politely, though she already knew why Laurel had voiced the sentiment. Contentment with one's life was like a banner—proudly displayed and obvious to all who cared to notice.

"She's a rock. Solid as they come." Laurel shook her head, chuckled softly. "When Dad had his stroke, it was Selena who took charge. She kept us on an even keel...kept Mom from driving us and the hospital staff nuts."

"She looks happy."

"She's delirious." Laurel leaned close, whispered, "except when someone dares to mention Lance Caldwell's name."

"Lance Caldwell?" Kylie swallowed hard, certain she would hear more than she cared to about Daren's younger, equally spoiled, brother. Did she dare hope to avoid further discussion that might also include her brief, scandalous involvement with Daren?

"The bastard jilted her." Frowning, Laurel nodded to acknowledge Kylie's wide-eyed look. "Selena had just bought her wedding dress, and had most of their wedding plans made when he broke their engagement. I tried to get her to sue him for half the expenses she'd already incurred, but you know Selena…" The attorney blinked hard, alerting Kylie to the fact Laurel had probably taken the set-back harder than her much calmer sister.

Uncomfortable with talk of broken engagements and disrupted wedding plans, Kylie said, "I know what Wyatt's up to, but I—"

"I doubt you know everything Wyatt is up to." Laurel sliced Tyler a withering look, then again glanced at Kylie. "He's studying for the bar. My money's on him passing his first try, too."

Kylie closed her gaping mouth. "I had no idea."

"I'm not surprised." Laurel's catlike smile made her eyes sparkle. "I doubt my oldest brother thinks of anything but you when you're together."

Kylie's cheeks flamed. Her gaze averted, she searched for an excuse to avoid further mention of her and Tyler. Their relationship was too new, their immediate future too unsure for her to know how to respond to the unasked questions surely on Laurel's mind. She didn't know what she'd say if Laurel did quiz her as to her and Tyler's plans, how she would answer questions she had yet to ask—or dare to answer—herself.

Strong hands came to rest on Kylie's shoulders, preventing her from having to resort to a lame ruse to escape. She looked up, into the familiar midnight blue eyes assuring her all would be well. Amazed at his ability to soothe her with nothing more than a look, his touch, she met his smile with one of immense gratitude. And, she feared, with all the love she felt for him evident in her gaze.

"Beat it, brat." Tyler softened the gruff command to his sister with a teasing grin. "You're monopolizing my woman."

"I know," Laurel stated flippantly, her expression as saucy as the wink she aimed at Kylie. "Took you all of two minutes longer than I thought it would to reclaim her."

"Meaning?" Tyler eased into the chair Laurel had vacated.

"I figured you'd come trotting over the second that trapped look drained the color from her face." Laurel smiled at Kylie, shrugged. "I have that effect on people."

"Your point, sister dearest?"

"You've got it bad, bro." Laughing hugely, Laurel strode toward the group of men sprawled beneath the branches of an elm taller and broader than the two-story house it shaded. "I'll be back to collect my debt, so don't think you're going to get away with the pauper routine again."

"I'm broke."

"You're a cheapskate." Laurel stuck out her tongue, looking more like a recalcitrant child than a respectable lawyer as she backed toward her male relatives.

"Beat it," Amos Wolfe admonished his son, a fleeting smile belying his gruff tone. His dark eyes brimming with affection, Amos hitched a thumb over his broad shoulder, indicating the path Laurel had taken a moment before.

Tyler spared Kylie a brief 'what can I do?' look, and then obediently rose from the chair his father obviously intended to occupy. Tyler followed Laurel, leaving Kylie and Amos alone, save for the trio of youngsters scampering around the stone-floored patio.

"I'm glad you came," Amos volunteered, his resonant tone sincere.

Like his forefathers, Amos possessed the stoic features and austere attitude that surely must have intimidated the first white settlers moving west. Both had caused Kylie many an anxious moment before she realized Tyler's father also possessed a keen sense of humor and a loving nature—a mixed bag of traits his strong, silent demeanor masked so well only a gifted few were aware of them.

"Marti's missed you."

"I've missed her." Kylie pushed her lips upward, held his steady look. "I've missed all of you."

"Same here." Amos searched her gaze, so long Kylie had to struggle to keep from squirming, then nodded as though pleased by what he saw there. "You make him happy."

Though she wanted to look away, Kylie refused to do so. Pretending she hadn't heard Amos' remark, or that she didn't know to whom he referred, was not an option. Like his middle daughter, Amos Wolfe seldom voiced his opinion. When he did, those within hearing distance heeded his sage advice and responded accordingly.

Kylie did so with only the slightest hesitation—trepidation that had nothing to do with her once inhibiting—and groundless—fear of Tyler's father. Like a superstitious old woman who believed a broken mirror would bring years of bad luck, Kylie was afraid voicing the truth might alter her and Tyler's fate, somehow curse their still tentative relationship. "He makes me happy too."

"Good." His smile mirroring Tyler's most endearing asset, Amos added, "It's past time the two of you realized that."

Kylie nodded, unwilling to risk speaking around the knot of emotion lodged in her throat. How could she respond? Amos obviously didn't know she and Tyler were together now only because some loony had vandalized her car and made her home the last place she wanted to be.

She doubted Amos would believe her if she dared to explain the circumstances. The gleeful light dancing in his brown-black eyes told her he wouldn't, that he'd made up his mind where she and his son were concerned. She desperately wished she could share Amos's obvious delight—and that she had a prayer of a chance at making her and Tyler's temporary relationship one that would fulfill her long ago dreams.

"Wish Alecia could have been here." He glanced at the children playing nearby. "Seems odd to have one of our youngsters missing."

"Where is she?" Kylie had hoped she'd have the opportunity to meet Tyler's daughter today, to at long last see the child he adored.

"She's on vacation with her other grandparents. They treat her like a little princess."

"And you and Marti don't?" Kylie asked, straight-faced. Pleased by his robust chuckle and the acquiescent shrug of his shoulders, she added, "she's a lucky girl."

"Granny has something for you," Amos stated matter-of-factly, changing the subject.

He pointed toward the elderly woman sitting in a ladder-back rocker, a lacy shawl drawn snugly around her narrow, stooped shoulders. Seated alone next to the ice cream freezers packed and awaiting Marti's call for dessert to be served, Amos Wolfe's mother loosened her grip on the shawl, raised one thin hand and motioned Kylie forward.

"I'll occupy the kids while you visit with her." That said, Amos stood and shuffled his way into the throng of children milling about. With quiet words Kylie couldn't hear and one small beckoning gesture, the stocky grandfather had the youngsters bouncing with excitement, eager to be led wherever he wanted them to follow.

Kylie crossed the short span of neatly mown grass, every bit as eager as the children trailing after the unlikely pied piper with a spring in his steps now. She couldn't recall ever having spent more than a polite minute or two with Tyler's grandmother. As quiet and staid as her aging son, Sadie Wolfe spared few words yet garnered much well deserved respect when she did. Kylie felt lucky to have been singled out by the Wolfe matriarch, and far too curious to delay their tête-à-tête.

Sadie patted the carpenter's bench beside her hand-made rocking chair, then tucked her gnarled hand beneath the snowy white shawl. "Have a seat, child."

Kylie did as she was told, entranced by the wisdom evident in the older woman's small, dark eyes, the map of lines wreathing her features. Sharp and shrewd, Sadie's piercing gaze left no doubt as to the wonders and disappointments she'd witnessed in her nearly one-hundred years. Her life's story, tragedies and triumphs alike, was written there, as was her desire to impart a fraction of her experience to those willing to listen.

"I hear you're having a bit of hard luck," Sadie remarked, her voice much stronger than her frail appearance indicated it would be.

Kylie hid her surprise, both at Sadie's no-nonsense tone and choice of topic. Far as she knew, Tyler and Wyatt were the only ones present aware of her ongoing strife. She doubted either of them had mentioned her stalker in their grandmother's presence. "You could say that."

"I just did." Sadie cackled, reminding Kylie of the wicked crones depicted in fairy tales. She reached for Kylie's hand, gripped it more firmly than most people half her age. "Don't let it get the best of you. You're a strong girl. A good girl."

"Yes, Ma'am."

"Don't ma'am me. I'm Granny, plain old Granny Wolfe."

"Yes, Ma—Granny." Kylie smiled, warmed by the older woman's terse reprimand.

"I made something for you."

Granny Wolfe leaned forward, drew her other hand from beneath the shawl and thrust it toward Kylie. Kylie stared at Sadie's wrinkled palm, at the tiny, intricately beaded cradleboard lying there. A perfect replica of the apparatus in which Native American mothers once carried their babies, the delicate miniature looked far too precious to touch.

Moved by the older woman's generous gift, Kylie raised her gaze to the dark one looking back at her, observing her with a keen, analytical regard she could not interpret.

"It's lovely," Kylie managed, powerless to look away. She felt as though

114

she were staring through a one-way mirror, able to see all things yet incapable of understanding what was occurring right in front of her.

"It's a talisman," Sadie explained, raising the expertly crafted miniature until a silver ring dangled free. "A key chain, too."

"Oh!" Kylie exclaimed, laughing at her absurd discomposure. "I'll treasure it. Always."

"Keep it with you." The old woman placed the talisman in Kylie's hand, patted her knuckles as if she were a favored child. "Always. Tyler's never without his, and look what a fine, strapping rascal he's become."

Kylie followed the direction of Granny Wolfe's gaze, to the tall, handsome man standing just a few feet behind her. Kylie's cheeks flushed with heat, as did her chest. The sight of him, close enough to hear every word they'd said and looking as if he dearly wanted to be included in their conversation, took her breath away.

Apparently too eager to await an invitation, Tyler joined them, an affectionate smile adding to his appeal as he bent to kiss his grandmother's weathered cheek.

"How's my favorite Granny?"

"Fit as a fiddle," Sadie replied, a saucy lilt to her voice. "How's my oldest grandson?"

"Fine as a frog's hair." Tyler sat on the bench beside Kylie, reached for her hand as though years hadn't passed since he'd automatically done that each time he was near.

Sadie rattled off something in her native Cherokee tongue—words that made her grandson's darkly tanned face suffuse with color. Despite his obvious embarrassment, Tyler responded in the same language, causing Sadie to laugh and shake her bony finger in his direction.

"I don't believe you!" Sadie gave Kylie a sidelong look, shook her head. "I taught him a lot of what he knows, but I never taught him how to lie."

"I'm not lying," Tyler defended himself, a gentle quality to his voice. "Why would I?"

"I don't know," his grandmother said with a dry chuckle. "Why would you?"

"I wouldn't."

"Then you're deceiving yourself." Sadie glanced at the table across the yard, still laden with an array of uneaten treats. "I could use a glass of water," she said, struggling to rise.

"Stay where you are," Tyler admonished kindly. "I'll get it."

Tyler was half way to the table, intent on securing the requested water, when Granny Wolfe again snagged Kylie's attention.

"Don't give up on him this time."

"What?" Kylie swallowed hard, afraid she would not care for Granny's words of wisdom on this subject.

"His wife gave up on him." Sadie pierced Kylie with a hard look. "She's the one who taught him to lie...to his family and to himself."

"His wife died." Kylie frowned, not understanding the older woman's critical remark. "I don't mean to sound disrespectful, but death doesn't amount to giving up."

"Connie gave up on their marriage long before the cancer claimed her," Sadie said gently, quietly. "She put a grievous sorrow in my grandson's heart, a burden he carries to this day that has little to do with *her* deceitful ways."

Tyler rejoined them then, preventing Kylie from asking the suddenly misty-eyed grandmother to complete her thoughts. Though she wanted to believe otherwise, Kylie sensed Sadie Wolfe hadn't intended to voice her concern for Tyler.

Why, when they had seldom exchanged more than a few courteous words, would Sadie think Kylie worthy of such a confidence? Why, when Kylie had no claim on Tyler, would his grandmother encumber her with a challenge of this magnitude?

Sadie had to know Kylie wouldn't rest until she knew what Connie had done to cause a serene woman such as her to speak so unkindly of the dead.

Kylie doubted she would realize a moment of peace until she knew Tyler hadn't been unduly hurt by anything his late wife had said or done.

Thinking he might have been made her own heart ache.

* * *

"I enjoyed it. I really did." Kylie coaxed her lips into a smile, though she feared the puny effort failed to convey her sincerity.

She couldn't push Sadie's cryptic words out of her mind. Nor could she fathom their meaning.

"Good." Tyler set the boots he'd just removed in his massive walk-in closet and shut the door. He turned to face Kylie, his expression neutral. "You needed the outlet."

"Now there's a new name for it."

His quick smile made her heart lurch. "I hope you didn't mind the inquisition. Laurel sometimes forgets she isn't in a courtroom."

"She behaved well enough." Kylie looked away, not quite sure she should mention Sadie's concern for her grandson. She didn't want to make Tyler uncomfortable, or force him to discuss something his grandmother felt was deeply troubling.

Truth be told, Kylie didn't know if she wanted to hear whatever deep, dark secret it was that had made Sadie confide in her. Though she doubted Tyler had skeletons of any consequence in his closet, she feared broaching the subject would lead to discussion of her own shortcomings.

She had enough problems without adding those to her growing list of woes.

"Are you nervous about tonight?"

Kylie snapped her gaze up, to the somber blue one watching her with a cautious reserve. "Should I be?" she asked, her forced smile weak, wobbly. The large, overtly masculine room seemed to shrink around her, crowding her inside the small space she occupied next to the distressed leather chaise.

"That depends."

"On what?"

"On whether or not you think I'll rush you…or force you to consider something that probably hasn't crossed your mind."

"Such as?"

"Staying here—with me—until we find out who's stalking you."

"What about your daughter? How will it look if—"

"Alecia won't be home until the end of next week. Connie's parents are taking her to Yellowstone, all across the upper Midwest. They regard the first end of school vacation as their special time with her."

"And if we don't resolve the situation by then?" Kylie swallowed hard, afraid to hope a date would not be set. She dreaded to think how empty her life would be once Tyler resumed his.

"You'll stay here until we do," he stated, his chin set at a stubborn angle. "There's plenty of room, and I'm sure you and Alecia will find something in common to occupy you once she returns." He shrugged, flashed her a grin. "Women usually do."

Kylie chuckled, but couldn't quite allay her misgivings. He'd said nothing about wanting her to stay for any reason other than her safety. If that were his only concern, shouldn't she just hire a bodyguard and prevent herself from weaving more into his actions than he planned?

"I want you to stay, Kylie." He moved closer, gathered her hands in his two strong ones. "I want to know you're safe."

"I understand," she said, her voice little more than a whisper of sound.

Tears of disappointment stung her eyes, clogged her throat. Kylie blinked them away, willed herself to weather the storm of despair brewing inside her. Though she hated to admit it, she longed to hear him say he wanted *her*, that the companionship she'd come to depend on mattered as much to him as her safety.

She truly didn't need love words, didn't want to hear the promises that would follow. Though she knew only a trusting child would build their hopes on such foolish fantasy, Kylie feared she was dangerously close to believing his gentle touch and constant care meant more to her than Tyler intended. Thinking it did made her chest ache, and also bolstered her determination to keep their time together in the proper perspective. To think of it as a temporary solution to her current situation, and nothing more.

"I don't think you do." Tyler urged her forward, held her in a loose, undemanding embrace. "I want you here, in my house. *In my bed.*"

He sounded sincere, his sweet words so close to those she'd hoped to hear, that Kylie's heart pumped a rapid staccato, hammering her chest with each painful thud.

"I want that, too," she admitted. Freed by the truth, she wet her lips, looked up, at the man she'd loved so long. "I want that, more than I could have imagined possible."

Tyler hugged her, so tightly Kylie felt her ribs creak in protest.

"I'll keep you safe, Kylie." He sealed his solemn pledge with a slow, gentle kiss that stole her breath. "I'll make sure you're comfortable." He punctuated the vow with another, deeper kiss that rocked her senses. "And I'll try not to push you, or rush you into making decisions until I know you're ready."

"And if I am ready?"

Her pulse speeding wildly, Kylie welcomed the heat building inside her.

She feared she might melt and pool at his bare feet if he didn't kiss her again—now! She felt powerful enough to move Heaven and Earth if he asked her to, so weak she was certain she'd wither and die if he didn't make love to her this instant.

In response to her husky inquiry, Tyler clasped her hand, lowered it with a slow and deliberate purpose to the rigid proof that he, too, wanted this time together.

"Does that answer your question?" He pressed her palm more fully against his need. Apparently amused by her sudden gasp, he smiled and said, "I'll take that as a 'yes'."

He kissed her again, stirring the passion making her tremble to a blazing need. Kylie slid her hands around his neck, smiling with accomplishment as he lifted her in his strong arms. She burrowed her nose into the downy cotton of his shirt as he crossed the short space separating them from his massive bed. The fabric smelled of the aftershave he favored, and of the man whose strength made her feel fragile and protected. Feminine. The combination played upon her rioting senses like an aphrodisiac. Heady. Powerful. All-consuming.

"Kiss me, Tyler." Kylie followed her whispered demand with a gentle tug of his hair now fisted in her shaky hands.

"In due time." He teased her lips with the feather-light touch of his, tempting her and denying her at once. "We have all night, babe…nowhere to go and hours and hours to get there."

Faithful to his word, Tyler did not rush her. With tender care and a methodical sensuality paced to increase her pleasure, he showed her the true meaning of giving. Of the love she'd so often dreamed of claiming.

And a bitter taste of the loneliness Kylie knew she would endure if Tyler did not remain a vital part of her life.

Twelve

Tyler slid out of bed, careful not to wake Kylie. He stared down at her, a wave of tenderness tightening his chest. She looked young and innocent curled on her side, the thick crescent of her dark lashes shading the upper curve of her sleep-rouged cheeks. Her small, delicately boned hands folded beneath her head and the curtain of tawny hair fanning his pillow made her look even more angelic. Untouched and almost too tempting to resist.

He smiled to think he could imagine the beauty slumbering in his bed anything but innocent, yet his vivid memories of the night just past were evidence enough of her skill as a lover. She'd touched him in ways no other woman ever had, physically and emotionally. Deeply. Completely.

With an adept generosity that seemed to add a fevered intensity to her loving, Kylie's soft hands and sweet kisses had stirred him to the depths of his soul, swept him to the brink of a sensual insanity that, even now, made his body ache for more. More of her caresses that had heightened his senses and fostered the incredible, insatiable madness that kept them up most of the long, glorious night. More of the kisses he knew he'd crave till his dying day.

Shaking his head at the erotic nature of his thoughts, Tyler gathered the clothes he needed and quietly left the room, tamping down the temptation making him want to climb back into bed and once again fan the flames of desire burning stronger each day.

Though appealing, and almost too powerful to resist, the physical attraction gnawing at him like a pesky mosquito also added a measure of melancholy to his musings. Their need for each other hadn't proved a sufficient reason to keep Kylie in his life before. Nor had their common interests and shared beliefs been enough to allow the understanding he'd hoped for when he married Connie. He hadn't expected Kylie to patiently wait in the wings while he honored his obligations. He had thought Kylie would allow him to explain, that she would, at least, accept his decision as the only valid choice he had once she knew the circumstances.

Instead, she'd left town with Daren Caldwell, lending credence to the gossip that fueled many of Tyler and Connie's most heated arguments. The rumors circulating included unfounded tales of Kylie also being pregnant with his child, and mention of his marriage to Connie as the sad result of Tyler acting on the rebound.

It had taken Tyler months to convince Connie he was committed to their marriage, that he no longer harbored feelings for Kylie. It had taken him much longer to actually believe he had put thoughts of Kylie behind him, and that she would not be part of his future.

Seeing her again had alerted Tyler to the fact he hadn't succeeded at all, that he'd never given up the hope of sharing his life with Kylie. Knowing she could once again walk away, and that she likely would once they apprehended her stalker, made him edgy. Other than her stepfather, Kylie had no family nearby, no reason to remain in Tahlequah. Her career demanded travel and convenience, amenities best found elsewhere. Kylie would, no doubt, soon realize that and once again choose to live somewhere other than the only place Tyler wanted to call home.

Logistics aside, Tyler wanted more from Kylie than a few precious memories this time around. More than the mutual passion that made sex with her as much a spiritual odyssey as a physical act. He wanted to treasure her sweet smiles every day, to know she would spend at least a portion of each minute they were apart dreaming of the next time they would have together.

He wanted her love, solely and completely devoted to him.

Aware of the selfish turn of his thoughts, Tyler descended the stairs, determined to improve his mood. And equally resolved to strengthen the bonds that would convince Kylie her home should also be his.

Soon showered and dressed, Tyler poured himself a cup of coffee, stepped outside. He braced a hip on the deck rail and watched the sun rise above the trees banking the far side of the lake, content and rested despite the scant amount of sleep he'd gotten. Chief trotted onto the planked floor, raised his broad head for the greeting his master gladly provided.

"Ready for breakfast?" Tyler chuckled at the dog's eager yelp. "Okay, okay. Find your bowl while I fetch the grub."

He watched the large dog amble down the stairs, lope around the corner of the house. Since a pup, Chief had made a habit of carting his empty dish from one area of the yard to another. The game of hide-and-seek, as well as the loyal pet's propensity for digging holes large enough to bury himself in, were traits Chief seemed determined not to break. No amount of training or coercing had proved successful and, since those two activities were Chief's only irritating characteristics, Tyler had long ago decided to tolerate the behavior.

The loveable mutt had always been a link between Tyler and Kylie, a faithful companion and a constant reminder of the woman who'd tearfully asked Tyler to care for the stray puppy her stepfather refused to allow her to keep.

Scowling at that sour recollection, Tyler grabbed the sack of specially blended dry food he kept in the patio closet, and then followed the sound of Chief's barks to the front of the house.

Amused to see the sizeable bowl setting next to the concrete steps, Tyler toed it farther from the lowest stair and filled it. When the animal failed to dive into it as he usually did, Tyler looked up, to where Chief sat near the entry. The pet stared back at him, emitting a low-pitched growl that rumbled like faraway thunder.

Puzzled by the ominous sound and Chief's refusal to budge, Tyler set the sack aside and mounted the stairs. He was reaching to scratch the dog's head when he noticed the white scrap fluttering in the early morning breeze. Frowning, he pulled the neatly folded paper from beneath the brass doorknocker. Tyler read the brief message, the hair along his nape prickling. He glanced down the long graveled drive, and then slowly dragged his narrow, searching gaze back along the sidewalk separating the sections of lawn he'd recently mowed.

Seeing no new tire tracks or any sign of footprints, he again looked at the note. *'Moving her won't help'* scrawled in a bold, childlike print told him little of the person who'd left it on his door. The rage building inside of Tyler because of it, however, left no doubt as to what he must now do to put an end to the danger threatening the woman he loved.

"You don't know it yet, pal, but you've just declared war." Aware he'd added his fingerprints to those of the writer that might remain on the paper, Tyler carefully folded the note, tucked it into his shirt pocket. Staring down the vacant driveway, he snarled, "and I'm the one-man army who'll soon make you regret it."

* * *

His boot heels tapping a staccato beat, Tyler marched down the corridor separating the small rooms buzzing with early morning activity. Uniformed deputies gathered hats and file folders, preparing to make way for the replacements reporting for the day shift. Intent on reaching the sheriff's office, Tyler paid little attention to the men and women milling about, officers and support personnel he knew well.

He had no time to spare for cordialities, and doubted he would have a minute's rest in the next few days. Discovering the identity of Kylie's stalker before the psycho had a chance to harm her further would occupy him fully. Tyler couldn't wait to slam the jail cell door shut once the creep was apprehended.

Wyatt rounded the corner ahead of Tyler, his wheel chair motor humming softly. Obviously surprised to see his brother—or concerned by Tyler's dark scowl—Wyatt spun the chair sideways, blocking Tyler's path.

"What's got your dander up?" Wyatt peered up, his expression mirroring the concern Tyler figured would be evident in his own.

"The bastard knows Kylie is staying with me." Tyler deftly plucked the note from his shirt pocket, holding it at one corner to preserve whatever evidence may have escaped his earlier handling. He shook it open, thrust the paper toward his wide-eyed brother. "I want to know how he knows."

Wyatt scanned the sheet of paper Tyler held aloft. Emitting a soft, astonished whistle, he looked up. "We need to get this to the lab, have it dusted for prints. Paper holds an image longer than most other material—"

"Yeah, yeah." Tyler slashed the air with his hand, dismissing the advice and revealing the frustration gnawing at him. "I doubt the bum's dumb enough to screw up now."

"If not now, soon," Wyatt stated calmly. "I think it's worth a shot anyway. Unless he wore gloves, there should at least be a partial print."

"Want to lay odds against it?" Tyler dropped his chin, ran a hand along the back of his neck. Frowning, he massaged the tension drawing his shoulders taut. "I don't know where to turn, Wyatt...what rock to look under to find him."

"Or her," Wyatt commented dryly, earning a glower Tyler didn't attempt to restrain.

"What the hell do you mean?"

"Assuming the stalker's male is both sexist and foolhardy. Ruling anyone—male or female—out at this stage is dangerous, as well."

"I haven't ruled anyone out." Tyler moved toward his brother, aimed a finger at the broad chest daily trips to the gym and Wyatt's determination to remain fit had honed to impressive proportions. "Do you know something I don't?"

"Only that I can still think rationally."

"Meaning?"

"You're too close to this...to Kylie." Wyatt shifted in his seat. "You should call in someone you trust to continue the investigation.

"No way," Tyler snarled, his ire rising even more. "I don't trust anyone enough to risk Kylie's safety."

"I'm not suggesting you ask someone else to protect *her*, just that you hand over the reins long enough to get a grip on your emotions." His sage advice tempered by a smile, Wyatt added, "you look like hell."

"Thanks." Tyler yanked off his hat, ran his fingers through the hair flattened against his head. "I knew I could count on you to cheer me up."

"You didn't make the trip down here to be cheered up." With a nimble grace, Wyatt twirled the chair around, squeezed the handle putting it into motion. "Let's get to it. I'm hungry as a grandfather grizzly and ready to find my bed."

"Lair's a more accurate term."

"Whatever."

Tyler chuckled in spite of his sour mood. Never a morning person, Wyatt had reason to grouse and grumble. Pulling a double shift whenever he could, attending classes and reading the law books Tyler had seen piled up ten high a time or two would wear down the strongest of men. Though hale and hearty despite his physical limitations, Wyatt occasionally looked weary, harried. Tyler knew his brother's dependency on the motorized chair frustrated him, and that Wyatt often camouflaged his aggravation with a wry humor.

"Sounds like you need cheering up more than I do."

"What I need is for you to keep a cool head."

"That's easier said than done. Finding that note on *my* front door put a whole new spin on fury. I never knew I could get so mad..." Tyler uncurled his fisted fingers, afraid he might punch a hold in the wall if he didn't get a grip on the anger spoiling for an excuse to erupt. He hated feeling useless, but knew he would until he'd located the shred of evidence needed to identify Kylie's stalker.

"Just try to remember Kylie is safe. Despite the bastard's propensity for keeping track of her, I doubt he'll risk your wrath for a chance to harass her while she's with you."

"I wish he would."

"I don't. The last thing we need is for the perpetrator to have a valid reason to escape the justice he deserves. Besides, time is on our side now. The trace on Kylie's phone will log all calls received. As we discussed yesterday, the phone company has also installed call forwarding, so she can take care of business from your house." Wyatt glanced over his shoulder and added, "Provided you can keep your hands off of her long enough for her to work."

Tyler slammed his teeth together, clamping down on his urge to dispute his brother's mildly dispensed charge. Unwilling to admit he had trouble keeping his hands to himself when Kylie was near, Tyler settled for a withering look—a glare Wyatt apparently found humorous.

Laughing heartily, Wyatt led the way to an office cluttered with unfinished paperwork and stacks of files. Tyler watched from the open doorway, amazed by his brother's dexterity as he maneuvered the mobile chair behind the desk and began pilfering through the maze of material within reach. Acting as though the unorthodox filing system was somehow organized, Wyatt seemed to know exactly where to find the resources he wanted. The first drawer he opened produced an address book. The second pile of papers included the printed sheet for which he'd obviously been looking. While Tyler looked on in amused fascination, Wyatt perused the document and reached for the phone. He flipped through the tattered pages of the leather-bound address book in search of the number he dialed the instant he located it.

"Hey," Wyatt responded to the person at the opposite end of the connection. "This is Wyatt, Cherokee County. Not much." Wyatt scooped a handful of dark hair off his forehead, paying little heed to the untidy length. "I need a favor." Smiling, Wyatt gave Tyler a thumbs-up sign. "I'm counting on it. I'd like you to run through a list of parolees and tell me what, if anything, led to their arrest...no, it's a relatively short list. I'm aware it's Sunday morning, but this is important."

Wyatt motioned Tyler toward the chair in front of the desk. Tyler shook his head, too restless to sit. Instead, he stepped into the now vacant hallway, intent on locating the coffeepot he knew would be full and waiting in the break room. He soon had a steaming cupful in hand, and turned to rejoin his brother. Halfway through the door, Tyler bumped into Deputy Keets, sloshing hot coffee down the deputy's shirtfront.

"Sorry." Tyler stepped back, grabbed a handful of paper towels and handed them to the red-faced officer. He tossed the near-empty cup into the wastebasket. "I wasn't paying attention."

"Don't worry about it," Keets stated, his terse tone indicating otherwise. The younger man mopped at the damp brown stains, scowling when his efforts failed to diminish the spots. "Guess it's a good thing I keep an extra shirt in my patrol car."

"I'll get it for you," Tyler offered. "Where are you parked?"

"Next to the back door." Keets tossed the soggy wad of towels into the wastebasket. "The cruiser isn't locked."

Tyler hastened outside, to the gleaming County unit left at an angle in the reserved parking slot. Opening the back door, he snatched one of the three neatly pressed shirts from the clothes hook, moved to close the door. Surprised to see litter scattered over the rear floorboard, Tyler scanned the mess. Pausing only long enough to make sure Keets hadn't followed him, he leaned down, poked through the rubble.

Empty take-out containers and girlie magazines half-hidden beneath the seat were unsurprising, as was the flashlight, extra handcuffs and other work-related paraphernalia. The stack of brown jersey gloves, still banded together, as well as the skein of lightweight rope, sheathed hunting knife and survival manual were not.

Puzzled by the odd combination, and the deputy's obvious breach of the safety measures to which all lawmen adhered, Tyler peered over the seat. As neat and tidy as the uniform shirts, the front half of the vehicle was immaculate. Like the extra box of ammunition and packaged batteries visible in the pigeon hole, the tobacco pouch stored in the open cargo bin of the console appeared to have been stashed with care.

Scowling, Tyler eased back, shut the door and headed toward the stately building. He hoped Keets had a viable explanation for the lack of concern that could allow a suspect access to a weapon. Though not a unit normally used to transport criminals, one unguarded moment could lead to disaster if a suspect sought escape rather than a peaceable surrender.

Once in the break room, Tyler handed the shirt to Deputy Keets.

"I'd like to apologize for the mess," Tyler offered sincerely. "I usually don't share my coffee with just anyone."

The corners of the deputy's mouth kicked up, hinting at a sense of humor Keets had heretofore kept well hidden. "It's okay. You didn't hear me coming and I didn't see you until it was too late."

"Can I buy you a full cup?" Tyler inclined his head, indicating the coffeepot.

"Later, maybe." Keets turned toward the door. "I've got a solid lead on a hot case I need to check out."

"Related to Kylie Bennett's car?"

"Nope." Keets pivoted to face Tyler. "I doubt there'll be any leads there." Apparently reacting to Tyler's uplifted brow, the deputy continued. "The vandal left no evidence." The officer's full-fledged smile, a gesture as cold as the pale blue eyes staring levelly back at Tyler, made Keets look sinister rather than amicable. "We still have nothing to prove Kylie Bennett isn't the only person involved."

"You're way off base, pal."

"Maybe. Maybe not." Keets shrugged, behaving as though privy to information to which Tyler had no knowledge. Tyler did not care for the thought. "I'm beginning to think her psychiatrist friend's suggestion is right-on. Doctor Andrews thinks Ms. Bennett's state of mind is questionable. Add that to the lack of evidence, and it's reason enough for me to consider Kylie's unfounded reports suspect."

"And if both you and Liza Andrews are wrong?" Tyler asked, his tone cold, lethal.

"Liza's a respected professional. I trust her judgment."

"And if you're wrong?"

"I'll eat a little crow and hope the good doctor's honest enough to admit she pointed me in the wrong direction." Keets narrowed his eyes, making his tepid smile seem insincere. "I doubt I'll be the one apologizing."

"As I said, you're way out of line." Tyler forced open the fists he'd clenched at his sides, afraid he'd punch the infuriating smirk and the man wearing it with no further provocation. Tyler seldom disliked a person, but found it difficult to find anything about the arrogant deputy worth consideration of his respect. The man was an odd duck, disturbingly peculiar.

A fair hand at reading people, Tyler felt sure Keets was a man bound to fall and willing to take down anyone in his path when he did. Thinking the deputy's imminent tumble could endanger Kylie chilled Tyler to the bone.

"Kylie's case is like most we have to investigate, difficult and time-consuming," Tyler said, his clipped tone indicative of his irritation. "Voicing personal opinions does nothing to help us solve them."

"You're right." Keets raised his chin, thrust out his rounded chest. "And, like the information I have on the case I'm working now, the lack of evidence and character reference I mentioned is privileged."

"True." Seizing the opportunity to broach the subject almost as troubling as the deputy's opinion of Kylie, Tyler said, "Since you're so keen on protocol, you might want to take a good look inside your patrol car. Your life or that of a fellow officer could be endangered by the knife I noticed in open view."

"What I keep in *my* unit could also save a life. I don't take chances, Wolfe…and I don't appreciate meddlers." That said, the deputy exited the room.

Tyler stared after him, not quite sure what to make of the man's remarks or his pompous attitude. Baffled as to why the sheriff and Cherokee County Commissioners would hire someone so obviously lacking the compassion and cohesion demanded of public servants, Tyler filled another cup with the steaming brew he'd come in search of.

He trusted the hiring committee's judgment, knew their background check and decision to employ Keets had been based on sound proof of the younger man's training and ability to perform. Though Tyler didn't entirely share their confidence, he respected the policies in force and the individuals adhering to them enough to dismiss his misgivings. Disliking a man did not amount to sufficient reason to consider him inefficient.

Tyler headed down the hall, still troubled by Keets' flippant insensitivity. He hoped like hell the idiot and his seeming lack of concern didn't cause Kylie further torment—for the deputy's sake as well as hers.

Tyler hated to think what he would do if either Keets' uncaring demeanor—or a failure to perform because of it—harmed Kylie in any way

* * *

Kylie completed her morning routine in record time. Eager to find Tyler, she tidied the luxurious master bath where her toiletries were now arranged next to his. Her makeup bag set beside his shaving supplies. Her perfume stood alongside his cologne. Her shampoo and shower gel rested in the hanging bin where he stored his shampoo and bath soap.

Unaccountably moved by the domestic sight—how right her personal affects looked next to his—Kylie descended the stairs, smiling as she searched the lower floor for the source of her buoyant mood. Seeing no sign of Tyler, she entered the kitchen, intent on savoring a cup of the coffee filling the air with its heavenly aroma.

She found Tyler's bright yellow note stuck to the coffeemaker. Removing it, she read the brief missive. *Running errands. Hope you like frou-frou coffee—regular stuff is in the canister if you don't. Be back soon.* Amused by his 'to-the-point' message, and how very like Tyler it was to take time to see to her comfort before hurrying out to tend to his own needs, Kylie filled the mug he'd left next to the pot.

Relishing the rich, unmistakable scent of macadamia she loved, she stepped outside. Seated at the patio table, Kylie watched a speedboat zip across the lake, its white-capped wake receding to the tune of the mockingbird singing from its perch in a nearby tree. She leaned back in the chair, content to enjoy both the incomparable vista and the serenity encompassing her, filling her with a warm satisfaction.

"Now that's what I call a magnificent view."

Startled by the sound of Tyler's voice, Kylie jumped, yanked her head around to watch him come up the steps and across the patterned concrete to join her. "I didn't hear you drive up."

"I'm glad. Seeing you totally relaxed and waiting for me is a pleasure I could get used to…even when you have no idea I'm close enough to get turned on by the sight of you."

He leaned down, brushed her lips with his in greeting. Apparently unsatisfied by the light, sweet hello, he kissed her again. And again, leaving her breathless when he moved back, to the chair next to hers. Seated, he smiled and said, "Good morning."

"Good morning." Kylie cursed the wispy sound of her voice. And the heat rising in her cheeks, the telltale blush likely responsible for making Tyler's eyes glitter like Indigo diamonds. Aware he was the reason for her girlish reaction—and that he knew very well he was responsible for it—she raised her chin, held his sexy, somewhat cocky look with one of supreme nonchalance. "Did you finish your errands?"

Tyler sobered instantly, acting as though she'd mentioned a taboo subject. She struggled to keep from squirming, certain she'd sounded like a prying wife—and that Tyler had not appreciated her intrusion.

"Most of them." He looked across the lake, slowly dragged his gaze back to her wide-eyed one.

"What's wrong?" Kylie stiffened, unaccountably nervous due to his terse tone—and the sudden, shielded look making him appear so grave. "Has something happened? Is it Carl—"

"Carl's fine, far as I know."

"Has something happened? Did you find out who's stalking me?"

"No," he stated emphatically. He reached for her unsteady hand, clasped it firmly but gently between his two strong ones. "I didn't plan to start your day off with disturbing news, but you have a right to know."

"Know what?" Kylie leaned forward. "You're scaring me, Tyler! What's going on?"

"He knows you're here, Kylie."

"How?" Kylie shrank back, tugging at her hand Tyler refused to release. "How could he know?"

"I don't know...yet."

"We told no one I intended to stay with you. Not even your family!"

"He obviously either has access to information we're not aware of or he's close enough to observe your every move."

Kylie shuddered. "That's more frightening than the phone calls. Almost as bad as seeing him standing in my backyard." She swallowed hard, unable to separate the emotions churning inside her. The fear she'd mentioned was understandable, her anger because of it expected. The near-urgent need to escape her tormentor's reach, even if it meant leaving the man she loved, gained purchase, becoming almost as powerful as her desire to remain close to Tyler—safely within the protective circle of his strong arms.

"Wyatt's pursuing a couple of leads that may pan out." As though sensing her distress, Tyler squeezed her hand, raised it to his lips for a gentle, reassuring kiss. "I think it would be wise for us to pretend all is well for the time being. No reaction to a madman's tactics is often like gasoline on a wildfire."

"Doing nothing sounds dangerous, too." Round-eyed, Kylie added, "Sort of like teasing a hungry tiger."

"I'm counting on it to achieve the same results." Tyler winked, gave her a confident grin. "We'll catch him, Kylie."

And if he catches me first? she longed to ask, but quelled the impulse to voice her concern out loud.

She truly didn't want to know what would happen if her stalker found a way to get to her.

Thirteen

"You missed your calling. Ringling Brothers and Barnum and Bailey would pay a fortune for an animal trainer of your caliber." Kylie clutched her aching ribs, but couldn't stop the laughter causing her happy pain. She wiped a tear from her eye, chuckling giddily as she watched Tyler coaxing Chief to perform yet another trick.

"This is the best one." Tyler pursed his lips and smooched the air, making the big dog dance like an excited puppy. "Kiss, boy...come on, now...kiss."

Needing no further encouragement, Chief reared up on his hind legs, planted his front paws square in the middle of Tyler's broad chest, and gave his master a wet doggy kiss. Laughing, Tyler turned his head, avoiding the second lap of Chief's tongue.

"Down, boy," Tyler commanded, patting the dog's head as the pet dropped to the ground beside the master he obviously adored.

"That's the most amusing show I've seen in ages." Kylie took a sip of iced tea, and set the frosty glass atop the table. "How long did it take you to teach him that trick?"

"Long enough to know I'd starve if I tried to make a living training the likes of him." He gave the dog another well-deserved pat, and then joined Kylie on the patio. "Chief is stubborn, or I'm a lousy teacher. I can't break him from digging pits in the yard...or from dragging his food dish wherever the mood takes him."

"Perhaps he's testing your ability." Kylie tilted her head, studying her companion from beneath her lashes.

"Naw." Tyler dropped into the chair opposite hers and raised the glass of tea she'd poured for him to his lips. He quenched his thirst, the muscles of his neck flexing as he drank his fill, and then set the glass aside. Kylie swallowed hard, transfixed by how the natural, manly look of him doing something so ordinary affected her. Capturing her gaze with his, he smiled and said, "He's just stubborn."

Darkly tanned and beautifully masculine, he seemed more relaxed than he had since the day her car had been vandalized. The smudge of dirt on his white T-shirt and the sweat beading his brow did nothing to detract from his appeal. His easy smiles and the way he'd seen to her every comfort, however, made his traits she admired number too many to count.

Kylie had enjoyed their time together, more than a week now since she'd agreed to stay at his house. As they had this morning, they'd toured the lake in his speedboat each day while most of the campers and lakeside residents were still sleeping. Still and quiet so early, the calm water and mutually agreed upon silence that hallmarked their trip seemed perfectly suited to their needs. While Tyler steered the boat, occasionally pointing out a long-legged crane or a small deer watching them, Kylie spent the hour or so allocated for their daily trip mentally compiling the list of calls she had to make that day. Thus far, she'd easily completed all necessary business and written columns enough to allow her a few days free of work-related chores should she need time away.

Considering how pleasant her days had become, Kylie imagined her new, almost carefree attitude and more relaxed work ethic would pave the way toward a schedule conducive to keeping both intact. She liked knowing her best was enough, and that she could accomplish as much work in one short afternoon at Tyler's computer as she typically managed in an entire day in her own home office.

She didn't know whether to attribute her progress to Tyler's close proximity, or to her own relaxed state of mind she now treasured. Both were a welcome change, and a way of life Kylie know she'd miss when Tyler returned to work—something he had done little of since she'd been staying at his house.

She felt guilty for taking him away from the career he valued so highly, but not so remorseful she'd considered returning to her own home. She hated the thought of leaving him, yet knew the time would soon come when she'd have no other choice. His daughter was due back later this week, and Kylie feared the child's natural curiosity would lead to questions neither she nor Tyler were prepared to deal with. Tyler adored Alecia, and Kylie felt certain the girl's arrival would alter Tyler's opinion of his houseguest...or, more specifically, the habits they'd so easily fallen into during Alecia's absence.

Making love, as slow and luxuriously as their mood allowed, when they first awoke would not be appropriate with an impressionable youngster in residence. Showering together, taking time to massage each other with the fragrant lather of the bath gel Kylie favored until they were both breathless with desire, would no longer be acceptable behavior. Lounging about the house wearing little or nothing—other than the sappy smiles neither of them seemed able to shed—would be another taboo once Alecia returned.

Well aware married couples surely must have learned to cope with curious offspring and find ways to enjoy such small pleasures, Kylie still had doubts as to what to expect once Alecia arrived. Would the girl like her? Or would the presence of a woman not her mother or kin of any kind make her resentful? What if they didn't get along? Would Tyler ask Kylie to leave, or simply continue playing protector and leave that monumental decision to Kylie?

"Earth to Kylie...Kylie to earth." Tyler's joking remark snapped Kylie out of her anxious musings, lured her wide gaze to his speculative one. "What's on that fertile mind of yours?"

"Alecia." Kylie looked away, toward the lake sparkling in the distance. "How will you explain my presence?"

"Like I have the time or two a witness has spent the night here," Tyler replied matter-of-factly.

"Will she accept that?"

"Alecia loves company. She'll love you."

"And if she doesn't?"

"What's not to love?" Tyler chuckled, earning a narrow look Kylie hoped would relay her irritation. "I'll tell her you're my guest, Kylie. Nothing more. I've learned to leave the rest to Alecia. She seldom meets a stranger, and her likes and dislikes are as clear as Lake Tenkiller on a sunny morning. You'll know within minutes whether or not you pass muster."

"And if I don't?"

"You won't have a clue, unless she wants you to." He laughed again, the deep, rich sound of his humor annoying Kylie even more. "Despite her young age, Alecia is tactful...precocious to the extreme sometimes. The only indication she doesn't care for someone is a marked politeness. I've come to realize that's her manner of dealing with those rare individuals she'd rather not be around.

"So far, only one disagreeable teacher and a softball coach no one else liked have been the recipients of the starched '*Yes, Ma'ams and No, sirs*' she uses to address them."

"I'll make sure she knows my name." Kylie smiled. "And that I detest being called 'Ma'am'." She slanted him a look, narrowed her eyes. "Were the witnesses you harbored male or female?"

"Both." His expression rife with mischief, he added, "One was a bookie whose mob boss had put a hefty price on his head. Another was a reformed hooker needing to escape the clutches of the pimp who'd murdered her sidekick and threatened to do the same to her. Turns out she was a country girl, forced into prostitution to care for herself and the baby she's now raising, thanks to extensive counseling and a legitimate job."

"Weren't you afraid she'd corrupt Alecia?" Kylie knew Tyler wouldn't do anything to harm his daughter, but couldn't imagine bringing someone of questionable character near a ten-year-old child.

"Dawn's really a nice girl…a kid sidetracked by too much responsibility and nowhere to turn for help. Besides, she taught Alecia how to make a macaroni and cheese casserole to die for."

"Sounds like you think a lot of her." Kylie strived for a nonchalant look, but feared the green-eyed monster rearing its ugly head at the thought of Tyler caring for another woman would prevent her from achieving it. His knowing smile told her she had not succeeded.

"I did. Do." He took another sip of tea, set the empty glass aside. "She sends us a Christmas card each year, and school pictures of her third grade honor student. Dawn also promised to send us an invitation to her wedding to the minister who counseled both her and her daughter."

"That's a wonderful story." Feeling small for letting jealousy affect her so, Kylie smiled and said, "I'll bet you have a hundred others every bit as moving."

"At least." Tyler rose, extending his hand she slipped hers into without hesitation. He mentioned little of his work, and Kylie sensed this moment would qualify as one in which his vocation was far from his thoughts. His eyes, gleaming like those of a child about to tear into a brightly wrapped gift, held her gaze a willing captive. "How long will it take you to put on a pretty dress and your dancing shoes?"

"D—dancing shoes?" Kylie sputtered. "I haven't danced in ages. I'm not sure I still can!"

"Then I'd say it's high time we find out." He urged her up with a gentle tug of her hand, and turned her toward the wide glass doors leading into the house. "I'll give you half an hour of privacy."

"And if I'm not ready then?" She peered over her shoulder, no longer amazed to see the fiery desire in his eyes locked on her own anticipatory look.

"I'll probably undo everything you've accomplished before we leave the house."

His husky promise, like the heat pooling in her midsection, urged her to hasten—and gave her a reason to dally as she bathed and changed into the sundress she'd worn the night Tyler introduced her to Mackey's.

She couldn't think of anything more appealing than giving Tyler the time and opportunity to make good on his sensual threat.

* * *

As she had since they'd arrived at their destination an hour before, Kylie discreetly perused her surroundings, still slightly awed to realize the short drive to Arkansas had allowed her a new and altered opinion of the amenities to be found near her rural Tahlequah home. Accustomed to such luxurious establishments in Dallas and other large cities she visited, she considered the Fort Smith restaurant Tyler had chosen both cozy and trendy, a notch above many she frequented.

Soft candlelight lent the well-appointed dining areas a romantic atmosphere. The stringed quartet playing in another room added an elegant touch, as did the formally attired wait staff seeing to their every need. Their secluded corner table allowed privacy, and a good view of the diners enjoying a night out and the diverse menu even the most discriminating patron could appreciate.

Despite the welcome distractions, Kylie had no trouble focusing on her companion. Truth be told, she had difficulty thinking of anything other than the handsome man seated across the table from her. Wearing tailored black slacks, a white shirt and fashionable tie, sans the Stetson she'd come to think of as an extension of Tyler's magnificent body, her date looked both sexy and relaxed. She could easily imagine him behind a desk every day, pushing a pencil rather than flashing the badge she'd seen him slip into the pocket of the jacket now draped over the back of his chair.

"Are you finished?" Tyler looked at the plate of food still remaining in front of her. He'd polished off his own serving of tender prime rib and the steamed white asparagus she, too, had enjoyed—though she could consume only a small portion of the savory meal meant for her.

Kylie nodded. "Everything tasted fantastic, but I can't eat another bite."

Their smiling maitre d' arrived. "Would you care to view the dessert tray?" Removing her half-full plate and Tyler's empty one, the waiter accepted Tyler's softly uttered, 'No thanks,' and went about his duties.

A short time later, Tyler was leading her down a flight of sturdy wooden steps and onto the remodeled barge that served as an outdoor dance hall. Anchored next to the dock where boaters and fishermen purchase fuel and refreshments during the day, the crowded vessel looked festive, a perfect place for area residents and visitors of Lake Tenkiller to mingle and dance away their cares. Country music, provided by a local band gaining national recognition according to the announcer, blared from overhead speakers. Couples, young and old alike, filled the deck, swaying to the strains of a George Strait ballad penned for the slow dances lovers enjoy.

His warm hand at the small of her back, Tyler guided Kylie into the throng. He turned her into his arms, enfolding her with a practiced confidence that soon made her feel as though she were born to dance. They moved with a comfortable grace, an ease that helped Kylie relax, allowing her to follow his lead with a growing satisfaction she did, indeed, remember how to dance. And cognizant of the fact she could think of no place she'd feel more at home than in Tyler's strong, capable arms.

One mellow tune segued to another, dance after dance keeping her where she longed to remain: close to the man she loved. Free of the worries so prevalent in recent weeks, Kylie enjoyed every moment—even Tyler's occasional teasing when her need to hold him next to her heart forced him to adjust his steps to accommodate her snuggling.

"Are you having fun?" Tyler said, his mouth so close to her ear the warm rush of his breath tickled her flesh. Tendrils of hair that had worked free of the clasp fastened at her nape brushed her sensitive skin, heightening her reaction.

Shivering, Kylie managed a nod. "Yes."

"Ready to call it a night?"

Kylie looked up, into his eyes brimming with a sensual promise that stole her breath. "Not quite." She smiled at his inquisitive look. "We have hours left before dawn," she whispered, her husky taunt sounding as seductive as she felt, "and at least one more dance I'd like to enjoy before the sun rises."

Smiling hugely, Tyler clasped her hand and made a beeline for the stairs, careful to avoid the dancers stepping into a lively Texas two-step. They were on the first step when someone called out Tyler's name—and then Kylie's. Turning in unison, Kylie couldn't have said which of them seemed more surprised—her and Tyler, or the robust man rushing toward them. Though partially bald and sporting some twenty pounds more than his height could bear without looking pudgy, she instantly recognized Daren Caldwell, as did Tyler. Kylie felt Tyler stiffen, knew that he, too, dreaded rekindling the acquaintance.

"Wolfe." Smiling, Daren extended his hand.

Tyler accepted the gentlemanly greeting, but Kylie sensed he'd just as soon reach out to pet a rattlesnake. The square brace of his shoulders and stubborn jut of his jaw made Tyler look as unfriendly as Kylie had ever seen him, rigid and not the least bit pleased to see his old nemesis. Daren had been a thorn in Tyler's side in high school, a spoiled rich boy who thought nothing of lording it over classmates born to blue-collar parents.

"It's good to see you." Daren turned to give Kylie a thorough once-over. The slightly veiled interest gleaming in his light blue eyes made her skin prickle. "And you, Kylie. I hear you're doing well."

"Very." Detesting the breathless quality to her voice, Kylie stiffened her spine, strived for a more forceful tone. "How are you?" She couldn't have cared less if Daren were drowning in debt, suffering the depths of a debilitating depression or in the midst of an early mid-life crisis, but felt the inane small talk expected in a situation such as this warranted. And, perhaps, her only means of avoiding mention of her and Daren's brief uneventful history.

Considering the accusations Tyler leveled on her the night he responded to her first emergency call, Kylie feared Tyler thought more than her need to leave town had prompted her to accompany Daren so many years ago.

"Good. Good." Daren stepped closer, crowding the space Tyler had provided by nudging Kylie back down the stairs and into the vacant corner where they now stood. "I'm still selling cars," he said with a self-deprecating chuckle, "the bane of consumers who believe used car salesmen are like politicians—all a bunch of crooks."

"Are you?" Kylie clamped her wayward tongue between her teeth, aware she had no business asking such a question. To her surprise, Daren ducked his head, gave a half-hearted laugh that sounded as embarrassed as she must have looked.

"Not anymore." Daren gave Tyler a long, man-to-man look, then offered Kylie a smile too sincere for her not to accept at face value. "A brush with the Feds and a court battle with one very unhappy customer made me see the light...in more ways than one."

"How so?" Kylie tilted her head, shocked to realize she truly wanted to hear his response. Despite his arrogant manner, Daren had always treated her with respect—even when she told him leaving Tahlequah with him had been a mistake. And that she had no desire to become the type of 'good-time girl' he preferred. She'd left him at a roadside diner in Texas, and hitched a ride with a family of four to Austin and, eventually, the University of Texas where she'd earned her degree.

"I barely escaped a prison sentence for selling stolen cars," Daren admitted quietly. "The agents investigating realized I wasn't aware they were stolen, that I was only out to make a fast buck on what I thought to be a good deal." He glanced toward the crowded dance floor, smiling as he watched a slender blonde weaving her way toward them. "Lana sued me for selling a vehicle that had been doctored to make it look and run right long enough for me to dump it on her." Daren slid his arm around the attractive woman's waist, hugged her close.

"I won," Lana said, her smile tender as she snuggled into Daren's welcoming embrace. She gave Kylie a friendly once-over, as she did Tyler, and introduced herself simply as Lana, a consumer advocate. Following a brief, light-hearted recap of her first encounter with Daren, and the business deal that initially soured her opinion of him, Lana added, "Daren got his wings clipped, but conceded the end result was worth the hassle."

"I hated losing the case, and having to pay for the repairs that car needed." Daren shook his head, gave Tyler a steady look that spoke volumes. "Both taught me the value of honesty."

"I can't imagine you liked either lesson." Tyler's clipped rejoinder alerted Kylie to his tension still making this unexpected meeting worrisome. She hated feeling defensive, but knew she would until she discovered the reason Tyler seemed to think acting so standoffish constituted acceptable behavior.

"I didn't." Daren gave his beaming companion another hug. "But Lana showed me such minor losses are trivial, nothing compared to what I stood to lose if I continued my wicked ways."

"How'd she manage that?" Kylie didn't attempt to conceal her curiosity, or the smile lifting her lips in response to Lana's proud one.

"She took me under her wing, counseled me on the ways honor and fair business tactics increase a man's self-worth…not to mention how sound judgment affects the bottom line in any business." His eyes and affection clearly focused on the woman standing so close to him, Daren added, "she also married me."

"Congratulations!" Tyler and Kylie said at once, each sounding sincere.

"Thanks," Daren replied, "coming from you that means a lot." He gave Tyler a pointed look, and a smile rife with regret. "I envied you, Wolfe. So much so that I seized every chance I had to undermine your accomplishments."

"You weren't the only one taking potshots, Caldwell." Tyler shrugged, a ruddy tint to his bronze cheeks. "The only reason I ran for student council president was to keep you from being elected."

"I figured as much." Daren chuckled good-naturedly. "Why do you think I persuaded Kylie to leave town with me when I knew damn well she was in love with you?"

Kylie tensed, certain the fragile truce that had allowed her to relax was at and end. To her relief, Tyler laughed and said, "to get back at me?"

"Exactly." Daren glanced at Kylie and winked. "I should have known Miss Prim and Proper would leave me high-and-dry, which she did the minute she realized my reason for asking her to accompany me was anything but chivalrous." He slanted Tyler a look. "I'm glad to see you two have finally come to your senses. You belong together, always did."

"Too bad one of us isn't entirely convinced of that," Tyler stated, tension radiating like a palpable force around him.

The couples quickly parted with the half-hearted pledge to stay in touch former adversaries seldom intend to honor. Kylie rushed to keep up with Tyler as they headed for his Jeep, her aching feet protesting the pace. The drive to his house, fifteen minutes of stony silence made nearly unbearable by Tyler's uncharacteristic surliness—and her own growing irritation—seemed to last an eternity.

Her hopes for a loving end to the evening that had gone so well until Daren arrived dashed, Kylie ducked into the bathroom to prepare for the sleep she knew would prove difficult, if not impossible. Ready to seek refuge in the guest room if Tyler indicated he preferred she spend the night there, Kylie was ill-prepared for his transformation when she exited the bath.

Like Mr. Hyde to his previous Doctor Jekyll, his mood had changed—drastically. Tyler's sheepish expression—not to mention the bottle of wine and two long-stemmed glasses setting on the nightstand—told her he regretted his churlish attitude. Or that he'd come to grips with whatever had made him behave like a spoiled child out to make those around him suffer because of it.

"I'm sorry I acted like a jerk," he apologized.

"Before or after we left Daren and Lana?"

"Both." His cheeks flagged with color, Tyler closed the distance between them, clasped her upper arms in his palms that felt both warm and somewhat unsteady against her skin. "I don't like Daren, never have and probably never will. But he isn't the reason I treated you like a rowdy orphan sorely in need of a time-out. You did nothing to deserve the silent treatment."

Kylie angled her head, held his imploring look with one of equal intensity. "Why did you act as though I'd done something wrong? Tonight, I mean…not all those years ago."

"Because you did."

Stunned, Kylie shoved herself back, attempting to break free of the hold Tyler refused to relinquish. Annoyed by his firm yet gentle strength and her own futile efforts to escape the contact, she stilled. Settling for a hostile, down-the-nose glare instead—a look impeded by his above average height—she hoped he would realize how unfair his accusation seemed to her. And how angry she was because of it.

"You let me walk right into his trap." Tyler's sudden grin made her see red—the visible imprint left by her palm itching to slap it off his handsome face! "Both you and Daren knew I believed you were an item. I admitted as much when I accused you of consorting with the Devil the first time you called for help. You could have explained the circumstances and set the record straight then."

"You were out of line." Kylie relaxed her rigid spine making her back muscles ache. "Besides, my *tryst* didn't result in a wedding band."

"Touché." Tyler inclined his head, granting her the small victory that failed to ease the hurt his sudden marriage inflicted upon her then—pain that still made her wish she'd meant enough to him that interest in any other woman would have been unthinkable. "Years of frustration and misguided jealousy got the best of me, Kylie. I'm the one who betrayed you, but blaming you lessened my guilt. For much the same reason, it made me madder than hell when Daren cleared you of the charges I'd leveled on both of you."

"So…" A justifiable fury rising inside her, she said sotto voce, "I'm forgiven?"

Tyler shook his head. "I'm asking you to forgive me, Kylie. I was wrong to expect your loyalty then, and dead-wrong to falsely accuse you of deeds far more acceptable that what I did."

"I think it's high time we forgive each other." Unable to hold onto her ire, Kylie blinked back the tears stinging her eyes. While she would have preferred to hear the reason he chose Connie over her, Kylie felt his apology was enough—for now. "We can't change the past, but we can make our immediate future a lot more pleasant."

Needing no further encouragement, Tyler pulled her close, nestling her slim curves against the steely warmth of his muscular frame. The remainder of the night passed in a sensual fog, her needs beautifully met and far surpassed by the attentive man seemingly eager to make her heartfelt statement a loving reality.

Replete and near slumber when dawn arrived, Kylie hoped her future included at least a little more time with Tyler. She drifted off to sleep, certain this wondrous night would simply be one more sweet memory haunting her once her stalker was jailed.

With her safe from harm, Tyler would have no reason to remain a part of her life.

Fourteen

Annoyed to hear the phone ring yet again, Kylie glanced at the caller ID, perplexed when she recognized Matt and Liza's home number registered on the monitor. Their unlisted Arlington number hadn't shown up either of the two times Matt had previously called to discuss the upcoming Pittsburgh seminar.

Mentally reminding herself to mention the oddity to Tyler, Kylie picked up the receiver, hoping to quickly be done with the preliminary details making this event more trying than most.

"Tell me the hotel found the record of our booking, and that the bankrupt catering service we hired was pulling your leg when they asked for additional payment up-front." Chuckling at her half-hearted joke, Kylie pinned the receiver between her chin and shoulder. Her hands free, she continued rinsing the wilted plant she'd rescued from Tyler's den—one of two in dire need of a little TLC.

"Be careful what you wish for," Matt scolded mildly, his amicable laughter easing Kylie's growing irritation over the calamities plaguing the Pennsylvania retreat. Carefully planned and now in danger of being cancelled, the seminar geared for married couples working to resolve their differences seemed destined to become one of the few disasters they had encountered outside their own challenging divorce.

"So, what's up now?" she asked, expecting to hear the other shoe drop.

"All is well."

"Really?" Aware she sounded skeptical, Kylie added, "Let me guess, you waved your magic wand and our troubles are a thing of the past."

"If only it were that simple..." Matt hesitated, making her wonder if they were still on the subject of the Pittsburgh meeting.

"What's happened in the last hour? What did you do?"

"What most men do when faced with a situation they can't control. I whipped out my checkbook...credit card, actually."

"You paid the catering service again? I'm not sure I approve—"

"I hired another one that required the same hefty deposit we paid *Angie's Food For Thought*. This business comes highly recommended."

"By whom?" Kylie set the bedraggled plant aside and dried her hands. Again holding the receiver with her left hand, she mopped up the water dotting the kitchen counter with her other one.

"The hotel concierge who finally located our contract and is eager to make amends."

"Sounds like you've taken care of everything."

"Not quite." The annoyance evident in his tone alerted Kylie to her ex-husband's concern. Seldom one to show his anger, Matt sounded both upset and frustrated.

"What's wrong, Matt?"

"Liza's bowing out."

"Why?" Her brow puckered in consternation, Kylie tossed aside the towel she'd been using.

"Personal business she claims can't be postponed."

"What's more pressing than honoring a professional commitment?" Exasperated, more because of the short notice than by Liza's intentions to back out, Kylie sank onto the nearest chair. "How could she do this? She knows how important it is for the panel of experts we've assembled to present a strong front...how vital she is to our program. Like it or not, we are a team."

"My sentiments exactly." Matt heaved a weary sigh, hinting their current planning dilemma had little to do with his mood. "As for her reason for backing out, I don't have a clue."

"Is her mother okay?" Kylie asked, aware Liza's sole surviving parent was getting on in years, and that the Florida resident might need her only child.

"Amanda is great. Thanks for asking. She's on a seniors' cruise to Barbados, and definitely not the reason for her daughter's defection."

"Then what is?"

"As I said, I'm clueless."

"I'm sorry. I shouldn't have pressed for details." Her apology rendered, Kylie ignored her inner voice cautioning her to leave well enough alone and continued. "This just doesn't sound like Liza. She would never do something like this without good reason." Kylie shook her head. "She hasn't seemed...her usual self. She didn't make a single decision at the Dallas conference without first consulting you."

"I know," Matt agreed, "she nearly drove me nuts, asking—demanding— my opinion on everything. So often I got a little testy."

"I noticed." Kylie laughed, amused now that she knew Matt also considered Liza's needy behavior annoying.

"I didn't realize I was so transparent."

"Clear as cellophane." Feeling guilty for needling him, Kylie admitted, "It got to me, too, Matt." She tugged her lower lip between her teeth, worrying her tender flesh as she considered her next words. "Liza's always been so independent, so strong. This sudden need for direction seems..."

"Totally out of character?"

"Exactly," Kylie stated thoughtfully. "Our contractual obligations can't be any easier for her than our ongoing business relationship is for us at times. Even Grace thinks we're crazy for honoring the commitments we'd made."

"Sounds like our Gracie." Matt laughed softly. "We're lucky to have her."

"I agree. Very few administrative assistants would have remained on staff once the media started dogging our every move. Fewer still have the nerve to tell their bosses the unvarnished truth, no matter how delicate the subject."

"She does have a way with words."

"Words and that keyboard of hers. I'm surprised it doesn't start smoking five minutes after she's logged onto her computer." Kylie watched a red-throated hummingbird hovering near the feeder outside the kitchen window. Its wings moving so fast they were little more than a gray blur, the tiny creature reminded her of Liza. Small and dainty, Liza often zipped from one task to another, quickly taking care of business yet leaving nothing undone. Thinking her once good friend might be experiencing problems neither Kylie nor Matt were aware of was troubling. "Did you ask why she couldn't attend the seminar?"

"Of course. Liza got defensive when I pressed her for answers, so I told her we'd make do. I've managed to persuade a colleague to lend a helping hand." Matt named a respected counselor both he and Kylie knew well, a woman who had often taken part in their conferences.

"Denise will be great. She has a knack for making even the most stubborn participant see the error of their ways."

They discussed minor details still unsettled, and agreed to meet for dinner the night they arrived in Pittsburgh. Ready to hang up and continue nursing the plants she'd found in dire need of water and pruning, Kylie said, "Have Liza call me this evening. I'm having dinner with a couple of friends, but I should be home by eight."

Promising to pass along her message, Matt remained silent—so long Kylie wondered if something other than Liza also had him worried. She hated to think the man she admired despite their differences had suffered a professional setback of some sort—or another personal quandary so soon after their high-profile divorce. They'd always shared their concerns, and considered each other a trusted sounding board. Kylie hoped he still valued her friendship enough to ask her opinion, or at least seek her counsel if he didn't.

"Matt?"

"Sorry," he stated apologetically. "How are you, Kylie?"

"Fine." Puzzled, she said, "Why do you ask?"

"Liza and I were questioned by local authorities earlier this week."

"Let me guess," Kylie jested, "bank robbers matching your description—"

"I'm serious, Kylie." His no-nonsense tone told her he was, as did his next comment. "Stalkers can be dangerous...deadly. I don't want you to take any chances. Hire a bodyguard or, better yet, get your butt on the next plane to Dallas."

"I'm safe, Matt." And furious, Kylie realized. How dare Tyler consider either Matt or Liza suspect! She'd assured him neither of them would harm her, that he should mark them off the list of potential enemies they'd compiled. Doing her best to quell the anger causing her to tremble, she inhaled deeply. "I'm safe. Really."

"Good. You can't imagine how worried I've been, and not because someone obviously thinks I'm capable of hurting you."

"I know you would never hurt me, Matt. Not intentionally." So would Tyler, once she'd told the marshal what she thought of him having the police question Matt and Liza, and possibly other business associates as harmless as her partners!

Kylie closed her eyes, her thoughts straying to the evening ahead. She hoped she could maintain a measure of calm in Alecia's presence, but feared the dinner she and Tyler planned to welcome his daughter home would prove a trial due to the unexpected fury gaining force inside her.

She also hoped Tyler's trip to the airport in Tulsa and back would take longer than he'd thought it would. Kylie knew she needed time and a long hot bath to help prepare herself for the coming night, for the confrontation that would demand privacy—possibly a soundproof room!

It had been years since Kylie had shouted at anyone, and an eternity since anyone had been more deserving of her anger.

"Your trust means a lot, Kylie. I never meant to hurt you—"

"I know." Kylie rubbed at the frown creasing her forehead, attempting to ease the tension throbbing in her temples. She knew Tyler was simply doing his job, but could not quiet the voice inside her head reminding her that he followed his own set of rules—always had, and likely always would.

"I wish things could have been different...that I'd exercised more control and the sound judgment our books lead people to think I have in abundance."

"I'm not blameless, Matt. I left the door wide open, if not for Liza, then for any other attentive woman who might have come along. Friends make good partners, but not necessarily good spouses. I certainly didn't."

"Friends also apologize whether or not they're wrong, and especially when they are. I regret what happened, how it happened. Forgive me? Please?"

"Forgiven." Kylie chuckled softly, relieved to realize she truly meant it. How could she not when a man so highly respected seemed to consider her the faultless victim of their break-up?

"Thank you." Pausing, Matt added, "Heed what I said, Kylie. Be careful, and don't hesitate to call if I can help in any way."

"I will. And, Matt," she said, her throat tight, "go easy on Liza. Even the most enlightened woman needs a little time to herself now and again."

"I know. I keep hoping time and her growing reputation as a ground-breaking psychiatrist in her own right will help make our marriage work."

"I'm sure it will."

Kylie said goodbye and hung up the phone, not quite sure she shared Matt's seeming optimism. Trouble so early in a relationship didn't bode well, nor did Liza's defection. Never one to shirk responsibility, Liza apparently thought only she alone could handle whatever crisis had caused her to forgo attending the Pittsburgh symposium.

Knowing Liza as she did, Kylie figured something major—something other than the media's perception of her and her new husband—had to be responsible for her once best friend taking time off.

Something obviously important enough—or too personal—for Liza to consider her quest anyone's business other than her own.

Kylie couldn't help feeling hurt. She and Liza had been so close, more like sisters than college roommates sharing the limited space in their dorm. They'd become fast friends, two good students living too far from home and family to spend weekends, even most holidays, anywhere other than on campus. Kylie could confide in Liza, and often had. She thought Liza felt the same, but now realized she didn't.

The loss of Liza's trust cut like a knife through Kylie's heart, carving a space large enough to allow room for her anger at Tyler to grow unheeded.

Fifteen

"We saw Old Faithful, too," Alecia stated with enthusiasm, "and a mother bear with two cubs prowling around our camp one night." The fair-haired girl paused, the forkful of spaghetti in her hand poised in midair. "The park ranger told us bears have learned to 'so-shi-late campsites with food."

"Associate," Tyler corrected with a gentle smile. He shot Kylie a conspiratorial look and winked, then again focused his attention on the child who'd dominated the conversation from the moment they'd picked Kylie up for their dinner date.

Unlike she'd imagined, Kylie found it difficult to concentrate on anything other than Tyler's adorable young daughter. Alecia's nonstop chatter and the lively tales she told of her Yellowstone adventure had allowed Kylie to let go of her anger—most of it, anyway. Holding onto her ire until Tyler had had a chance to explain himself seemed petty, and contrasted sharply to the anger management training she'd developed for her seminars. She knew better than to let emotions get the best of her or to worry about matters over which she had no control.

Kylie also knew that venting, when she had an opportunity to vent properly, would rid her of the remnants of anger—and her guilt because of it—making her feel uncomfortable, antsy. Her irritation on a back burner, she sought to quell the envy watching father and daughter interacting so beautifully stoked to a harsh reality. Had she possessed magical powers, Kylie would have granted herself a more active role in their byplay: the part that rightfully belonged to Connie.

148

Kylie felt certain Tyler's wife would have been proud to claim their affections, had Alecia's mother survived long enough to enjoy what must, to the casual observer, appear to be a joyous family outing.

"We visited Jackson Hole, Wyoming," Alecia said around a mouthful of pasta. "You'll never guess who was sitting at the table next to ours in the restaurant!"

"Ricky Martin?" Reacting to Alecia's negative head-shake, Tyler mentioned another of his daughter's favorite celebrities, and then said, "I give up. Who?"

Alecia rolled her eyes, acting as though her father's quick concession displeased her. "Harrison Ford." She gave Tyler a cheeky grin. "He helped rescue a Boy Scout who got lost in the mountains the day after we left Wyoming."

"Sounds like you enjoyed your vacation." Kylie smiled at the pretty girl who'd directed only a few of her remarks to the new kid on her block.

"Every minute of it!" Alecia exclaimed, sounding much older than her ten years. The little girl smiled at her father, and Kylie could easily see why Tyler loved her so dearly. The smile suddenly gone, Alecia wrinkled her short upturned nose. "Except when the motor home got a flat. Grandpa George had to change it. Nana Joyce said the heat made him grumpy, but I don't think that's what made him gripe at me."

"Do you know what did?" Kylie asked, pleased to realize Alecia's comments were aimed at her, as was the mischievous look so like her father's.

"The stink from the road kill." Alecia pursed her lips in disgust, and just as quickly set loose the smile lighting up her gray-green eyes. "I didn't mean to make it worse."

"How did you make it worse?" Tyler interjected, his look mildly chastising.

"I turned it over." Alecia ducked her head.

"You touched a dead animal?" Tyler leaned forward, fatherly concern etching his brow. "You know better, Alecia Nicole. How could you—"

"I didn't touch it." Alecia set her fork aside, gave her father an entreating look. "I used a stick."

"Why would you even think—"

"—I was going to bury it, but Grandpa wouldn't let me."

"Thank God he didn't." Tyler shook his head, looking as though he wanted to laugh—and knew he shouldn't. "I wish I could have seen Mr. Mahoney's face."

"Nana said it was worth a thousand pictures." Alecia giggled. "She told Grandpa she thought we had a flat about a dozen times just so his face would turn red again. I did too…until he threatened to stop every time we passed another road kill. He said he was going to buy a shovel and let me bury so many of the smelly, unfortunate critters I'd never think of doing anything like that again."

"Remind me to thank your Grandfather the next time I talk to him." Laughing, Tyler excused himself, leaving woman and child alone at the table.

"Do you like spaghetti?" Alecia inquired, once again busy eating.

"Yes, I do." Kylie hated to think what the starchy pasta would do to her waistline, but could fault neither the zesty sauce nor the quantity and variety of food available on the buffet.

"You aren't eating." Alecia raised one pale brow, an affectation that again reminded Kylie of Tyler. Other than an occasional look and the mannerisms very like his, few things about Alecia resembled her father.

Unlike Laurel, whose Indigo eyes and chiseled features were a feminine version of her brother's handsome attributes, Alecia appeared to have inherited none of Tyler's physical traits. Her dark blond hair and gray-green eyes had to have come from her mother's gene pool, as did the petite yet athletic build that hinted of future success at whatever sport captured her fancy. The freckles dusting her nose and cheeks, as well as the sun-kissed skin still too fair for anyone to guess she was of Native American descent, were not evident in any of Tyler's young relatives.

Though she'd seen the many pictures of the angelic child Tyler had in every room in his house, none prepared Kylie for the sprite who called him Daddy. Alecia did not resemble her father, but she definitely could lay claim to the Wolfe charm that made Tyler so irresistible.

"Aren't you hungry?" Alecia asked, regaining Kylie's attention.

"I'm saving room for dessert."

"Me, too." The girl looked toward the line forming along the dessert table. "We'd better hurry. I'd like a turtle brownie, if there's any left."

"That sounds yummy…and fattening."

"You're not fat." Narrowing her eyes, Alecia tilted her head, studying her tablemate with a childish fascination Kylie found both alarming and complementary. "You're pretty. Almost as beautiful as my mother."

"Thank you." Having also seen pictures of Alecia's attractive mother, Kylie considered the proclamation high praise. Inordinately pleased, she said, "So are you."

"I've got freckles." Wrinkling the nose where most of those freckles were located, the girl added, "Daddy says they're angel kisses, but I know they aren't."

"How do you know they aren't?"

"Cause Mommy's an angel, and I'd know it if she kissed me."

Unable to think of a response—and positive she wouldn't be able to speak around the lump in her throat—Kylie glanced at the dwindling line of patrons still next to the dessert table. She swallowed hard. "Do you think I should brave the crowd and see what's left?"

"Yes," Alecia stated with an emphatic nod.

"You want a turtle brownie, right?"

"Anything chocolate's the best." Alecia flashed a grin so like Tyler's Kylie couldn't help but respond in kind. "Do you like ice cream?"

"I love it."

"I'll ask Daddy to stop and get some on the way home."

"Stop and get what?" Tyler looked from his daughter to the woman he loved.

"Ice cream," Alecia and Kylie chimed at once. "Chocolate almond?" Alecia said, causing Kylie to laugh aloud.

"It's my favorite," Kylie remarked, her smile mirroring that of the little girl he'd missed so much. "I knew there was something about you I liked—other than those adorable freckles."

Standing, Kylie winked and said, "I'll be right back."

Tyler watched her make a beeline for the buffet table, her trim hips swaying with a feminine purpose. Stunned by the powerful rush of desire that nearly buckled his knees, he eased into the booth, using the table to shield that part of him most affected by Kylie's unintentional appeal.

"I like her."

Snapped to attention by his daughter's declaration, Tyler smiled. "So do I."

"She likes my freckles."

"So do I."

Alecia rolled her eyes. "I'm serious."

"And you think I'm not?" Tyler teased.

"We should marry her."

Out of the mouths of babes, Tyler mused, aware he should caution Alecia against voicing his fondest wish. Until he knew Alecia and Kylie could get along, and that Kylie would welcome the role of mother as well as wife, Tyler did not dare dream of asking her to marry him.

He refused to pose *that* question without knowing whether or not Kylie wanted to remain in Cherokee County, near where they'd grown up and close to Alecia's many relatives. Home and hearth mattered to him, as did Kylie's feelings. He wanted her to consider Tahlequah home, especially if he and Alecia were at least a part of her reason for choosing to stay.

He didn't want to think of the alternative.

* * *

Later, soon after tucking Alecia into bed and locking the house, Tyler and Kylie strolled down to the lake. Hand-in-hand, they walked along the moonlit path, words unnecessary as they traversed the forested trail.

Once they reached the dock, Tyler moved to secure the boat he'd insisted they check out before also retiring for the night. Kylie watched him lower the canopy and fasten the tarp in place, her chest as tight as the stays he hooked with a practiced ease. Fascinated, Kylie couldn't help but admire the muscles in his arms bulging as he worked, flexing and straining like those beneath his white cotton T-shirt illuminated by the moonlight.

Always handsome, he looked especially attractive tonight. The sight of him moving about the boat, his attention focused on the task at hand, took her breath away.

And made her even more cognizant of the concerns weighing heavily on her mind.

Kylie needed to talk to him, ask why he'd ignored her wishes and had Matt and Liza questioned like common criminals. She hated to spoil his good mood and put a damper on what had been a very enjoyable evening. Aware her view of the police inquiry, as well as the anger she felt because of it, would likely make her sound like a shrew when she dared to voice her opinion, she forced her thoughts to other things—the appealing man making quick work of the chore she'd helped with none at all.

"Is there anything I can do?"

"As a matter of fact, there is." Tyler slanted her a look, flashed a grin made more brilliant by the bright starry night. "Come over here."

Dazzled, Kylie matched his smile with one of equal pleasure. "Aye, aye, Captain."

He waited until she'd stepped onto the boat, and then grasped her about the waist. Lifting her high, he spun around, forcing Kylie to cling to him or risk causing them to tumble as he danced her across the carpeted deck.

"Tyler!" she exclaimed when he continued, making her dizzy. "You're going to drop me!"

"Definitely." His laughter decidedly sinful, he fell onto the padded bench at the back of the boat, careful to cushion her fall with his big, warm body.

Sprawled atop him, Kylie lifted her head, only slightly amazed she could do so without reeling. Striving for a stern look, she pursed her lips, drew her brows together. "What was that all about?"

"Joy," he said with a smile, "pure joy."

"And here I thought you were showing me a new dance step."

"I was." He kissed her slowly. Thoroughly. "It's called happiness."

Kylie's heart swelled and did a little dance of its own, making her chest so tight she could scarcely breathe. "I'm happy, too."

"Are you?" His frown indicated the doubts responsible for his simple query.

"Very." *Delirious,* she mused. With his arms around her, the steady thud of his heart so close to her own, she could think of nothing or no place that would please her quite so much.

Smiling, Kylie trailed her finger over the crease marring his brow, easing the shallow lines of worry etched there. Her anger suddenly seemed frivolous, considering he was only doing his job—a job for which he'd been honored many times. She knew he'd never do anything to purposely hurt her, and that he would do everything necessary to put an end to the harassment with which she'd been dealing.

She had to trust him, allow him to pursue all leads—even if those meager avenues resulted in him questioning her business associates. Kylie knew he'd realize soon enough that Matt and Liza were innocent of any wrongdoing; that the stalker both she and Tyler wanted to see behind bars was in no way connected to her ex-husband and his wife.

"You seem...distant." His frown returned, deeper now that he'd mentioned the torment Kylie thought she had concealed. She forced a smile, but sensed it fell short of soothing his doubts.

"Really?" She squirmed, fitting her body more fully against the rock-hard wall of flesh so warm beneath her. "And here I thought I was about as close as I could get with my clothes on."

"That's the trouble." His smile so wickedly tender she felt tears sting her eyes, he raised his hips, cradled the heart of her femininity. "You're wearing way too many clothes."

Much later, naked and sweating and entirely too content to care, Kylie laid her head on Tyler's damp chest. "You're far too good at this for me to think you haven't had a lot of practice."

His chuckle caused her head to bob. The bear hug with which he squeezed out the little air remaining in her lungs made her feel cherished. "Are you bragging or complaining?"

"Just stating fact."

"Are you jealous?"

"Curious, actually." She gave him a serious look. "I imagine you have your pick of women—beautiful women."

"Do you really want to discuss them now?"

"No." Aware she truly meant it, she smiled and added, "I should probably be grateful, anyway."

"Because I've gone so long without I can't get enough of you?" He cupped her chin in his palm, gently raised her head so he could kiss her again, softly. Completely. "You're the only woman who matters, Kylie."

His loving touch and the skill with which he moved her beyond words, to the magical plateau of a passion too wondrous to consider anything but exceptional, made Kylie believe he meant what he said.

Kylie wanted to think she mattered to him, but feared that would not be the case when he no longer felt the need to protect her.

Knowing their time together was limited, and that the love she felt for him would continue to grow stronger, caused her heart to ache at the thought of leaving him once her stalker had been arrested.

* * *

"I like it." Alecia angled her head, studying her reflection in the mirror. A bit of a perfectionist, she adjusted one of the multi-colored butterfly clips fastened to the narrow plaits holding her fine straight hair off her face. "Thank you for fixing my hair."

The girl fairly leaped off the vanity stool, and just as quickly embraced her startled hairdresser.

Watching from the doorway, unobserved by the women in his life, Tyler felt the corners of his mouth kick up. As he'd hoped, Alecia and Kylie seemed to like each other. Despite the reservation he'd sensed in Kylie, a somewhat standoffish attitude seemingly directed solely toward him, she appeared to be totally enthralled with Alecia. Delighted to be the recipient of the attention that had, heretofore, been his alone.

The thought of sharing his daughter with the woman he loved appealed. Almost as much as his dream of slipping his ring onto Kylie's finger and knowing she would always be a part of his and Alecia's life.

Tyler's growing fear that something—or someone—would prevent him from realizing his fondest desire seemed uncontrollable at times, like a windswept wildfire on a drought stricken Oklahoma prairie. His ability to put an end to the worry and think positively had become increasingly difficult. Almost impossible.

Keeping a grip on his emotions, and doing his best to protect Kylie from the unknown predator who seemed to know everything about her, was taking a toll on him. He didn't know which he considered worse, his nagging doubt Kylie might not share his hope of a future with him and Alecia or the very real possibility he might not be able to keep her safe. The thought of Kylie choosing the allure of her high-profile career over the country life Tyler preferred left him feeling bereft. The thought of losing her due to a madman's fixation filled him with fury—a rage no law enforcement officer should recognize in himself.

"You're welcome." Kylie returned the child's embrace, her warm smile reflecting her pleasure.

Releasing her hold, Alecia spun toward the mirror, her heart-shaped face beaming. "I'd like to try the French braid you said would look good."

"We'll work on that tomorrow, provided you have the patience to allow me to practice. It's been a while since I've braided anyone's hair."

Like a ball of twine unwinding as it rolled free, the tension inside Tyler ebbed, allowing him to more fully enjoy the 'girl talk' so new to him—and, he knew, to his daughter as well. He couldn't recall ever having heard Connie speak to their child as an equal. Caught up in her own selfish games, his late wife spent little quality time with Alecia, and seemed to consider the everyday demands of parenting tedious. Tyler couldn't help but think his daughter's journey to womanhood would be much smoother if Kylie were nearby, guiding her along the way—and at least a little rockier if she wasn't.

"Now we'll see what we can do with mine." Smiling, Kylie reached for the brush.

"Do you want to borrow some of my clips?" Alecia leaned over the vanity laden with little girl pretties and the varied treasures she kept there. She grabbed a handful of glittery clips and held them out to Kylie. "These would look good."

Tyler doubted Kylie would consider silver ladybugs appropriate accessories for a woman her age.

"I believe you're right." Kylie clamped one shiny clip above her ear, and then shook her head. "I think I'll save some time and wear my cap instead." She brushed her tawny hair up and secured it with a colorful band, then tugged on the khaki hat she'd apparently set on the vanity earlier. "What do you think?"

Kylie made a show of posing for Alecia, acting as though the child's opinion were of vital importance. The slim shapely legs revealed by her tailored shorts made Tyler wish she were posing for him, and that he could whisk her away long enough to explore every appealing inch of her golden, sun-kissed skin.

"Cool," Alecia said with a smile, "really cool."

"Time saved here gives us more time to shop, right?" Kylie kidded, making his daughter's smile even brighter—almost as wide as the sappy one Tyler felt plastered on his own mug. He could get used to their feminine chatter. Quickly.

"Can we stop for ice cream?"

"What would a day of shopping be without our favorite treat?"

"Bor—ing."

"Shall we head out?" Kylie asked, subdued laughter making her voice quaver.

"Yes." Pausing to admire her hair one last time, Alecia leaned toward the mirror. "I really like my hair. Would you teach my Daddy how to fix it like this?"

"Of course," Kylie replied, "if he wants to learn. Until he does, I'll be glad to help you experiment with a few styles."

"He needs to learn how to do it," Alecia stated matter-of-factly. "He's a good daddy, but he doesn't know much about things like hair and makeup."

"Most men don't, though a scant majority of them think they know it all." Kylie's comment worried Tyler—until she completed her thought and added, "Luckily for us, your father is one of the rare few I've known who isn't full of himself."

"My daddy does know everything," Alecia said with conviction. "Nana Marti says he's smart as a whip and so handsome it hurts to look at him."

Kylie's laughter bubbled like sparkling champagne, and had the same effect on Tyler. The sound of it made him lightheaded. And also elated to think how alike she and his daughter were.

"I wouldn't tell him that," Kylie said in an aside as she caught Tyler's look. She winked, and his heart took flight. "Flattery such as that can give a man the bighead."

"I won't, cross my heart." Alecia giggled as she did just that, her small hand slashing across her narrow chest to seal her vow. "Promise you'll teach him how to fix it just like this?" She patted her hair, took one last look in the mirror, and then turned to face Kylie. "So he can do it for me when you're gone."

Tyler's heart plummeted, dropping like the crestfallen expression on Kylie's face. She forced a smile, so bittersweet it, too, seemed somehow connected to the organ making his chest ache with each hard thud.

"I promise," Kylie said brightly.

Too brightly. Tyler felt the pain she fought so valiantly to conceal. It ripped through him, arcing like white-hot steel thrust deep inside him. He wanted to tell her she never had to leave, that he wanted her here, now and forever. Always.

Prudence held him silent. Until he knew she also shared his dream, he didn't dare say anything lest he influence her. The decision to stay or go had to be hers.

"What are you so all-fired eager for me to learn?" Tyler stepped into the room, turning his attention to the child dancing his way.

"How to do this!" Alecia waved her hands above her head. "Isn't it pretty?"

"Beautiful." Tyler picked up his daughter and, with her balanced on his hip, pulled Kylie into their group hug.

Kylie hesitated only a moment, and then slid her arm around his waist. He gave her a moment to adjust to the third party in the embrace, then kissed her soft sweet lips as he'd wanted to from the moment he stopped outside his daughter's room.

"Hot dog!" Alecia exclaimed. "I knew you liked her."

"Did you now?" Tyler set the squirming girl on her feet.

"Yep." Smug and smiling, the child wagged a finger at her father. "I know a secret...I know a secret." She turned to Kylie. "Don't we?"

Kylie nodded, but Tyler had a feeling she didn't have a clue as to what secret his daughter seemed to think they shared.

"What is it?" he asked, aware Alecia would soon tell all. Alecia's fondness for saying too much, especially near Christmas and birthdays, was common knowledge his family found vastly amusing—and occasionally annoying.

"I can't tell." Alecia looked at Kylie and giggled. "We don't want you to get the bighead."

"Is that so?" Tyler moved toward his daughter, waving his fingers as he neared her. "Perhaps the tickle monster can make you talk—"

"Noooooo! You'll mess up my hair!" Squealing her protest, Alecia bolted from the room, leaving both adults shaking with laughter.

Tyler took advantage of the time alone with Kylie. He had her in his arms, and his mouth on hers, so fast Kylie had no chance to dodge him. Soft and sweet and far too giving for him to believe she intended to resist, her ardent kiss fueled his desire, the urgent, heated need never far from his mind.

Easing away from her, Tyler drew a shaky breath. Her dewy-eyed look and the emotions simmering there nearly buckled his knees. *I love you* hovered on the tip of his tongue, but he stayed the words. "You look beautiful."

"I can think of at least a dozen words that more accurately describe the way I look." Kylie rolled her eyes, playfully batted her lashes as she straightened the hat dislodged by their previous activity. "Casual. Comfortable. Stylishly slouchy, to name a few."

"Beautiful is the only one I can think of." Tyler pulled her close for one last kiss, and then moved back. The sultry daze dilating her pupils and making her green eyes look as soft and inviting as the plump curve of her lips still parted and moist from his kiss pleased him. Smiling with satisfaction, he said, "You'd better get moving, otherwise we'll both have to face the music. Alecia isn't the most patient child."

"She's adorable." Kylie pushed a lock of hair from his forehead, stared at him so long Tyler began to worry. The uncertain, almost wary reticence now filling her gaze rocked his senses.

"What's wrong?" he asked, not quite sure he wanted to know.

Kylie had been so quiet—too quiet—since they'd returned home the night before. He didn't want to think Alecia had anything to do with Kylie's odd behavior, but couldn't help believing she did. Except when they'd walked down to the lake to secure his boat and enjoy a moonlight swim—and while making love beneath the stars—she'd acted as though something troubling had occurred. As if she were simply marking time, waiting for an opportunity to announce her departure. Even thinking she might leave him rocked Tyler to the depths of his soul.

"Nothing." Kylie pushed her lips upward, though Tyler would not have called the halfhearted curve a smile. "Really."

"Would you tell me if something is bothering you?"

"Of course," she stated, her gaze averted. "Why wouldn't I?"

"To keep me from worrying," he stated, "or to avoid bruising my tender feelings."

"You're a big boy, Tyler. I wouldn't hesitate to tell you what's on my mind if I feel we need to talk about it."

"You're a terrible liar." Tyler placed his finger beneath her chin, gently urged her to raise her head and again look at him. "Your nose turns red when you fib…and you refuse to look at me."

"That's nonsense!" She batted his hand away, but continued to hold his steady gaze with her slightly irritated one. "There is something I'd like to discuss with you, however—"

"Kylie?" Alecia called from the hallway. "Are you coming?"

"Now isn't the time." Kylie grabbed her purse from the bed and turned to go. Pausing, she spun around and quickly closed the distance between them. Standing on tiptoe, she cupped his face between her palms and pressed her lips to his. "It's nothing major. We'll talk when Alecia and I get home."

Tyler watched her go, the sweet taste of her kiss lingering like the hazy fog of a vision too real to forget. He hoped the shopping trip wouldn't last too long. And that whatever it was putting that strained unhappy look on her face had nothing to do with him.

Or his daughter.

Sixteen

Tyler used the time Kylie and Alecia were shopping to catch up on the household paperwork he'd neglected of late. The phone rang as he was stuffing the last utility bill and payment slip into an envelope.

He glanced at the caller ID, scowling when he recognized the Dallas area code and number registered. Despite thinking he should let the answering machine pickup and record the message obviously intended for Kylie, he lifted the receiver, intent on jotting down the information.

"Wolfe residence," Tyler ground through clenched teeth. Talking to Kylie's ex-husband did not appeal.

"May I speak to Kylie?" the feminine voice inquired politely.

"She isn't in, may I take a message?" he asked just as graciously. Glad to know it wasn't Matt Andrews at the other end of the connection, he said, "I'll make sure she gets it."

"This is Liza Andrews," she stated, "I had a message to call her."

Intrigued by her somewhat defensive tone, Tyler seized the opportunity to quiz the psychiatrist. "I wasn't aware she'd called you. Is there anything particular you'd like me to tell her?"

"No—yes." Apparently at odds over what she wanted to say and what she intended to relate, Liza paused. Long enough to pique Tyler's curiosity. "Tell her I'm fine...and that I appreciate her concern."

"I'll do that." Tyler hesitated a moment, unsure as to what, if anything, he might gain by pressing the obviously irritated woman. Positive he had nothing to lose, he continued. "I'd like to apologize for the inconvenience you and your husband endured because of me."

"I assume you're referring to the inquisition." Liza's low-pitched chuckle sounded more derisive than amused. "I can't believe anyone would consider either Matt or me capable of such reprehensible behavior."

"Until we catch the person responsible for the *reprehensible behavior*, no one is above suspicion." Aware he was dangerously close to breaching protocol, Tyler added, "Even you."

"You're wasting your time, Marshal." A tapping sound punctuated her cool remark, making Tyler think Liza was drumming her fingers on the receiver. "Kylie and I are friends. I want only the best for her."

"And for yourself?"

"Of course. Doesn't everyone?" Liza chuckled again, though Tyler felt certain she wanted to shriek. The tension in her voice sounded thick enough to slice.

"How did you get my number?" He punched the caller ID, bringing up the numerical information.

"Kylie must have given it to Matt," she responded matter-of-factly, "it's written beneath the message for me to call her."

"That explains it." Though he was far from convinced, Tyler said, "How else could you have known she was staying here?"

"The process of elimination?" she replied dryly. "Kylie's frightened. It stands to reason she'd seek protection. Who better than you to provide that protection?"

A private guard, perhaps? Tyler considered silently, certain Kylie had told no one of her decision to stay with him—least of all her ex-husband's wife.

Though Kylie insisted their friendship had survived the recent upheaval, Tyler questioned the current status of their relationship. To his knowledge, Kylie hadn't spoken to Liza in weeks, nor had Liza Andrews phoned Kylie before. While Kylie and Matt talked and emailed each other daily, both women seemed content having little or no contact.

The lack of communication wasn't unreasonable, considering the circumstances. Still, Tyler couldn't help but wonder if Kylie hadn't misinterpreted the signs, causing her to believe Liza shared her unbiased outlook. To his way of thinking, Liza seemed cool and distant, not the least bit friendly. Very unlike Kylie.

"Don't get me wrong," Liza continued, "I'm glad you're helping her. I just wish you'd direct your attention to finding the miscreant responsible for her current dilemma. Neither Matt nor I appreciate your interest in our personal lives."

"Not even if poking my nose in your affairs helps solve the case?"

"I didn't say that!" Liza snapped, sighing as though she were dealing with a slow-witted child. "Forgive me for sounding waspish. I've had a long, tedious week, and I'm in no mood to discuss this. Please tell Kylie I called, and that there's no need for her to return my call."

Tyler's brows jackknifed at the sudden sound of the dial tone buzzing in his ear. He pressed the disconnect button, puzzled to think the woman Kylie obviously cared enough about to phone and request a return call had not once asked about Kylie's well-being. And equally baffled as to why Kylie would have given his number to anyone other than her assistant. The call forwarding installed on her home phone allowed legitimate calls to come through—and was intended to prevent all but those individuals who needed to know Kylie's whereabouts from learning anything they could use to pinpoint her current location.

Annoyed to think she may have given Matt his number, Tyler punched in Wyatt's direct line.

"Hello."

"It's Tyler.

"How's my favorite brother?"

"I'm not sure."

"What's up?" His tone concerned, Wyatt asked, "What's going on?"

"Probably nothing."

"Something obviously is. You sound like you'd like to rip someone's head off. Should I be worried?"

Tyler laughed, amused as much by Wyatt's teasing as by his perception. "Only if you refuse to give me a little help."

"I'll do what I can. What do you need?"

"Did your check of the parolees convicted of stalking or more violent crimes provide anything worthwhile?"

"Nada. None of the men and women living within a fifty mile radius is a career stalker. Each case involved one victim and cited reasons ranging from child custody disagreements to love affairs gone wrong." Wyatt paused, and then added, "There is one disturbing similarity we can't ignore."

"What's that?"

"Of the five parolees who were arrested for stalking a stranger, only one was identified prior to the first face-to-face confrontation with his victim.

What's worse, just one of the initial confrontations resulted in incarceration."

"In other words, we'll likely not know who's harassing Kylie until the bastard musters enough courage to confront her?" Frowning, Tyler snapped, "I'm not willing to give him that opportunity."

"You may not have a choice. Considering the number of incidents and the increasingly destructive nature of his high-jinks, our boy is likely chomping at the bit."

"Tell me something I don't know." Tyler raked his fingers through his hair. Seizing upon Wyatt's reference to a masculine perpetrator, he asked, "Are you sexually biased or suddenly sure our suspect is a man?"

"As positive as I can be without valid proof the jerk is a man. All five parolees I just mentioned are men. All but one chose their victim seemingly at random. The fifth claimed to have once dated the woman he stalked for three years before he got up the nerve to approach her."

"I take it she didn't substantiate his claim."

"She didn't have the opportunity to verify or deny his statement."

"Tell me she refused to file charges." Fear trickled down Tyler's spine, chilled his blood.

"In a manner of speaking, she did." Wyatt hesitated, and then quietly said, "She died from injuries suffered in a car accident—a wreck caused by excessive speed. The DA alleged she had been trying to escape the vehicle riding her bumper when her car spun out of control."

"A car driven by her stalker?" Unappeased by Wyatt's confirmation, Tyler growled, "Why isn't he still in prison?"

"His attorney plea bargained—two years served and an additional two of parole and counseling. The stalker is a decorated Vietnam vet whose questionable mental state is well documented. His own mother filed a protective order and moved out-of-state to avoid contact with her only son."

"Sounds like a real winner. Should we run a background check?"

"Already done, Bro. He works a swing shift and has an airtight alibi both on the night Kylie first reported a prowler and on the night she received the prank calls. I didn't pursue proof of his whereabouts the weekend her car was vandalized, but I will if you think we should."

"It doesn't sound like there's a need to." Tyler rubbed his jaw, contemplated his limited options. "Since you're on a roll, there is something I'd like you to check for me." Tyler related his request, relieved by Wyatt's wholehearted approval and vehement vow to act immediately. "Call me as soon as you find out."

"It shouldn't take long. Hang around."

Tyler dropped the receiver into its cradle, but remained behind the desk in his study. Discovering the ease with which anyone other than his family, friends or the supervisor he trusted implicitly could secure his unlisted phone number would tell him all he needed to know right now.

Provided he and Kylie found an opportunity to talk when she returned, he felt certain she would quickly confirm or deny the suspicion keeping him on edge.

He hated to think she'd disregarded the precautions they discussed and given Liza—anyone!—his number. Thinking she had provided information that could prove dangerous—deadly—to any person other than her assistant worried him—almost as much as the fact Liza seemed uninterested in Kylie's safety.

* * *

Kylie handed Alecia the last of the sacks from the trunk of her car, smiling as she surveyed the finish making the vehicle shine like new. The body shop Wyatt recommended had done a wonderful job repairing the damage. Anyone who didn't know it had been trashed would be hard-pressed to find a sign it had vandalized.

"Are you daydreaming?" Alecia asked, giggling as Kylie nodded.

"And admiring my new paint job." Kylie carefully stashed the talisman key ring Granny Wolfe had given her into her purse and trailed the child into the house, her arms laden with the bargains she'd found.

"Something smells good." The girl headed toward the kitchen, sniffing appreciatively. "Daddy's cooking. Yum!"

Tempted by the delicious aromas filling the air, Kylie followed Tyler's daughter, anxious to discover the source of the delightful smells. Tyler stood over the stove, a wooden spoon in one hand and his attention focused on the open cookbook lying atop the counter. Kylie couldn't recall ever having witnessed a more appealing domestic scenario—nor a man who looked so out-of place and determined at once. Considering the variety of heat-and-eat dishes in his freezer, she doubted he made a habit of cooking from scratch.

"What are you fixing?" Alecia stood on tiptoe, attempting to see into the two steaming pots before her.

"Indian tacos." Tyler bent to buss Alecia's cheek, and then offered Kylie the same greeting as she joined the duo in front of the island range. "It's Mom's recipe from the reunion cookbook."

"My favorite!" Alecia hugged her father, then hastened from the room, obviously eager to sort through the purchases she'd made.

"It smells Heavenly." Kylie set aside the bags she'd carried in. "Is there anything I can do?"

"I have everything under control." Tyler slanted her a satisfied look. "Almost. We'll be ready to eat as soon as I figure out how to prepare the fry bread."

"What about it has you puzzled?"

"The temperature of the peanut oil." Tyler shook his head. "The recipe says to cook the tacos fast, but not so fast as to crisp the outside and undercook the middle."

"Allow me," Kylie said, grinning as she nudged him aside. She glanced at the neatly rolled circles of dough rising atop the counter, and then at the bubbling pot of oil. "I believe it's ready."

While Tyler looked on, taking into account the care with which she transferred the bread to the oil, Kylie soon had the Indian-style tacos cooked. She was scooping the last piece from the pot when Alecia rejoined them.

"Why don't you set the patio table, squirt?" Tyler tugged a lock of his daughter's hair, earning a mock ferocious glower.

"You're going to mess up my hair."

"Sorry," he apologized, smiling as the girl gathered the dinnerware and headed outside.

"You're going to have your hands full in a few years," Kylie warned. "At least four boys stopped what they were doing long enough to say hello to her today. One looked like an adoring puppy when she offered to help with the English homework he's been assigned to complete for summer school."

"Sounds like Brandon Cooper." Tyler grinned. "I think he purposely fails at least one class each year so Alecia will help him during regular and summer school."

"So, he's smarter than he appears?"

"He routinely makes straight A's."

Kylie shook her head, amazed by the logic of youths. And by how adorable Tyler looked wearing an apron. "Besides cooking for us, what did you do while Alecia and I were out?"

"Routine stuff. The boring little chores I'd put off so I could enjoy every minute I had with my houseguest," he said with a smile. "I also talked to my supervisor. Sounds like I'll be out of town later this week." Frowning, he added, "Unless I can persuade him to send another marshal in my place."

165

"You can't do that." Kylie turned to face him. "Altering your daily routine and putting up with me twenty-four-seven is sacrifice enough. Postponing trips or asking someone else to fill in for you on my account is above-and-beyond the call of duty."

"Have you heard me complaining?" Tyler gave her a smacking kiss, and a gentle swat on her backside that made her feel wonderfully domestic—and somewhat chastened.

"No."

"I like having you here…and I don't always appreciate assignments that require last minute travel to unknown destinations." *Which comprise the bulk of my duties,* he mused, frowning as he pondered the days Kylie would be alone if no one else was available to make the pickup in San Antonio.

"I'll be okay." Kylie slipped her arms around his waist, smiling. "I'm a big girl, Tyler. I'll manage. I have enough work to keep me busy at least a week."

"That reminds me…" he said, "Liza returned your call. She said to tell you she's fine, and that there's no need to call her back."

"Rats!" Frowning, Kylie continued. "I wanted to talk to her. Matt's worried about her."

"Because she isn't going to Pittsburgh?" He asked, aware of the trouble she and Matt were having with the Pennsylvania conference.

"Partially." Kylie shrugged. "But not entirely. He thinks something's bothering her…something disturbing enough to cause her to cancel attending the seminar with no explanation."

"And he thinks she'll tell you what's going on?" Tyler shook his head. "Their relationship sounds…odd, to say the least."

"I'm sure it has been difficult. Starting a new relationship that's been the focus of too much media attention and unkind speculation none of us deserved is enough to put a strain on the best marriage." Seeing Tyler's thoughtful, albeit dubious look, she asked, "Is there something you haven't told me that I should know?"

He gave a jerky nod indicative of his concern. "The call came through on my private line. It wasn't forwarded from yours."

"That's odd…" Kylie eased back, turning to check the taco filling still on the burner. "Their home phone number registered on the caller ID when Matt called, too. I intended to mention it but—"

"The table's set." Alecia sashayed past them and began filling glasses with ice.

Tyler and Kylie shared a look, silently agreeing to continue their conversation at a more convenient time.

A short time later, the trio remained on the shaded patio. Tasting as good as it smelled, the food disappeared in no time. Both Alecia and Kylie complemented the cook. Obviously pleased by their accolades, Tyler promised to try his hand at another of the dishes he'd discovered while searching for Marti's taco recipe. They had just finished clearing the table when Alecia noticed Chief slowly moving their way.

"Look," the girl cried as she dashed toward the dog. Now near the edge of the unfenced backyard, the pet appeared too tired to move at his normal pace. "Chief's limping!"

"She's right." Kylie watched the weary animal lumbering across the lawn, his dark fur damp and dirty. Though Chief often accompanied her and Tyler to the lake, she'd never seen the dog enter the water.

"Alecia, stay back!"

Pausing, Alecia peered over her shoulder at her father. "Why?"

"He may be injured. Chief's gentle, but any wounded animal should be approached with caution." Tyler strode toward the dog, speaking soothingly as he neared the pet.

"Chief loves me." Her lower lip quivering, Alecia obeyed her father. "He loves me."

"I know he does, honey. Right now he's hurt and probably a little scared. That could make him forget you're his best friend."

Hoping to ease Alecia's upset, Kylie hastened to where the child stood, slid her arm around the narrow shoulders stiffened by an admirable show of courage. "He'll be okay, sweetie. Your daddy will take good care of him." Nodding her agreement, Alecia remained silent, tears trickling down her cheeks as she clung to Kylie.

"Easy, big boy." Kneeling, Tyler stroked Chief's broad back. "Let me have a look at your leg."

As though understanding his master's request, Chief raised the left front paw he'd been favoring, set it atop Tyler's knee. Kylie could see blood oozing from what appeared to be a small wound high on the dog's leg. Frowning, Tyler gingerly touched the area surrounding the circular cut, and then applied a gentle pressure to the furry leg above and below the injury. Chief whimpered, but made no effort to pull free. Easing the paw back down, Tyler ran his fingers along the inner side of the pet's leg, again making the dog whine.

"Do you think it's broken?" Kylie tucked an errant strand of hair behind Alecia's ear, glad the girl now seemed to be handling Chief's injury with a calm few children could manage.

"I don't believe it is." His features taut with concern, Tyler stroked the matted fur along Chief's wide chest. Though Tyler's touch was infinitely gentle, Kylie sensed a tense undercurrent, a measure of restraint indicative of anger or, more likely, the same helpless frustration making her feel useless. "But the wound extends through the fleshy tissue."

"Do you want me to get the first-aid kit?" Alecia strained forward, but Kylie held her back, kindly persuading her to remain where she was until her father answered.

"We need to take him to the vet." Tyler stood, casting Kylie an unreadable look as he slipped his fingers beneath Chief's collar. "Will you phone the pet emergency center while I load Chief?"

Nodding, Kylie reached for Alecia's hand, intent on leading the wide-eyed girl into the house. Alecia shook off her hold, choosing, instead, to accompany her father.

"I can use her help. Chief doesn't care much for car trips." Sparing Kylie an apologetic look, Tyler said, "You'll find Doc King's number in the Rolodex next to the phone in my office."

"I'll take care of it." Kylie rushed into the house, to Tyler's office. She found the number and alerted the care center, but had scarcely set the receiver in place when the phone rang, startling her. "Wolfe residence." Frowning, Kylie acknowledged the caller, wishing her stepfather's home health nurse had chosen a more convenient time to contact her. "Oh, no!"

"What's wrong?" Tyler entered the room, scowling as he approached her.

Kylie covered the mouthpiece with her unsteady hand. "It's Carl. He's in the hospital. His nurse says he isn't doing well…and he's asking for *me*."

Pausing only long enough to reassure her with a quick embrace, Tyler lifted the phone from her hand and, once he'd announced his identity, secured the information needed to allow Kylie to determine her course of action. The call disconnected, he tucked Kylie's head beneath his chin, hugged her close. His voice as firm and comforting as his hold, he related the nurse's opinion of Carl's condition; a prognosis Kylie truly hoped would prove unfounded. Much as she disliked her stepfather, she hated to think he might not survive.

"I'll take you by the hospital if you want to go, and come back there as soon as I drop Chief off at the vet's."

Tyler rocked her from side to side, ran his strong hands up and down her spine, calming her. And alerting her to how much she wanted him by her side when she faced Carl Bennett for the first time in six years.

"We should take care of Chief first. There's nothing I can do to help Carl."

"Carl obviously feels differently, otherwise he wouldn't have asked for you." Tyler leaned back, raised her head with the gentle nudge of his fist beneath her chin. "I'll call Wyatt and have him meet us at Doc King's. He and Alecia can stay with Chief while I drive you to the hospital."

"Thank you." Kylie blinked back the tears threatening to overflow her lashes and coaxed her lips into an upward curve. "I don't want to go there alone."

"You don't have to." Tyler dipped his head, brushed her lips with his. As though dissatisfied by the brief contact, he kissed her again, stealing the last of her nervousness along with her breath. Easing back, he urged her from the room. "Let's get moving."

Eager to comply, Kylie grabbed her purse and headed for the door. She dreaded seeing Carl, but knew she could handle most anything life tossed her way so long as Tyler stood beside her.

She hated to think how she might react to situations such as this if he were not near enough to lend her his support, his strength that also made her feel stronger.

Seventeen

Kylie paused outside Carl's hospital room, her mouth dry and her palms damp. Queasy from the medicinal smell, she pushed open the door, prepared to endure her stepfather's company—and for what she hoped would be a brief visit.

She wished Tyler were here with her, at her side. He'd agreed to stay in the family waiting room, as she'd asked him to do when he offered to pay his respects along with her. Knowing he would have walked her down the corridor and stood beside her as she faced Carl proved enough to bolster her courage.

Aware she had to do this alone, that she must confront her misgivings and the man she wanted nothing to do with, she'd insisted Tyler relax and enjoy a cup of coffee while she bearded the lion. Smiling his understanding, Tyler had kissed her and told her to take all the time she needed, that he'd be waiting when she felt ready to leave.

Still tasting his kiss, Kylie stepped into the room, her lips tingling from the brief contact. Forcing a smile, she moved toward the bed, more in control despite the trepidation causing her stomach to churn.

Unmoving, Carl appeared to be sleeping, totally unaware of the constant hum and occasional beeps of the many machines monitoring his condition. His eyes were tightly shut, the hollows of his once round cheeks sunken and deeply lined. Creases wreathed his thin lips, fanned out from the corners of his eyes, and bisected his broad forehead, making him look much older than when she'd last seen him, too pale and fragile to pose a threat.

Tears stung her eyes, and Kylie blinked them away. Carl Bennett did not deserve her pity. He'd made her life much harder than it should have been, and caused her untold grief. Knowing her mother, too, had been forced to deal with his surly attitude and domineering ways, Kylie refused to grant him the empathy responsible for her sudden emotional state.

The innocent result of a teenage love affair gone wrong, Kylie had been made to feel worthless and guilty due to her mother's bad choice. Carl seemed to consider it his duty to mold Kylie according to his own design, to treat his stepchild like the sinner he considered his wife to be because of her past indiscretions.

Neither Kylie's efforts to please him, nor her mother's occasional intervention, had been enough to thwart the browbeating and sometimes extreme methods of control to which Carl subjected both mother and daughter.

Not even Kylie's good grades or the stringent obedience she strived to maintain at all times pleased him. Her hair and clothes and friends were subject to ridicule; her every act reason to scold her, discipline her. Finally, aware she would never live up to Carl Bennett's expectations, Kylie learned to cope with his moodiness, learned to keep her distance and tolerate his criticism.

With a feigned indifference, Kylie had also accepted her mother's nonpartisan role, knowing there was little Ruth Bennett or anyone else could do to change Carl's opinion of his wife's daughter.

Kylie's relationship with Tyler had helped tremendously, granted her the ability to build upon the courage she lacked when dealing with Carl. Her confidence had grown along with her feelings for Tyler, allowing her to accept the inevitable and alter her outlook as she matured. As it had in the past few weeks, Tyler's unconditional support gave her the strength to overlook the actions of others and attend to her own business without undue concern as to how others viewed her efforts.

As she had so long ago, Kylie flourished in spite of the circumstances beyond her control.

And, as she had back then, Kylie loved Tyler as much because of his unshakable support of her as for his solid character and many appealing traits. She knew no other man would ever measure up to the standards by which he lived.

She also knew no other man would do, that her love for Tyler was of the special, everlasting kind no woman could resist.

"Kylie?"

Kylie stiffened at the sound of her name, whispered so softly she thought for a moment she'd imagined hearing it. She looked at the man lying so still, a hint of a smile curving his colorless lips.

"Is it really you?"

"In the flesh," she replied, her tone less tart than she would have liked. She refused to give an inch, lest he steal a mile. She knew how quickly he could turn the table and make her feel inconsequential, defensive.

"I can't believe you're here." Carl shifted, attempting to sit up. His breath came in short, uneven gasps, the rasping sound indicative of the effort required to fill his diseased lungs with life-giving oxygen.

"Stay where you are." Kylie moved forward, to the foot of the bed. "I don't intend to stay long."

Nodding, Carl eased back down, tugged the sheet higher. "How are you, girl?"

"Fine." Hearing herself referred to as *girl*, the no-name person he seemed to consider her, raised Kylie's hackles. She hated knowing he still wouldn't routinely use her name; that she mattered so little not even that small courtesy counted.

"Glad to hear it." He drew a shaky breath, settled back in the bed. His dark eyes were dimmer now, less piercing than she recalled. "You've done well, Kylie. Your mother would be proud."

Kylie glanced at the nearest monitor and nodded, unable to speak around the lump suddenly lodged in her throat. Seldom supportive, her mother had seemed indifferent most of the time; so often Kylie figured her only child's achievements and happiness meant little to the woman who gave birth to her. Unlike Tyler, who responded to his daughter's every word and deed with a fatherly pride, Kylie's mother acted as though her parental duty amounted to providing the basic necessities. Ruth Bennett seldom offered advice, and almost never asked her daughter's opinion of anything.

Kylie couldn't help but feel cheated—and at least partially guilty for failing to do more to make their relationship stronger, more normal.

"I owe you an apology." Carl's remark, much louder and seemingly sincere, snapped Kylie's gaze to his. He smiled as though her wide-eyed look amused him. "More than one if you're of a mind to hear me out."

"That depends," Kylie said, her heart pounding like a jackhammer. She wouldn't promise to forgive him, but found she truly wanted to know what he had on his mind.

Carl chuckled, making her smile despite her intention not to. "You always were a stubborn child…unyielding sometimes."

"I had to be." Kylie squared her shoulders. "You taught me that giving in would gain nothing, except more criticism."

"I know." Carl blinked hard, causing her to think he, too, felt the sting of the unwelcome tears burning her own eyes. "I didn't make it easy on you."

"No, you didn't." Kylie clenched her teeth, clamping down on her desire to expound and mention any of the many times he'd caused her heartache. His refusal to allow her to try out for the cheerleading squad her senior year had hurt, as did his stubborn insistence she dump Chief in the alley where she'd found the small, fuzzy pup Tyler adopted.

She wanted to tell him he'd been wrong to try and control her every move, how deeply his hateful words had affected her. Willing herself to put the past behind her and keep their visit brief, she took a deep breath, forced a smile. "You definitely didn't."

"I've come to terms with that." He shifted sideways, reached for the final book of Kylie and Matt's series from the bedside table. "This helped." He held up the *We Will* title that had enjoyed a three-month ride at the top of the best-seller lists. "It helped a lot."

"You've read my book?" Aware she sounded skeptical, Kylie added, "I can't imagine you enjoyed it."

"I've read every one of them." He thumped the cover with his index finger, a digit as thin and sickly looking as the rest of him. "This one twice. You put a truckload of advice in there, girl…and a simple explanation for why we act the way we do for no good reason."

"That was our goal. Determining the underlying cause for unacceptable behavior is vital to those who hope to put an end to the destructive habits that prevent them from interacting normally. We wanted our readers to know behavior modification is possible, and that it doesn't always require an extraordinary effort."

"You did that." Setting the book aside, he cast her a steady, imploring look. "I didn't know what to do with you, girl."

"What to do with me?" Kylie shook her head, unable to comprehend his meaning.

Carl nodded. "You were such a little thing, sweet and loving like any toddler. I couldn't wait to get home after work. Knowing you'd meet me at the door, smiling like an angel, made me feel like a king.

"That meant a lot to me, more than I realized until it was too late to go back to those happier times."

"I don't remember many good times," Kylie said quietly, her thoughts on the near constant conflicts that made her teen years so difficult.

"I can understand why." Carl ducked his head, acting as though shaken by his admission. He inhaled deeply, wheezing as his narrow chest ballooned. "I blamed you for everything that was wrong in my life. The job I hated...your mother's indifference...the fact we couldn't have kids, was your fault."

"You wanted more children?" Stunned, Kylie said, "I had no idea."

"I'm not surprised. We never really talked much." He chuckled dryly, a sound as rusty as a seldom-used hinge creaking open. "The way you used to look at me, like I hung the moon and stars, made me want a son...a child of my own who'd also think I was worth loving.

"Then you grew up, and I realized I'd never measure up. Suddenly, you were too smart for me to fool—too bright to trust a dropout to know what's best. I hated not being able to afford piano and dance lessons, so I made your mother account for every dime I earned. I hated not being able to take you places, so I refused to let you go the few times you had a chance to discover the world outside this town. I was a tyrant, plain and simple."

"You were that." Kylie sighed, not quite sure she should believe what she was hearing. She doubted Carl Bennett could change so dramatically, but could not deny she truly wanted to think he had.

The thought of anyone—even Carl—being so miserable simple joy was beyond reach, made her heart ache.

"I wanted to be a good to you, but I didn't know how. Instead of trying harder, I gave up. Criticizing you and your mother helped me overlook my own faults. By acting like I didn't care, I was able to convince myself you didn't give a hoot what I did, and that my attitude was justified." He gave her a solemn look. "Truth is, I did care. I didn't realize how much until I nearly missed out on the only chance I had to make things right."

"How so?" Kylie asked, slightly amazed to think she wanted to know what changed his mind, what had occurred to make him want to change. She'd counseled abusive spouses often enough to know nothing anyone said or did made a difference unless they were willing to accept the new set of guidelines needed to improve their life.

"I didn't take your mother's threat to leave seriously." He smiled, obviously amused by the shock Kylie figured would be evident in her expression. "She'd packed her bags and was headed for the car when I came to my senses. I coaxed her back into the house and, with my usual hardheaded approach, demanded an explanation. Ruth gave me a piece of her mind and issued an ultimatum: act like a man or give her a divorce." Carl looked away, swallowed hard. "That was the first time she'd ever raised her voice to me."

"I can't imagine Mother yelling at anyone, least of all you."

"She told me she'd wanted to many times," he said quietly, "and how much she hated the way I treated you." He looked at Kylie, not attempting to hide the tears misting his eyes. "I thought you were the reason she married me, girl. I had a hard time coming to grips with that. Fact is, I was wrong about that, too. Ruth said she loved me, had since I met her at the diner where she was working to support the two of you." He shook his head, shrugged. "That alone made me feel ten times a fool…"

"When did this happen?" Kylie shifted sideways, her interest piqued. She'd sensed a calm in her mother shortly before her death, a strong, almost bold, acceptance of the cancer rapidly stealing her health. She had attributed the peaceful demeanor to her mother's usual meekness, but now wondered if it had been the result of finally expressing her true feelings—emotions Ruth had kept well hidden from both her husband and her child.

For the first time, Kylie realized her mother had also cheated Carl, withheld the love and attention he obviously wanted as much as Kylie had.

"Right after she got sick." Carl rubbed a tear from his cheek, sought a more comfortable position. "Even knowing she would have a hard time on her own, she was willing to sacrifice what little comfort I could afford her to make her point." He inhaled deeply, rattling his chest, and met Kylie's somber look with one of beseeching sincerity. "I ended up begging her forgiveness, and promising to never again take her for granted. I also told her I'd make things right with you, that I'd make you understand why I was such a miserable failure.

"Your books showed me why I acted the way I did. Ruthie's love and the strategy outlined in each of your books helped me put my priorities in order. I'm the one who made things rough, and it's high time I shoulder the blame."

While not exactly a deathbed confession, Carl's words rang true. Despite her lingering reservations, Kylie sensed the same calm in him she'd noticed in her mother, an accepting strength that would continue to grow no matter what she said or did because of it.

Aware she wanted to take his words to heart, that she no longer felt the need to lash out, made her feel much better. Thinking she would not have to avoid him in order to protect herself, also improved her outlook. They might never be friends, but she could at least offer some assistance in his time of need.

"I agree," Kylie said with a smile. "And, since we're on the subject, I have to accept at least a portion of the blame."

"No way." Carl waved his hand in a dismissive gesture. "You were a child, Kylie...the innocent victim of an unhappy man who wanted everyone around him to bow and scrape. Your mother wasn't brave enough to put me in my place, and your attempts to reason with me fell on deaf ears. Instead of praising you for the being a good kid, I seized every chance I had to belittle you. I'm surprised you didn't rebel and give me the excuse I wanted to boot you out."

"I did rebel." Kylie shrugged. "In my own way."

"Your way was right," he said with a smile, "'Cause I had no idea you were rebelling."

"Perhaps it was." Kylie chuckled. "My occasional defiance certainly made me feel better."

"Enough of that." Carl coughed, his face drawn as though the effort taxed his strength. "I wanted you to understand, but that isn't the reason I asked Helen to call you."

"Why did you ask for me?" Kylie looked away, certain the old Carl would emerge, spoiling what had been a reasonably amicable visit.

"To make sure you're okay."

"Why wouldn't I be?" she asked, positive he would prove her right to think he hadn't changed at all; that he would again give her reason to avoid him no matter how ill be became.

"I heard about your troubles. I don't want you to take any chances."

"How—"

"—I can't do much anymore, Kylie. Watching TV or listening to the police scanner is about all I can do without getting winded." He gave her a solemn look. "This is a small town, and news travels fast. If I hadn't been listening to the scanner the night you called for help, I'm sure Helen or someone else would have told me what was going on."

"Your nurse does seem a bit talkative." Uncomfortable knowing she was likely the subject of speculation and small town gossip, she added, "Everything's under control."

"Would you tell me if it wasn't?" he asked, his expression as hard and unyielding as she remembered.

"Probably not."

"That's what I figured." His smile sudden and warm, he said, "Would you at least take an old man's advice?"

"Possibly."

"Be careful...and trust Tyler Wolfe to keep you safe."

"Tyler?" Positive she must look as shocked as she sounded, Kylie shook her head. "You hated Tyler. You said he was a bum out for a good time, that he was using me!"

"He proved me wrong. I shouldn't have judged him so harshly. Your books showed me why I had." Carl gave her a weary smile. "I apologized to him, too."

Stunned, Kylie opened her mouth to ask when, but quickly closed it and turned to see who had just rapped on the door. Tyler poked his head in through the opening, and said, "Mind if I come in?"

Upon hearing Carl's surprisingly hearty welcome, Tyler joined Kylie at the foot of the bed. He reached for her hand, threaded his fingers through hers. The two men chatted briefly, and then Tyler glanced her way, his expression unreadable. "Are you ready to go?"

Kylie nodded, bid Carl goodbye, as did Tyler. Promising to visit him again soon, they hastened from the room. Once in the corridor, she paused, forcing Tyler to also stop since he still held her hand. "What's wrong?"

"Chief's out of surgery and—"

"—Surgery? Is he okay?"

"He'll be fine, just a little sore for a few days." Pulling his hand free, Tyler continued down the hall, his fists clenched as he walked beside Kylie. "We have to pick him up. Doc had another emergency, and Wyatt can't load Chief without my help."

He'd give a month's wages to know who'd shot his dog—what kind of two-legged animal would purposely harm another man's pet.

Tyler had suspected the injury might be the result of a bullet, but had hoped his fears would prove unfounded. The smooth, circular entry and ragged exit had appeared consistent with the manner in which a projectile would rip through flesh. Aware a sharp stick or some other cylindrical object hit with enough force could also inflict such an injury, Tyler had kept his fears to himself, unwilling to upset either Kylie or Alecia any more than they already were.

Wyatt's call telling him Chief required minor surgery, and that the wound had, indeed, resulted from a gunshot, put the match to Tyler's temper. He had no doubt Kylie's stalker was responsible. Thinking the sick bastard might soon confront Kylie, and that the jerk was obviously prepared to use deadly force to gain her attention, filled Tyler with a profound fear.

Aware both Kylie and Alecia would have to be warned of the danger—or kept out of sight entirely—and that even he would have to exercise greater caution, Tyler vowed to do everything within his power to find the man responsible for wounding Chief.

He hated to think what he'd do once he knew who was behind the vicious attack, the potentially deadly game that made the previous incidents to which Kylie had been subjected even more frightening.

Legally, Tyler was limited as to what he could do without serious ramifications. Excessive force was not a foul he intended to grant Kylie's stalker. He'd turn in his badge before he allowed the bum to claim entrapment, yet setting the bastard up appealed. No matter how clever, few criminals were above a little well-planned temptation.

Tyler knew he'd do everything within his power to see the psycho tried for his crimes and jailed to protect the woman and child he loved. As an officer of the law, he also knew he'd act accordingly—hopefully, within the boundaries of professional protocol.

Though he doubted Kylie would appreciate what he now knew they had to do, he felt certain she would welcome the outcome. She treasured her independence, and would likely relish once again being free to come and go as she pleased. He hoped she would choose to stay with him and Alecia, but couldn't help but wonder if she would do so when given a choice.

He slanted her a sideways look as they neared the Jeep, praying she would forgive him if he failed to keep her safe. Fearing she might not—and even more afraid she would not have the chance to—he unlocked the passenger side door, blocking the entry long enough to cause her to look up.

"What is it, Tyler? What's wrong?" she asked, her wide green eyes filled with concern.

"I'm just feeling a little neglected."

Tyler lowered his head, covered her soft, sweet mouth with his. He kissed her as though it were the last time, with all the love and longing he could muster. Kylie responded in kind, making his head spin as she gave in to the desire making them both tremble.

Needing air, Tyler forced himself to end the kiss. Still wanting the contact, he pulled her close, angling his body to accommodate the slim, yielding curves tempting him to chuck his half-hatched scheme and whisk her away. Knowing he could do that, give her a new identity and take her so far from the madman plaguing both their lives she'd have no reason to fear her stalker again, gave him the courage to stick to his plan.

Aware she might soon hate him, Tyler urged her into the vehicle. He hastened to the driver's side door, hoping he had the guts to accept her decision, whatever it happened to be. Life without her held no promise.

The thought of Kylie with no life at all speared his soul with a pain too intense for him to describe.

Eighteen

Kylie waved as Marti and Alecia climbed into the minivan Amos had parked in front of Tyler's garage. Though their trip to Branson, Missouri, to visit a popular Ozark Mountain theme park seemed sudden, it had also been cause for celebration. Alecia had been so excited when Tyler relayed his parents' invitation for her to accompany them, the girl had used every excuse in the book to stay up late the night before. Kylie doubted she had slept more than five hours, and figured the anxious child had slept even less.

"I miss her already." Tyler looped his arm around Kylie's waist and drew her nearer.

"They'll only be gone three days." Kylie snuggled close, tears threatening as she watched the van drive away. Knowing the child would enjoy the trip as much as her grandparents would relish the time away made Kylie feel a little better. Alecia wasn't her daughter, but Kylie, too, felt the misery parents everywhere must deal with when their offspring leave the nest—even for a brief excursion such as this.

"I know," Tyler whispered next to her ear, his breath warm against her skin. Turning Kylie to face him, he smiled and said, "I can't imagine what we'll do to occupy ourselves now that we have the run of the house."

"Can't you?" Kylie batted her lashes playfully. Delighted by the wicked promise darkening his eyes, she slid her arms around his neck and wriggled her body even closer. "I can think of at least a dozen things we could do."

"Such as?"

"We could dust your office. We could hang the picture Alecia bought for her playroom. Or..." Kylie raised her mouth to his, kissed him lightly. Unsatisfied by the chaste contact, she deepened the kiss. Soon breathless, she pulled away, hoping her smile looked as seductive as she felt. "We could give each other a massage and see where that leads..."

"To hell with the massage." Tyler scooped her into his arms, kicking the door shut behind him as he headed for the stairs. "For now."

* * *

Despite the work each of them needed to do, Kylie and Tyler spent most of the day in bed, enjoying each other and the hours alone as only lovers can. Exhausted and content, they'd raided the kitchen a short time before, putting together a simple feast of deli meats and cheeses, fruit and buttery crackers to savor along with the bottle of wine Tyler had snatched from the liquor cabinet.

Kylie plumped the pillows beneath her shoulders and eased back. Bare, save for the burgundy sheet draped across her midsection, she sighed as she sought a more comfortable position. Her body ached in a most delightful way, her muscles and private places reacting to each move with the tingly tenderness experienced in love's aftermath. She couldn't recall ever having felt quite so satisfied—physically or emotionally.

She knew the only thing that could complete her happiness would be the knowledge this day was one of many to come. Her certainty it would be one of the few she would never forget once Tyler had no reason to protect her added a bittersweet quality to the blissful lethargy immobilizing her.

"Tired?" Tyler set the silver platter aside and topped off each of the two goblets with the last of the wine. Handing one glass to her, he stood, looking down at her as she raised the crystal rim to her lips.

"Mmm—hmm."

Kylie savored the crisp white wine, her mouth suddenly dry despite the liquid washing over her tongue. Obviously unconcerned by his naked splendor rendering her speechless, he seemed totally unaware of how his masculine beauty affected her. The desire to touch him was so strong her fingers burned because of it. She wanted to again feel the supple power of the well-defined muscles bisecting his broad chest and giving his limbs the undeniable male shape that made him so appealing.

Knowing she could fulfill the fantasy making her head spin from just looking at him, that a single word or the most innocuous action from her would trigger the need he, too, seemed unable to control, enabled her to resist the temptation—barely. Staring into his eyes, seeing the desire blazing there, lit an answering flame deep inside her—the rapacious fire of a passion so powerful her ability to control it melted like a candle left untended.

Amazed to think she wanted him again, needed him—so badly tremors of heat were coursing through her like rivers of molten lava—she tugged the sheet higher. Stunned to realize she'd lost not only her heart, but also that most vital part of her being—her soul—Kylie shifted beneath his heated look, uncomfortable now that she knew the cost of loving him.

The price seemed ungodly, much higher than she'd expected. She hadn't counted on losing herself so completely in the bargain.

"Too tired for that massage you mentioned?"

Kylie opened her mouth, intending to tell him she was too weary to consider even a therapeutic massage appealing; that his strong hands skating over her bare skin was the last thing she needed just now. Instead, she said, "Definitely not."

"Stay put." He flashed a grin—a sexy, knowing look too damn self-satisfied for her to consider anything but devilish—as he turned and walked into the master bath.

Unable to tear her gaze away, Kylie watched him move, entranced by the flex of his muscles rippling with each step. Broad shoulders tapered to an incredibly trim waist that also called attention to his narrow, perfectly rounded buttocks. His legs were long and lean, powerfully built despite their slimness. Beautifully tanned from head to toe, his skin looked like smooth bronze, as sleek and solid as the firm foundation of strength beneath it.

Anticipation hummed inside Kylie, a growing excitement nurtured by the visual feast making her hunger stronger. Unable to quell the ravenous need causing her to tremble, she gladly relinquished control, nourishing her rising desire with a spirited freedom that made the sensations zinging through her even more powerful.

She wanted to touch him again, feel the leashed fury of his passion; experience the rush of her own unfettered release. Her inhibitions unchained, the emotional potpourri assailed her, warming every cell, pooling where her body had become achingly aware of her feminine need.

A potent mix, the feelings rioting inside her seemed right, a just reward denied her so long ago. Kylie doubted she would ever be the same, yet knew she would not trade these last few days with Tyler for all the lonely years to come.

She would enjoy this time together. She would survive the outcome, stronger and happier because she had allowed herself this freedom, more alive than she'd ever been due to the man unwittingly wreaking havoc upon her senses.

* * *

Tyler grabbed a bottle of scented oil from the top shelf of his medicine cabinet and closed the mirrored door, catching a glimpse of his reflection— and the woman watching his every move from the rumpled bed. With her hair sexy and wild, her full lips swollen from his kisses, she looked well loved— and anxious to make love again. Emotion knotted his stomach, spread as the all too familiar heat of desire seared his loins, tightening his body.

Staring into her hot green eyes, seeing the hunger burning there, made his head spin. Like an intimate touch, the need blazing in those wide beautiful eyes touched him as nothing else ever had, humbled him.

He couldn't imagine why his tousled hair and five o'clock shadow didn't repulse her, or how she could still have the strength to want him—so much her desire was evident, palpable. Praying his average looks and the passion he felt for her would continue to please her, he turned, holding her avaricious look as he neared the bed.

"You first, sweet lady," he said, amazed he could speak. His throat felt parched, no doubt due to the fiery need sweeping through him.

Kylie shook her head, held out her hand. "You first."

She pushed up into a sitting position, the sheet forgotten as she uncorked the bottle he'd handed her. Her breasts swung free, each small, perfect globe beckoning him, tempting him to forgo the massage and fill his hands with the flesh still rosy from his touch. Instead, Tyler lay facedown across the bed, his teeth clenched as Kylie quickly got down to business.

Pausing only long enough to set aside the bottle, she straddled his hips, pressing her warm thighs against him. Tyler inhaled sharply, stunned by the intensity of the sensations spearing him. Fiery prickles lapped at his skin, radiating from her body to his each place they touched. A sweet tension gripped him, making him throb like an untried teen too inexperienced to realize the pleasure-pain causing him such torment would soon subside, that his release would rocket higher because of her sensual torture.

Apparently unaffected, Kylie spread the oil across his upper back with sure methodic strokes, gently kneading his taut muscles. Tyler groaned as she

183

worked her magic, her soft hands brisk and efficient as she smoothed the scented liquid over his skin. The smell of cloves, clean and spicy, titillated his senses, adding to his heightened awareness of the feminine heat brushing against his backside.

As though alerted by his focus on the contact, she scooted back, her hips poised above the backs of his knees as she massaged his buttocks. The steady motion of her hands slower now, Kylie continued, seemingly fascinated by that portion of his anatomy closest to the rock-hard desire causing him such pleasant misery.

Unable to relax, Tyler remained still, unsure as to how much more he could endure. The silken pressure of her palms gliding over his hips was almost more than he could stand. Soothing yet gently probing, the feel of her fingers exploring the sensitive space between his thighs pushed him over the edge, snapped his control.

"Enough already!" He flipped over, careful to keep his wide-eyed masseuse above him. Cupping the rounded curve of her derriere in his palms, he dragged her closer to the rigid proof of his need. "More than enough!"

"I'm not finished," she protested. Her sultry smile that of a siren caught in her own seductive net, she whispered, "I want to touch you. I need to touch you!"

"Later." Holding her gaze, Tyler lifted her up, guided her onto his aching arousal. Her lashes drifted down as the hot moist folds of her femininity surrounded him, completed him.

Ensnared by the sensual power of her acceptance, Tyler felt as though he were watching from somewhere high above, able to sense every fragment of his being as Kylie took over, loving him as he'd never been loved. Wild and free, she gave of herself, sealing his fate as well as her own long before sweet satisfaction claimed them, calmed them.

Aware a part of him would forever remain with her, Tyler held her close, his breathing as ragged as the need ever present because of her.

* * *

"When are you leaving for Pittsburgh?" Tyler handed Kylie the napkin she'd asked for, and leaned back in his chair.

Kylie swallowed the last juicy bite of peach that suddenly tasted like cardboard, and dabbed at her mouth, delaying her answer to his question. She stared up at the starlit midnight sky, wishing she could tell him she wasn't going, that she wanted to stay here with him and never face the registrants eager to learn how to better their relationships.

What she wanted and what she had to do seemed worlds apart, yet also intimately linked due to her bond with the man waiting to hear her response.

"Wednesday afternoon." Sensing his gaze, she glanced his way and smiled. "Grace booked a three o'clock flight so I'd have time to settle in before dinner."

"She sounds like a gem."

"She is. I'd trust her with my life."

"You definitely did that."

Kylie stiffened, alarmed by his terse comment. "What do you mean?"

"I asked Wyatt to scan the reverse directories on the Internet. Using my name, all he could access was the address of the apartment I rented while building this house." He gave her an odd look, one as vaguely accusing as his tone. "Using your name, he was able to access not only my phone number—the unlisted number I asked you to give no one other than your assistant!—but my current address as well. With a click or two of the mouse, he also had a detailed map any fool could follow to my door."

"How?" Kylie shook her head, "Grace wouldn't give your number to anyone without first asking me if she should...and I've only been staying here a week. That's far too short a time for misleading information such as that to be posted anywhere, even on Internet sources."

"How doesn't matter. Finding out who is responsible, does."

"Do you think I did it?" Kylie swallowed hard, her throat so tight it hurt. "Do you think I purposely put you and Alecia in danger? That I care so little I'd risk your safety?"

"I don't know what I think or what I can do to lessen the damage," he stated solemnly. "I do think you should reconsider going to Pittsburgh."

"That's impossible." Kylie wadded the napkin she'd shredded into a ball, her thoughts as mangled as the damp paper. "How long have you known about the map?" *How long have you suspected I betrayed your trust?* she wanted to ask, but curbed the urge. "Since yesterday? The day before?"

"Long enough to establish a few precautions."

"Precautions that include limiting my travel plans?"

Nodding, Tyler looked toward the lake, his expression cloaked by the night. His hands atop the table were fisted, as tightly drawn as the apprehension trickling down her spine. Kylie didn't know if he was upset due to the ease with which Wyatt had accessed the information regarding her

185

whereabouts or because she'd insisted upon maintaining her schedule.

She couldn't help but wonder if she'd displeased him some other way. Had she overstayed her welcome? Was the desire so abundant this whole wonderful day one-sided? Thinking she'd misread his interest made her queasy, antsy. Doubts assailed her, mounting along with her irritation.

"I have to go, Tyler."

He turned to face her, his dark eyes as laser bright as the shaft of moonlight illuminating them. "I never expected you to stay."

Kylie's heart plummeted, landing in the pit of her stomach with a resounding thud. "I see," she said, wishing she truly did understand his abrupt about-face. Had she anticipated a declaration of love, she would have been sorely disappointed, far more distraught than she felt thanks to the anger shielding her from the imminent heartbreak.

"I don't think you do." Tyler leaned forward, his features as hard as his tone. "We both have commitments, Kylie…a life that has nothing to do with each other. I put mine on hold to see you through a rough time, yet you aren't willing to sacrifice one trip to help me settle this once and for all."

"What you're asking is unreasonable. I didn't ask you to stop working or to baby-sit me!" Kylie stood, willing her wobbly knees to stop shaking. "For the record, I'd never expect you to turn down an assignment."

"What did you expect of me, Kylie?" Shoving out of his chair, Tyler rounded the table and moved toward her, so close his shadow enclosed her. "Flowers and pretty words? A commitment?" He shook his head, chuckled as though amused by his hateful behavior. "Been there, done that, babe. That route isn't for me."

"I appreciate you pointing that out." Furious, Kylie squared her shoulders. "And since we're on the subject, perhaps I should let you know my expectations weren't that high."

She glanced down, at the buttoned fly and obvious masculine shape of him that would have caused her heart to race a short time ago. Looking at him now had the same effect, but she forced herself to feign the cold acceptance she desperately needed to overcome the loss gripping her with equal intensity.

Pushing her lips upward, she raised her gaze to the hard blue one glaring back at her. "Confusing honest affection with lust is the first mistake most women make. As you so eloquently put it, 'I've been there, done that'…and once was more than enough for me."

Kylie spun around, tears threatening as she hastened toward the door.

"Kylie—"

Pausing, she glimpsed her dark reflection in the plate glass entry. Hating the hollow look of the woman staring back at her, and the man whose expression mirrored that of the lost soul watching both of them, she reached for the levered knob.

"Don't make it worse, Tyler."

Though she doubted he could make her feel worse than she already did, Kylie sought the relative safety of the guest room. The thought of spending another night here, so close and yet so far from the man she loved, filled her with dread.

The thought of returning home, to the house where true danger lurked in every shadowy corner, chilled her to the depths of her being.

Nineteen

Tyler shouldered the carryon bag holding his essentials and skirted the clusters of travelers waiting for their baggage to appear on the conveyer. He usually enjoyed the hubbub of a busy airport, seldom felt claustrophobic as he now did. The joyful looks and warm hugs that greeted newcomers and old acquaintances alike didn't put a smile on his face like they normally did. The signs of anticipation and affection simply served as a reminder of the gaping hollow in his life, the equally monstrous ache in his chest.

Far from his family and estranged from the woman he loved, Tyler felt more alone than he ever had, a solitary being in a world where a group of two seemed far more appropriate than a party of one.

Thoughts of Kylie filled his head, as they had since he'd watched her walk into the house last night. Head high, her spine stiff, she'd closed the door softly, shutting him out as surely as she had moments before when she'd refused to consider his request that she bow out of the Pittsburgh conference.

Throughout the seemingly endless night, he'd vehemently damned her stubborn pride, and his own steadfast resolve to not follow her. He should have talked to her, made love to her as he'd wanted to. Planned to.

Had he explained his reason for asking her to delay travel plans and expressed his fear her stalker would soon confront her, Tyler felt sure she would have understood, that, perhaps, she would have been more agreeable…and less apt to encounter the danger that could ensue when her stalker made his next move.

Knowing Kylie would likely be alone when—if—the bastard harassing her made his presence known, filled Tyler with dread. Thinking she might not survive the confrontation chilled him to the depths of his soul, made him too angry to focus on anything other than what he'd failed to accomplish. He had shielded her from the unknown creature causing her so much trouble. He had not been able to convince her the threat remained, outside his jurisdiction and too real and frightening for her to go about her business as usual.

Tyler knew it was beyond the norm to think he'd be near enough to protect her at all times, yet couldn't help but feel he could have done more to convince Kylie she needed to exercise caution still—and more to persuade her she should remain with him. At his side and in his life where she should have always been.

Scowling, he pushed aside the stormy self-recriminations and made his way past the baggage claim area to the exit. Giving the taxis lined up outside a cursory glance, he scanned the lanes of traffic crawling toward him. Pausing, Tyler searched for the familiar gray SUV Rob Owens had driven since long before the roomy vehicles became popular. Tyler spied the battered Ford Explorer and his waving friend a second later.

"Took you long enough." Tyler stashed his bag in the backseat and climbed into the passenger side. As friends went, Rob counted among the best. Always able to lighten the darkest mood, Rob's ability to help put things in the right perspective made Tyler very glad to see him—that and needing a ride.

"I'd have piddled longer if I'd known you'd be in a pissy mood." Rob jabbed his fist into Tyler's upper arm and feigned a second poke along with a head duck indicative of the moves he'd learned in the ring. The Golden Glove champion had long since hung up his trunks, but stayed in shape by boxing at the gym a deceased uncle had left to him.

Tyler doubted Texas Rangers half Rob's age were conditioned so well—or half as dedicated to their career. Since losing his wife, Rob had spent most of his time working and attending the baseball games he loved almost as much as boxing.

"You talkin' about me?" Tyler returned the comradely greeting, already feeling better.

"Where to?" Rob guided the SUV into the slow-moving traffic, heading for the freeway.

"Any motel near the Garden Villa rest home." Tyler rattled off the address of the retirement home where he planned to meet Victoria Candelera early the next morning. The young woman scheduled to enter the Federal Witness Protection Program would soon become someone else, leaving behind all things familiar to escape the drug king who'd vowed to kill her for testifying against him.

Unlike his fiercely independent Kylie, Ms. Candelera knew the face and name of her nemesis, and was willing to make the sacrifice necessary to protect herself from harm's way.

"I know just the place." Rob chuckled. "And exactly what you need to wipe that scowl off your ugly puss."

"I'm not in the mood for a blind date," Tyler protested, but couldn't hold back the smile pushing his lips upward. "You can keep Barb and the party animals she calls women to yourself."

"Hey, now!" Rob cast him a sour look. "How was I supposed to know those girls worked the streets?"

"By looking at them?" Tyler asked tongue-in-cheek. "Skin-tight leather and sequined belly shirts are a dead giveaway—not to mention the bottled blonde shades of hay piles they call hair."

"They weren't all that bad. You had a good time, didn't you?"

"The vague recollections I have of that night don't rank high on my list of memorable occasions." Tyler shook his head and grinned. "I had a hell of a hangover the next day, and about the only thing I remember is climbing into a taxi after you refused to give me your keys."

"Designated drivers don't give a drunk the keys to their only means of transportation." Rob slapped the dashboard affectionately. "The Paddy Wagon will be ten years old this fall and I've yet to invest a dime in the old gal."

"Ten bucks worth of wax every year or so wouldn't hurt."

"Can't afford such luxury." Rob maneuvered the vehicle onto the entrance ramp, glancing over his shoulder as he merged with the heavier traffic. "Retirement is looming sooner than I care to think about."

"Retirement?" Despite the gray winging Rob's once dark temples, Tyler couldn't imagine anyone less suited to leisurely travel and playing bingo. Forty-five seemed far too young to hang up the badge Rob had proudly worn for twenty-some odd years. "You?"

"Yup. Been thinkin' about it for a while now." A shadow crossed Rob's rugged features, the result, Tyler knew, of images and thoughts of his late wife. The painful memories seemingly gone in a flash, Rob glanced at his passenger and grinned. "I sold the gym last month and bought a new business to see me through my golden years."

Tyler closed his gaping mouth, sure he'd misheard his long-time friend. The gym where the native Texan had honed his boxing skills and spent time with the only male role model in his life meant a great deal to Rob—so much so that Tyler figured something dramatic must have occurred to make him willingly part with it.

"The offer I got was too good to refuse," Rob explained, "and I've discovered a cause more important than training boxers or hunting violent criminals."

"What's that?" Intrigued as well as shocked, Tyler asked, "what could be more important to you than catching the bad guys?"

"Catching the bums who prey on kids. I've decided to devote my time and whatever expertise I've accumulated to hunting the perverts wanted for crimes against kids." Rob winked and grinned. "I bought a detective agency."

Tyler lifted a brow, more curious than surprised by his friend's admission. Rob had a soft spot for youngsters, had wanted children of his own. Tyler had long felt Rob and Della's inability to have a baby together had affected Rob almost as deeply as the loss of his wife. Though he'd never said as much, Rob seemed unable to share the camaraderie generated by Tyler and others in their circle of friends when their offspring were mentioned.

"In San Antonio?" Tyler shot him a quizzical look, almost certain Rob was feeding him a line. The Ranger had never mentioned retirement, not once hinted he considered any other kind of investigation work a career option.

"In your backyard."

"Oklahoma?"

"A small town just outside of Tulsa."

Tyler whistled, unsure which announcement amazed him more—the fact Rob was about to leave one of the nation's most elite law enforcement groups or that he'd be living close enough Tyler could actually visit his old friend more often.

"Never thought I'd see you speechless." Rob wheeled into the driveway of the home he'd shared with his wife, his expression hinting at the good humor for which he was known.

"You should probably note it and get ready to talk," Tyler offered, "'cause you're damn well going to tell me what's going on."

"I just did, didn't I?" Rob shook his head, puckered his brow with a feigned puzzlement. His brown eyes were bright as a shiny new penny—a portent of things to come. "On the outside chance I didn't, I'll gladly highlight my plans again…provided you fess up to whatever it is that's put that black cloud over your head."

"What makes you think I've got anything other than business as usual on my mind?"

"The creases making your mouth droop," Rob stated matter-of-factly. "The scowl you were wearing when I picked you up—not to mention the five times you've checked your watch since you climbed into the Paddy Wagon." He shoved the gear into park and killed the engine. "If I were sensitive instead of so damn good looking, I'd be hurt to think you weren't tickled pink to be riding in such a fine four-wheeler."

"The transportation isn't a problem." Frowning, Tyler stepped out, hefting his bag as he slammed the door. "It's the driver I'd just as soon avoid."

"Is that any way to talk to your best bud?" Rob loped around the front bumper, slowing as he fell into step with Tyler. "And here I thought we were friends."

"Remember that when I throttle you." Snarled in warning, Tyler's threat served only to amuse his companion.

"That bad, huh?" Laughing, Rob unlocked the front door. "Is she a looker?"

Though he wanted to pretend he'd misunderstood Rob's unsubtle remark, Tyler knew better. Faking a massive brain failure or refusing to answer would only prod the Texas Ranger to question him further or, worse yet, spur him to action. Tyler knew from experience how quickly Rob could ferret out the truth and get to the root of a problem. And how far he'd go to learn what he wanted to know.

"Gorgeous." Tyler slanted the lanky man beside him a grin. "Smart, too."

"Anyone I know?"

"Someone you'll soon know very well if you're serious about moving to Oklahoma and becoming a P.I."

"Dead serious." Rob took the duffel from Tyler and tossed it in the nearest corner—the vacant space next to a sofa that had seen its better days. "Kick your feet up while I fetch the brew. I have a feeling this bull session will take a while."

Tyler did as he was told, and was soon glad he had. They talked until midnight, downing a six pack of beer and pizza Rob ordered in long before they'd come to a decision as to which of them faced the greatest challenge. Hearing Rob's enthusiasm for the career change he planned improved Tyler's mood. Seeing the concern on his friend's face when he related his fears for Kylie's safety—and after Rob's mention of a similar, disastrous case he'd once worked—rekindled Tyler's worry.

He needed to get home and talk some sense into Kylie.

He wanted to be near her, and not solely because some lunatic considered her fair game.

Tyler loved her too much to risk not telling her how he felt. Losing her because he hadn't made his feelings known was no longer an option.

Despite Rob's vow to lend a professional hand, Tyler's fear for Kylie's safety hadn't diminished. The manner with which Tyler intended to ensure her protection, however, had changed. Whether or not she approved, he planned to shadow her every move.

* * *

Stopping to see her stepfather wasn't in Kylie's plans. Having slept none at all the night before, she debated the prudence of visiting Carl Bennett. Never at her best around him, Kylie doubted her ability to deal with him was up to par, which amounted to reason enough to delay her courtesy call.

Despite the reservations causing her to question both her timing and intent, Kylie drove past the Cherokee County Courthouse as she had so many times before, to the tree-lined street where she'd grown up. The small white frame house looked much the same, a little lonelier somehow. Marigolds no longer bloomed in the flowerbeds flanking the stairs leading up to the porch. The window boxes weren't overflowing with petunias. Devoid of the small touches her mother added, the house looked different and familiar at once.

Kylie walked toward the entry, her thoughts on the stately redbrick structure she'd left early that morning. She wondered if Tyler had also spent a sleepless night; if he'd tossed and turned as she had, as tormented by her closeness as she'd been by his. Her anger with him had lasted no time, scant minutes. Her ongoing need for his touch, his body lying beside her in bed, had diminished none at all, making the long hours of the night seem unending.

Knowing she should have let him explain why he'd insisted she cancel her travel plans nagged at her, forced her to acknowledge the validity of his concern. She knew he didn't intend to curtail her responsibilities or demean the importance of honoring commitments; that he only wanted to ensure her safety. Still, he could have suggested something more reasonable, offered another plan of action—anything less autocratic than simply telling her she shouldn't attend the Pittsburgh conference.

The seminars comprised a major portion of her livelihood, and were a source of pride she could ill afford to lose. Her self-worth had been battered enough already, would likely not withstand an assault so personal as losing touch with participants looking to her for guidance. Offering others the help needed to improve their ability to cope boosted her morale, and also bolstered her own coping skills.

He could have told her he loved her, and put to rest the uncertainty distressing Kylie more than their disagreement.

His touch told her he cared for her, at least a little. His kisses, warm and tender or hot and wild, told her Tyler, too, felt the soul-deep emotion that had kept her up all night, alternately tossing in bed and pacing the floor, careful to keep her steps light, her restless meandering less noticeable.

Instead, he'd said he didn't expect her to stay, letting her know he considered their time together a fleeting glimpse of what might have been—and a sure source of torture in the years to come. Kylie knew she'd never forget him, that her love for Tyler would forever haunt her, an ever present reminder of the joyful bond she would not find in another man's arms.

Her heart aching, Kylie rapped on the front door, determined to ensure Carl's well being and be done with this last unplanned task. Carl opened it a moment later, smiling as if he'd been expecting her.

"Come in, come in." He stepped back, rattling the oxygen tank cart beside him in his haste. Looking much better than when she'd last seen him, save for the mask feeding oxygen into his diseased lungs, Carl seemed stronger, less fragile. "Sorry 'bout the mess." He waved his hand toward the array of medicine bottles littering the coffee table in front of the sofa, the Sunday paper strewn aside for later reading.

"How are you?" Kylie settled on one end of the floral print couch—the same divan that had occupied most of the small room since her high school days. She glanced around the living area, surprised to see youthful pictures of herself still hanging on the walls—and even more shocked to note a framed newspaper article detailing her success as an author.

"Not bad," Carl replied, wheezing as he plopped down in the chair opposite her. "Glad to be home."

Kylie's throat tightened. *Home* sounded so appealing, yet her own yielded no comfort. The thought of living alone in her rented house no longer filled her with pleasure, merely a deep unending dread. She swallowed hard, aware her feelings for the man who brought such joy to her life—and inspired a purpose the career she loved no longer promised—would make returning home even more difficult.

"It's good to see you again." Carl's statement redirected her attention. "But I can't help wondering why you're here."

"To mend fences," Kylie said. *Because I can't go where I want to be.* With Tyler—in his heart and in his bed every night. "To make sure you're okay."

"Fine as I can be, all things considered." Carl chuckled dryly. "Better than you, I'd wager."

Kylie stared at her stepfather, amazed to realize he'd seen through her charade. She did want to ensure his well being, though that was only a small part of her reason for dropping by unannounced. She couldn't recall ever asking for his advice, yet somehow knew she needed his confirmation she'd made the right decision. "I'm leaving for Pittsburgh the day after tomorrow."

"And you don't want to go?"

"I have to go. The seminar is booked solid. Matt could handle the extra duties if I didn't go, but I can't dump the extra load on him. We're a team."

"But you want to?"

"More than I've ever wanted anything," she stated. *Except the one thing I'll never have*—Tyler's love. Kylie blinked hard, forestalling the tears threatening to flood her eyes.

"Are you afraid?" Carl stood and crossed the room, dragging the wheeled cart after him. Seated beside her now, he peered at her solemnly. "Has something happened?"

I've lost my heart, if that counts, she thought but said, "Not really. I'm just a little unsure as to what I should do, stay home or go on as before."

"What does Tyler think you should do?"

"Stop working. Put my life on hold." *Share his bed with no hope of sharing his life.* Kylie stiffened, alarmed to realize she'd set the rules for their relationship, that her own misgivings had contributed so greatly to her current dissatisfaction.

She hadn't told Tyler how she felt about him, hadn't given him the opportunity to reveal his feelings had he wanted to do so. She hadn't insisted on knowing why he so strongly suggested she curb her activities, why he'd taken her to his house when he could just as easily have stayed with her. He wanted her with him and Alecia, a part of their life and safe as well!

Elated by her sudden certainty Tyler loved her, and that he would surely tell her what she so wanted to hear, Kylie stood. "I've got to go. Thanks."

"For what?"

"For proving that an apology is much easier when it is richly deserved. I'm sorry it took me so long to come to my senses." Amused by his confused look, she smiled and added, "I've been counseling others for years now, without heeding my own advice. Strength and happiness come from within, as does the joy of forgiving. When you realize there is so little, practically nothing, to forgive, overlooking the deeds that caused each of us untold anguish is simple.

"I blamed you for all that was wrong in my life, too. I never once considered what was wrong with yours. We were both cheated. Mother went to great lengths to make this house look warm and inviting, but she did little to make it feel like a real home. She saw to our physical comfort, but was never demonstrative. Though I sometimes doubted her love, I didn't once wonder how you must have felt when she was at her most distant self."

"Your mother was a good woman," he stated defensively, "she did her best."

"Yes, she did." Kylie moved toward the door, waving Carl back when he would have stood. "Unfortunately for us, she did little to make us a family. Going through the motions without reaching out to ensure the love and unity we both needed—deserved—caused us more grief than comfort. I should have realized that long before now."

"Better late than never," Carl said with a smile. "I'd like to see you once in a while...hear more about your work."

"You can count on it."

Kylie stepped outside, finally able to appreciate the summer sunshine making this day more beautiful than any she'd enjoyed before. Despite the storm clouds billowing on the western horizon, she felt all would be well; as if the purpose of her life and the happiness putting a spring in her steps were restored—and resting solidly on the broad shoulders of the man responsible for both.

Kylie felt sure she'd never doubt herself or Tyler again, that no matter how grave a situation she faced, one thing would remain constant: Tyler and the unconditional support that had once again made her life complete.

Twenty

Rob accompanied Tyler to the retirement home early the next morning. Though he usually rented a car to further shield the identity of the witness being relocated, Tyler knew Rob would do nothing to compromise Victoria Candelera's safety. With his thoughts and worry focused on Kylie as well as Ms. Candelera, Tyler truly appreciated the added support.

"Stop scowling and think of the time and trouble you'll save with me dropping you off at the terminal." Rob spread his hands in a dismissive gesture. "It's not like I'm some bozo you hitched a ride with. I don't know your little prisoner's name, and I'm damn sure her dazzling good looks won't keep me up nights thinking of ways to find her."

"If I do my job according to plan, no one will be able to find her." Tyler slanted his friend a confident look. "Not even you."

"You're lookin' at the twenty-first century version of Sam Spade. I intend to locate every Tom, Dick or Harry I set out to find."

"Since her name is nowhere near any of those, I have nothing to worry about, do I?"

"Not a thing…unless her name turns up on my desk somewhere down the line."

"It won't."

Frowning, Tyler stopped at room 121. He rapped on the door, ready to collect his charge and head home. Tension radiated through him, rigid prickles of doubt he couldn't quite put his finger on. He'd suffered misgivings before, usually when he'd missed a detail vital to solving a case—a clue that later seemed too obvious to have overlooked. But this wasn't a case that required a lengthy investigation or any effort beyond boarding a plane with a prisoner in tow—something he'd done countless times.

Escorting Victoria Candelera to her new home amounted to a routine assignment, which caused Tyler to question the source of his concern. He felt certain his edginess stemmed from his worry for Kylie's safety; that he'd somehow failed to link the meager clues her stalker had left behind.

Wondering what he'd missed, and why it suddenly seemed important for him to piece together the evidence—and get home posthaste—did nothing to improve Tyler's mood. Not even Rob's good humor helped.

The numbered door opened, and Tyler heard Rob's sharp intake of air. It was easy to see why his friend reacted as though he'd been punched in the gut. The auburn-haired woman standing before them would stop rush-hour traffic. Victoria Candelera possessed the classic beauty few men could resist—delicately chiseled features, peaches-and-cream skin and vivid hazel eyes currently wide and leveled on Tyler's own narrowed gaze.

Judging by her steady, assessing look and the small fists clenched at her sides, Tyler knew her fear must be nearly debilitating—too great for him not to at least try and put her at ease. Smiling, he introduced himself and the stone-still man at his side.

"It's nice to meet you." Husky and sincere, her voice matched her heart-stopping looks—too sexy for a sane man to consider anything but dangerous. Victoria managed a small, tremulous smile—a smile Tyler knew his pal would dream of despite his claims otherwise.

"Is there anything you need to do before we head out?" Tyler and Rob stepped inside the room, closing the door behind them.

"Not really." Victoria shook her head. "Nothing other than to say goodbye to my grandmother."

Both Tyler and Rob looked toward the bed, at the wild haired old woman watching them like a hawk circling its prey. She aimed a bony finger at Tyler's chest. "Take care of her, Mister."

"I plan to." Tyler moved to the bed, extended his hand. She ignored his greeting, merely continued to eye him as though he were pond scum. "Your granddaughter will be safe with me."

"You'll answer to me if anything happens to her."

"I understand," Tyler responded, aware how worried anyone would be knowing their kin was about to leave the fold...possibly never to return.

Contact of any kind with friends and family was strictly prohibited. Disobeying the rules wasn't unheard of, but he had a feeling neither Victoria nor her gritty guardian would abuse the policies intended to protect them both.

Joining him at her grandmother's bedside, Victoria leaned down to kiss the wrinkled cheek the other woman raised with a stubborn jut of her chin. "Take care of yourself, Nanna. Mind the nurses and eat what they bring you."

"Don't I always?"

Victoria chuckled, her laughter as rich and warm as fine brandy. "Let's not go there. I doubt Marshal Wolfe has either the time or desire to referee our argument."

"What argument?" Nanna glanced from her granddaughter to Tyler. "Are we fussing?"

"Not yet," Victoria said with a smile, "but we will be if I dwell on the many times you've hassled the nurses or refused to eat since you've been here."

"I'll mind my manners." The older woman glared at Tyler. "And so will you. Tory's a good girl."

"Yes, Ma'am." Tyler resisted the smile making his lips twitch. He couldn't help thinking Victoria's grandmother and his own would get along very well—or argue as frequently as Oscar and Felix of The Odd Couple notoriety if left together too often.

"I love you, Nanna," Victoria whispered, emotions making her voice tremble. "I'll miss you."

"I know." The older woman looked away, hiding the sheen of tears glistening in her dark eyes. "Keep your chin up, and your nose to the grindstone. Things will get better."

"I'm counting on that." Victoria straightened, her smile forced as she retrieved her purse from the bedside table. She briskly moved toward the lone suitcase next to the door, glancing at the still silent Rob as she reached for the handle.

"I'll get it," Rob stated, putting action to word. Unintentionally bumping Victoria aside, he steadied her, and dropped his hands as though burned by the contact. Tyler smiled, too amused by Rob's sudden clumsiness and his reaction to it to curb his own response.

"I'm ready." Standing at the door, Victoria met Tyler's steady look. "Shall we go?"

Nodding, Tyler moved to join her. Pausing only long enough to wink at the old woman still watching him as though he were contemplating murder rather than the safe escort of her granddaughter, he smiled and said, "Don't worry, Ma'am. I'll take good care of her."

"It isn't you I'm worried about." Glaring at Rob, the grandmother added, "It's that rascal I don't trust!"

"I'm trustworthy." Finding his usual strong voice, Rob added, "As reliable as that bum." He jerked a thumb in Tyler's direction, smiling at the woman unaffected by his gesture.

"I hope so, for your sake." That threat firmly issued, the elderly woman gave Rob a chilly smile. "I'd hate to have to come looking for you."

"I don't think I'd care much for that, either." Rob chuckled. "Rest easy, Nanna. I'm one of the good guys."

Nanna arched a thick, white brow, apparently unconvinced by Rob's sincerity. Tyler urged Victoria and his friend out the door, frowning as they made their way down the long corridor. Eyeing the patients and staff milling about, Tyler was satisfied no one other than those living or working at Garden Villa appeared to be present. Relieved, he concentrated on the task at hand, anxious to make their flight and get home.

Tyler didn't doubt the trip to Tulsa would go according to plan. He did harbor grave concerns as to what he would encounter once he arrived home— why he felt such a driving need to be there now.

Fear for Kylie's safety was only a small part of his worry. His gut feeling something was about to happen accounted for much of it—that and his growing certainty he'd soon discover what had been right under his nose all along.

Tyler hoped like hell it turned out to be something of little importance or, hopefully, the undisputable evidence that would finally allow him to identify the man stalking Kylie—and not a major oversight that could prove to be a fatal mistake.

* * *

Foul weather in Houston delayed their flight just over four hours. Soon after Rob bid them farewell, Tyler and Victoria grabbed a bite to eat and bought magazines to make the time pass more quickly. Despite the distractions, Tyler was fit to be tied long before they boarded the plane. Finally airborne, he knew it would be late when they arrived in Tulsa, and at least another hour after landing before he'd be able to head home.

He'd have to get Victoria Candelera, now Tory Candle, settled into her new home, and make sure his Tulsa comrade was in place to watch over her the next few weeks. Tyler dreaded taking the time needed to ensure Tory's well being, but could in no way compromise her safety. While he hoped Kylie's ordeal would soon be over, Tory faced a lifetime of looking over her shoulder, always alert to the danger that could be lurking nearby. He'd never lost a participant, and did not plan on letting Tory become the first.

"I'm sorry for all the problems." Tory's apologetic tone sounded both sincere and incredibly sad.

"You can't control the weather." Smiling, Tyler glanced her way, once again awed by her beauty. Had he not been head-over-heels in love with Kylie, it would have been next to impossible to ignore Tory's appeal. "Unless you're a witch."

"David sometimes accused me of acting like one." A teasing light danced in her hazel eyes, a misty brightness that also looked bittersweet.

Tyler's heart knotted, tightening with empathy. He admired Tory's courage, the strength evident in her uplifted chin. Unlike many seeking protection in the program, she radiated an inner sweetness, a goodness that made relocation doubly difficult. Tory didn't seem the type to shirk responsibility, and he figured leaving her grandmother's care to strangers must weigh heavily on her mind. On her spirit.

Satisfied no one on the half-full plane was near enough to overhear their conversation, Tyler asked, "Your brother David?"

"My one and only sibling." Tory nodded, concern creasing her brow. "He's the reason we're in this pickle."

"According to your file, he's only part of the reason." Tyler fielded her inquisitive look with his neutral one. "My guess is neither of you had a clue as to what he'd gotten himself into…or how vicious a man like Espinosa can be when crossed."

"I certainly didn't, and I'm positive David knew little more than I." She pushed her lips into a semblance of a smile. "He did know the cars he was driving to San Antonio from all over the country were hot, but that's the extent of his involvement. He knew nothing about what happened to the stolen cars…and he had no idea he was a major cog in the drug cartel that accounted for Espinosa's primary payload."

"He wouldn't be in the program if he'd been more deeply involved. Helping convict the higher-ups responsible for luring him into the operation went a long way toward convincing the judge he deserved a second chance."

"David's a good kid," she said, tears glistening in her thick, dark lashes.

"He wanted to buy Nanna a house, and help me and my husband get on our feet."

Tyler patted her hand, already familiar with her family history. Espinosa's goons had killed her husband, and both Tory and David were lucky to have escaped the pre-trial attack. Tory and her brother testified against Gorge Espinosa, helping the prosecutor win a conviction that would keep the drug lord behind bars the rest of his natural life. Unfortunately for Tory and David, Espinosa's reach extended far beyond the prison walls, and his army of miscreants would leave no stone unturned in their quest for revenge.

Now also in the Witness Protection Program, David, like Tory, would forever have to stay on guard, watchful of those too interested in the little things most Americans take for granted. Personal questions and nosy neighbors were suspect, as were the simple joys of life—like spending holidays with family and making new friends.

Tyler hated to think how difficult it would be to leave his rowdy relatives behind, or to ditch the career he loved. He knew people who could manage it without a second thought, and a few who'd probably even welcome starting over; individuals with no ties to a community and no real sense of home. Men who seemed to live for their work yet didn't pour their heart into the effort required to make a good impression.

Orvil Keets's round face leaped to mind. Frowning, Tyler contemplated why the deputy's demeanor irritated him so much. He figured it was the young officer's disrespectful attitude. Or, perhaps, the caustic remarks he'd made regarding Kylie's state-of-mind.

Keets acted is if he knew Kylie well enough to make such a judgment, and had even gone so far as to suggest she could be behind the stalking incidents a time or two. Accusing Kylie of making up the entire fiasco had been a step over the line, far as Tyler was concerned. The deputy's defense of Liza rankled, too.

"*Liza's a respected professional,*" Keets had boasted, surprising Tyler with his vehement tone. "*I trust her judgment.*"

Tyler stiffened, apprehension trickling down his spine as he recalled the arrogance with which the deputy had mentioned Dr. Liza Andrews—a woman he should not have known any better than he knew Kylie. And certainly not well enough to tout her skills. In his mind's eye, Tyler pictured the gloves and knife he'd seen on the cluttered floorboard of Keets's police cruiser. Clearer still, the neatly stashed tobacco pouch he'd noticed in the pigeon hole.

The discarded tobacco ashes Tyler had found near Kylie's house suddenly made sense, as did the near total lack of evidence and unclear motive behind the stalking.

"Dear God," Tyler muttered, alarming Tory as he lurched forward in his seat. The real proof *had* been right under his nose—as close and unmistakable as the man likely responsible for tormenting Kylie!

"What's wrong? What is it?"

Tyler yanked his head around, glaring at the obviously nervous woman looking at him as though he'd sprouted horns. Forcing a calmness he hoped would ease her concern, he replied, "Nothing…yet."

"You're scaring me." Tory peered around, eyeing the near empty section of the plane as if she doubted his word.

"I'm scaring myself." Tyler forced a smile, praying the fear jumbling his thoughts would prove unfounded. *And there isn't a damn thing I can do about it*, he realized—until they landed!

He glanced at his watch, scowling when he noted the time. It would be nearly seven when they arrived in Tulsa, at least eight before he could leave for Tahlequah. He reached for his cell phone, and then shoved it back into his pocket. He didn't dare call the Cherokee County Sheriff's Department. The outside chance Orvil Keets might intercept the call was a risk Tyler could not take.

Giving the deputy a head start greater than the opportunity he now had to confront Kylie with no one—other than Tyler—wise to his game, presented Keets an advantage Tyler was not willing to grant him.

Phoning Wyatt was out of the question since that, too, could result in Keets getting wind of Tyler's suspicions. With his parents out of town, even that unlikely avenue led nowhere.

"You're on your own, Wolfe," he said aloud, causing Tory to again give him a wide-eyed look. *Just like Kylie.* Tamping down his fear, Tyler offered Tory a tight smile. "Everything's okay, Tory. I was just thinking out loud, mulling over the details of another case."

Facts not even a rookie would have overlooked. Failing to piece together the small but unmistakable clues that would have pointed a finger at Keets weeks before was unforgivable—a mistake Tyler knew would haunt him forever if the price of his oversight caused Kylie further harm.

Knowing she'd have to face Keets alone if the bastard realized he had the time and opportunity to act chilled Tyler to the bone, and prompted him to breach the rules of etiquette. He again reached for the cell phone, determined to contact the one person who could protect his love: Kylie.

The phone rang ten times before he disconnected, scowling as he held the worthless device in his unsteady hand. He wondered where she was, why she hadn't answered. Tyler remained tense, afraid Kylie couldn't pick-up her phone, and that Keets had already implemented whatever evil plan he had in store for her.

Warning himself not to go there, Tyler eased back, determined to do all he could to safeguard Kylie—and praying he'd have the chance to help her.

Thinking he might not didn't merit consideration.

Twenty-One

Kylie saved the file she'd just edited, the last of the columns due this week. Harvey would be pleased, she knew, when the faxed copies arrived ahead of his deadline.

Thunder boomed, rattling her office windows. Lightening flashed, streaking through the early evening sky already darkened by the roiling clouds that had grown heavier throughout the day. Rain pattered the glass, sliding down the pane in uneven streams whipped by the rising wind.

Kylie stared at the trickles crisscrossing the glass, shivering as she imagined how cool it would be outside. Glad she had no reason to go out, she smoothed down the khaki shorts rumpled from sitting so long and tugged her tank top into place. Normally uneasy when storms threatened, she felt none of the usual qualms: fear a tornado might strike, doubts as to her readiness if one did touch down. She was too happy to let such an unlikely occurrence dampen her mood. She'd accomplished so much today it would be foolish to consider it anything but a success—regardless how stormy the end.

Smiling, she looked at the clock, surprised to have taken so few hours to complete her work. With a little luck, she'd finish reading the research material Matt had faxed earlier that day before ten o'clock. Now half past eight, she felt certain she could spare a few minutes for a light snack before tackling the last pre-seminar preparation she'd planned.

So thinking, she hastened to the kitchen and set about making tea and building a sandwich. With the teakettle on the burner, she turned to the refrigerator, but stopped in mid-act. Frowning, she glanced at the wall phone, wondering why Tyler hadn't returned her call.

Thinking he might have while she'd been watering the outside plants, she dashed back to her office to check the answering machine. The red light wasn't blinking; wasn't shining at all.

"Nitwit!" She rolled her eyes, irritated to have forgotten to turn the blasted machine back on after she'd cleared it of messages that afternoon. Punching the ON button, she returned to the kitchen, determined to enjoy her brief break and quickly read the articles Matt had asked her to review.

She'd just retrieved the last of the sandwich fixings and set them on the counter when the doorbell rang. Certain Tyler had gotten her message—and that this night would be the first of many wonderful nights to come—she hurried to the front door.

Smiling, Kylie flipped on the porch light, and peered through the peephole. She gasped, shocked to recognize a visitor other than Tyler standing outside. She cracked open the door, hesitant despite her immediate concern for the bedraggled woman staring back at her.

"Liza?" Kylie stepped back, opening the door wider to allow her unexpected guest to enter. "What's wrong? Liza, are you okay?"

Kylie had never seen Liza look so weary. So lost. Aside from the wrinkled pantsuit dappled by the rain now coming down more heavily, Liza's short hair was a tangled mess, her normally neat brunet curls as damp and untidy as her clothes. Her dark eyes were unusually bright, wide and wild looking. Haunted.

"Yes. No."

Liza's lower lip trembled, indicating the depth of her disquiet. In the ten years she'd known Liza, Kylie had not once seen her cry, not even when her beloved father died their sophomore year in college.

"Is Matt okay? What's going on?" Shutting the door, Kylie moved closer, her worry mounting. She embraced the smaller woman, sure something dreadful had occurred to cause Liza such distress. "Liza, you're scaring me...I—"

"Nothing's wrong...everything's wrong," Liza admitted quietly, "I don't know what's wrong."

"Come into the kitchen with me. The tea I was brewing is almost ready. I'll pour you a cup, and then see what I can find for you to wear." Kylie managed a smile, though she feared it would do nothing to ease Liza. "Soaked as you are, you must be chilled."

"I am," Liza stated, smiling oddly. "I couldn't find my umbrella."

"That's a first." Kylie led the way to the kitchen, glancing over her shoulder to speak. "I can't recall you ever having misplaced anything. You always had the course notes and pertinent data I needed to help keep my grades up when I couldn't find my own."

Kylie motioned Liza into the nearest chair, and then quickly prepared each of them a steaming cup of the beverage. That done, she hastened upstairs, soon found leggings and a sweatshirt small enough to fit her petite guest. While Liza changed in the downstairs bathroom, Kylie made sandwiches, her thoughts on the woman who seemed close to the breaking point; more distressed than Kylie had ever seen her.

"Thanks."

Liza sat down, her expression solemn as she watched Kylie put the finishing touches on their impromptu meal. Kylie felt as though she were under a microscope, her every move suspect. Discomfited, she focused on the task, unsure as to why she found it so difficult to relax. Despite their recent differences, Liza had always been a calming influence; a source of comfort— which made Kylie's reaction doubly upsetting. She needed to be the strong one now, not a foolish ninny allowing her friend's uncharacteristic distress to trigger her own inappropriate misgivings.

"I didn't mean to impose. I should have called, and at least given you a chance to tell me this wasn't a good time to visit."

"You know I would have told you there is no bad time for you to drop by...however unexpected." Kylie set the loaded plates on the table and joined Liza. No longer hungry, she stared at the sandwich, then looked at her troubled companion. "I doubt you're of a mind to eat any more than I am."

"Not really." Liza shook her head, blinked as if desperate to hold back the tears glistening in her eyes. "I'd like to talk, get your opinion on something."

"I'm all ears." Kylie pushed the plate aside and braced her elbows on the table. "What do you want to talk about?"

"Matt. My marriage."

Kylie stiffened, certain discussion of her ex-husband and his current marital problems would be a subject she wanted no part of. Despite her and Liza's friendship, past and present, advising the woman responsible for her and Matt's break-up seemed...unprofessional. Unthinkable.

"I'm not sure that's a good idea," Kylie ventured, her trepidation mounting.

"But it is!" Liza leaned forward, her brown eyes gleaming strangely. "You know Matt better than anyone. I know you can help us mend our rift. Matt values your opinion. He'd be open to any suggestions you have."

"I don't think so." Kylie squared her shoulders, bolstered by her certainty Matt would not have encouraged Liza to come to her for guidance. A skilled counselor in her own right, Liza also knew Kylie's relationship to each of them would make her an unwise choice.

"I need you, Kylie!" Liza pleaded, tears overflowing her lashes. "We both need you!"

Weakened by Liza's emotional state, Kylie relented. "I know Matt's worried about you. He—"

"You've talked to him?" Liza straightened, instantly reclaiming the control Kylie had always admired. "About me?"

"Not about you specifically," Kylie hedged, unsure as to how she should respond. Despite the restraint making Liza appear more like her old self, Kylie sensed the hold on her emotions remained fragile. "Neither of us understands why you decided not to attend the Pittsburgh seminar. He expressed concern as to why you hadn't confided your reasons or, at least, offered an explanation."

"He wouldn't have listened if I had!" Liza slapped her hands on the table, propelled herself up. Glaring, she added, "He's too wrapped up in your current dilemma to give me or our marriage a second thought."

"Our next book isn't due on our editor's desk for another three months," Kylie said, confusion furrowing her brow. They had plenty of time to complete the final draft and revise the chapters and subjects on which they'd disagreed—a scant two entries that had caused neither of them much concern. "We're well ahead of schedule."

"That isn't what I'm talking about!" Liza spun around, began pacing in front of the patio doors like a caged tiger anxious to escape. "Matt's so damned afraid you're going to get hurt, he seems totally unaware how shaky our relationship has become." She turned to face Kylie, her eyes narrowed, accusing. "You'd both be in trouble if I were the jealous type."

"Thank goodness you aren't." Kylie straightened, attempting to quell the apprehension twisting her stomach into a knot. She had no reason to fear Liza; no reason to think her statement anything but an idle comment intended to lighten the gloomy mood making Kylie increasingly uneasy.

Despite Liza's seeming sincerity, Kylie didn't believe her, not entirely. Truth be told, Kylie had been jealous too, when she first learned Liza and Matt were involved. She'd had a hard time controlling the emotion, until she realized her own sense of failure caused her to envy the woman Matt chose over her—and not her former best friend who truly was better suited to Matt than Kylie had ever been. That perception helped Kylie accept their marriage and wish them well—and also gave her reason to hope she, too, would someday enjoy a relationship so seemingly fated.

"Will you talk to him?" Liza asked, regaining Kylie's attention. "Will you help us work things out?"

"I'll do what I can, but I can't promise a miracle. The end result is up to you and Matt."

"Thank you!" Liza smiled, apparently grateful to have secured an ally. Kylie felt more like a traitor. "How soon can you be ready to leave?"

"Tonight?" Kylie shook her head. "You want to drive in this downpour?" She pointed toward the glass doors. "The rain is coming down in buckets!"

"It'll let up sooner or later…besides, the resort is less than two hours away. If we leave right away, we'll be there before Matt turns in for the night." Liza named the resort where Matt was staying, enjoying a brief golf vacation before heading to Pennsylvania.

Thinking about the winding two-lane highway leading to the Arkansas resort bothered Kylie. Treacherous even when dry, the road would be far more dangerous wet. Kylie hated driving at night, seldom set out anywhere so late. Still, if she could help Matt and Liza overcome their difficulties, the relatively short trip would be worthwhile. The risks seemed a small price to pay for her own peace of mind, and the satisfaction she'd glean from helping two people she cared about.

Nodding, Kylie stood. "I'll grab my purse and be ready. If it's okay with you, I'll drive my car so I can come home tonight."

"No!" Liza rounded the table, clasped Kylie's upper arms in her firm grip. "I'll drive, and you can use my car for the return trip. I'll feel better if we ride together…just in case we have trouble."

"Fine," Kylie agreed, feeling anything but convinced. Liza's suggestion sounded reasonable, though the inconvenience of having to reclaim her car made no sense whatsoever. Shrugging, Kylie shook off her growing concern, positive she had no cause to worry. Liza needed her, and also wanted to ensure her safety…nothing more.

"Let's go then." Liza beamed, obviously relieved by Kylie's response. "I can't wait to get things settled…once and for all."

Not of a mind to argue, Kylie retrieved her purse and moved to the foyer, Liza on her heels. Locking the door behind them, Kylie pocketed the talisman key ring Granny Wolfe had given her, oddly calmed by the ancient Cherokee symbol. She opened the umbrella she'd also grabbed, shielding them both as they dashed toward the luxury car parked nearby.

Holding the umbrella, Kylie waited while Liza climbed in behind the wheel, and then hastened to the passenger side. She opened the door, so intent on escaping the heavy rain she almost fell when her foot landed on something too hard and unyielding to mistake for the carpeted mat. Reaching to steady herself, Kylie looked down, at the dark gloves and ominous pistol lying on the floorboard.

Kylie froze, half in the vehicle, afraid to move—and even more frightened by what held her spellbound! Wide-eyed, she stared at the small gun, fear rippling down her spine in waves as cold as the rain drenching her clothes. She looked at Liza, suspicion nagging at her. Kylie had known something was up, that her usually disciplined friend was not acting like herself.

Sure she must be wrong to even think Liza intended to harm her, Kylie remained still, willing her heart to slow down. And hoping the woman watching her like a judge about to pass sentence would say something— anything to crack the unnerving silence broken only by the rain pounding the damaged umbrella with its relentless patter.

Instead, Liza smiled, a cold, arrogant smile that triggered a deep, immobilizing fear unlike any Kylie had experienced before. Understanding dawned, its clarity as harsh and forbidding as the bolt of lightning zigzagging through the sky, illuminating the face of the stranger staring back at her. A pungent sulfurous smell filled the air, seeped into Kylie's burning lungs. The weeks of terror she'd endured seemed less frightening and more dangerous at once; her ongoing ordeal a test she'd passed only to realize failure loomed one step ahead of her—as real and as close as the woman she'd considered a friend.

"It was you…" Kylie whispered, then more firmly accused, "You!"

Liza quirked a brow, but said not a word as she lunged for the gun. Grasping it too quickly for Kylie to counter the move, she raised the weapon, forcing Kylie to act.

Dropping the umbrella, Kylie ran toward the house, Liza's furious screams propelling her. Aware she would not have a chance to unlock the door and get inside before Liza caught up with her, Kylie changed direction, rounding the side of the house so fast her feet nearly slid out from under her. Slowing somewhat, she glanced toward the outbuilding, instantly decided no place near the house would provide a safe haven.

"Tyler!" Kylie whispered raggedly, praying he'd somehow hear her, help her.

Strengthened by the sound of his name, Kylie shoved open the backyard gate and flew over the uneven ground, hoping she'd be able to locate the rocky path leading to Tyler's house. With no light to guide her, the pitch black terrain appeared the same no matter which direction she looked, the dark surface of the lake the only identifiable landmark she recognized. Following the nearby shore, high above the shimmering depths leading her to safety, Kylie ran, her breath coming in short, shallow gasps.

Lightning flashed, granting Kylie a brief glimpse of the trail she sought. Clutching her side to stay the pain knifing through her ribs, she ran toward the path, her canvas shoes now as wet and slick as the grass and rocks making the journey more hazardous.

A gunshot rent the air, echoed through the forested ravines. Kylie screamed, and immediately clamped one hand over her mouth. She couldn't give herself away, refused to do anything to help Liza find her. In control again, she forced down her hand, unwilling to yield to the fear gripping her.

Doing her best to breathe more quietly, Kylie rushed ahead, pushing aside the limbs slapping at her skin. She narrowed her eyes, trying to avoid the stones large enough to see through the sopping, tangled strands of hair hindering her vision and clinging to her cheeks stinging from the abrasions.

Her legs were burning, her muscles tightened by fear and weakened from her pace. Kylie ignored the pain, too intent on reaching Tyler's house to allow anything to slow her. Through the maze of trees she could see a dim light, the most beautiful sight she'd ever seen.

"Thank God!" She spared a glance to her right, frightened to realize how close she was to the edge of the cliff—and how far it was to the murky water below.

She surged forward, stumbling in her haste to avoid the added danger. Her foot slid sideways, causing her ankle to buckle. Searing pain shot through her lower leg, compounding her misery. Listing precariously, Kylie teetered, unable to do anything to avert her imminent tumble. She slid over the edge, hands stretched out before her searching for something—anything—to break her fall. She felt nothing but cold dark air, and the unyielding hardness of the boulders and trees battering her body as she rolled down the embankment.

Yanked to a sudden stop, Kylie glanced back, surprised to see her fingers wrapped around a sapling. The slender tree looked ready to snap, the bowed trunk so small she doubted it would support her weight much longer.

Noticing the equally narrow ledge just behind her, she drew her knees up, back-crawled her way to the more steady perch.

Uncomfortably crouched and still clinging to the tree, Kylie peered down, toward the white-capped waves fifty feet or more below her. Shivering, she looked up, to the cliff top from which she'd fallen, also at least that far.

The wind whipped at her rain-soaked hair, but Kylie couldn't have cared less. She was alive and safe—or at least as safe as she could be given her current, precarious position.

Heaving a sigh of relief, she eased back, determined to weather the storm and make her way up the rocky cliff at first light. She had escaped certain death. A few hours of agony presented no cause to worry. She'd deal with Liza then, face whatever she had to in order to see this through.

"Hello, down there!"

Kylie cringed, fear rocketing through her. She looked up, at the demented woman staring down at her.

Well and truly trapped, Kylie could do nothing but watch Liza, her fate in the pale, amazingly steady hands aiming a gun at her hard-pounding heart.

* * *

Tyler leaped from the helicopter before it landed, causing the pilot he'd hired to shout a warning.

"Are you nuts?" the man asked, scowling.

"Call the Sheriff's office, tell the dispatcher an officer needs backup. Now!" Sparing time to provide the address, Tyler charged toward Kylie's house, brightly lit and inviting despite the rain streaming off the porch roof.

Seeing the unfamiliar car parked out front, Tyler hoped whoever had come to visit this dark, stormy night was still inside, a deterring factor neither he nor Keets had counted on. He rapped on the door, frowning as he listened for approaching footsteps, anything to calm his ragged nerves. Hearing nothing, he tried the door, rang the bell and again pounded the damp wood. Unable to stay the fear clawing at his stomach, he shoved his shoulder against the entry, moved back and kicked open the barrier.

"Kylie!" Tyler raced inside, pausing only long enough to determine his course. He ran up the stairs, calling Kylie's name as he searched the vacant rooms. Apprehension spurring him on, he retraced his steps, peered into each of the downstairs rooms leading to the kitchen.

Frightened by the stilted silence, he rushed toward the back of the house, skidding to a stop when he neared the table. He stared at the plates, the second setting and untouched food that affirmed his fear to be well founded. Dread spiraled through him.

His stomach clenched, gripped by a debilitating pain sharper than the terror assailing him. *Too late!* He was too damn late!

"No, by God!" Tyler snarled, unwilling to accept the obvious.

Hands fisted at his sides, Tyler stormed through the house and out the front door. He circled the dark blue Lincoln, scowling as he memorized the license tag. Glancing toward the helicopter, its swirling blades slinging raindrops, he shouted, "Did you reach the sheriff?"

"Backup is on the way. Two units. Is there anything I can do?" His expression somber, the other man leaned out of the open door. Apparently sensing the tension radiating through Tyler, the pilot he had commandeered seemed eager to help.

"Call the dispatcher again, have the officer on duty run the Texas plates on that car. Search this side of the house, and then wait for my backup to arrive." Tyler reached for the gun holstered beneath his arm. He retrieved the weapon, hoping he wouldn't have to use it—but also prepared to use any and all means necessary to help Kylie.

He moved around the side of the house, scanning the soggy ground for a sign Kylie or Keets had gone this way. Muddy skid marks and a small footprint next to the patio alarmed him, mobilized him. Certain Kylie had chosen the rocky woods over death at the hands of a man sworn to protect, Tyler dashed toward the gate, careful to keep his booted feet beneath him as he ran.

The sound of a gunshot rent the stormy silence, echoing through the hollows and ravines with an eerie finality. Tyler faltered, unable to breathe as he paused to listen, praying something—anything—would prove his fear groundless. Deathly silence, a quiet punctuated only by the drumming rain and a distant rumble of thunder, was all he could hear—and all he needed to reinforce his determination to find Kylie. To protect her from the seeming insanity threatening her life.

Uncaring as to his own safety, Tyler sprinted along the overgrown trail, his heart pounding so hard his ribs ached. Imagining Kylie, her body broken and bleeding, lent wings to his feet.

Hell bent on reaching her, Tyler hoped he'd remember the code of ethics he had sworn to uphold. He doubted he'd be able to—or that he'd have a prayer of a chance of controlling the rage rising along with his bone-deep fear.

* * *

"Don't do this!" Kylie pleaded, praying Liza would come to her senses. "You're too smart to let—"

"Shut up!" Liza leaned forward, so close to the cliff edge Kylie wondered how she kept her balance. Waving the gun back and forth, she smiled, that same cold, arrogant smile that hinted of the madness surely behind her actions. "My need to talk things out is over…has been for some time now."

"Why are you doing this? What did I do to make you hate me so?" Kylie inched closer to the rocky bank at her back, trying to make her trembling body a smaller target. She heartily wished she were invisible, or at least brave enough to leap into the swirling waters below to escape the grisly death Liza obviously planned.

"Plenty." Liza caressed the gun with her free hand, then again aimed the short barrel at Kylie, using the potentially lethal cylinder much like a pointer. "You spoiled Matt, made him feel too guilty to appreciate what we have."

"I did nothing of the sort!" Kylie bristled, aware words were her only weapon—and her only hope. Convincing Liza she wasn't a threat would require a calm approach, total concentration. "I'd be lying if I said I wasn't hurt…that I didn't feel betrayed. You were my best friend, Liza. I trusted you!"

"That was your first mistake." Liza laughed, the shrill sound of amusement indicative of much darker emotions. "I fell for Matt the minute I met him. Fool that he is, he didn't have the courage to tell you we'd discussed our mutual attraction, that he knew how I felt before the two of you eloped."

Pain knifed through Kylie, the blistering hurt of a betrayal much deeper than that she'd felt when the media reported Liza and Matt's affair. How could Matt not have told her something so important? How could he have married her, knowing the woman she cared most about also wanted him?

"I second your opinion," Kylie said, fury making her voice shake. "Matt is spineless."

"Don't you dare criticize him!" Liza leaned forward yet again, swung the gun toward Kylie's aching heart. "Matt would be fine now, all mine and unconcerned by your recent troubles…if my plan hadn't backfired."

"What plan?" Kylie drew her knees closer to her body, prepared to jump if her ploy to keep Liza talking failed. She doubted even the searing pain of a bullet ripping through her flesh would hurt more than the treachery visited upon her. Once again she'd trusted blindly, only to reap the rewards of her foolish belief that others would honor her ideals, respect her rights. Angry at being duped, she demanded, "What plan?"

Liza gave her an odd look, one of imperial superiority. "Now who's playing dumb?"

"This isn't a game, Liza! Tell me what you've done." Kylie's heart pounded harder, battering her ribs as she debated the wisdom of forcing Liza's hand. Win or lose this deadly stalemate, Kylie needed to understand what had pushed her friend over the edge; had to know what Liza had done to make her behave like a card shark holding all the aces. "What have you done? Is Matt—"

"Matt's fine, safe and cozy in our Dallas home. He thinks I'm in Florida, visiting my mother." She glanced at the lake and straightened abruptly, acting as though she'd just realized the danger lurking below.

"He's not in Arkansas?" Kylie narrowed her eyes, fury edging her fear aside. She detested lies, almost as much as she hated knowing she'd fallen for the biggest deception of all—thinking Liza worthy of her friendship. "Why, Liza? Why would you risk the marriage you obviously treasure to hurt me? I'm not a threat to your relationship or anything else."

"Oh, but you are. Don't you see? He'll never be free, long as you're in the picture...never be mine entirely." Liza shook her head, scowled. "If that nitwit had handled this right, you'd be history...one of the many missing persons no one ever finds."

"Tell me what you've done!" Kylie snapped, no longer afraid she might further offend her tormentor. Had Liza already hurt Tyler? Somehow managed to locate Alecia? Fear rippled down her spine, raising gooseflesh in its wake.

Kylie swallowed hard, closed her mind to the images of Tyler, bleeding and lifeless, unable to return her calls. She couldn't go there, to a pain more piercing than any she had endured. She could bear living without him; she couldn't stand the thought of losing him to death.

"I used my head...the skill you've often complimented." Chuckling, Liza continued. "Remember the teenager I counseled years ago? The young man who'd been committed for assaulting his mother?"

Kylie nodded, vaguely recalling the victory Liza claimed when she convinced the courts her patient meant his mother no harm; that drugs had caused him to temporarily lose control. Liza hadn't mentioned him again, nor had Kylie thought to ask what had become of him.

"He's a simpleton, a puppet who dances to whatever tune I hum."

Realization dawned, infusing Kylie with a furor as intense and harsh as the lightning slashing the sky. "You convinced him to stalk me, didn't you? You took advantage of his illness and used him to taunt me!"

"I deserve more credit than that, dear." Laughing, Liza again leaned forward, raindrops streaming down her face like a parody of tears. "I helped him earn his GED, and train for the job critical to my plan."

Kylie expelled a shaky breath, aware Liza had obviously been scheming for years, waiting for the opportunity to see her wicked plot through.

"Unfortunately for me, the bastard thinks his job is more important than our agreement. Orvil seems to have discovered the conscience missing when he attacked his mother."

"Orvil?" Kylie felt numb, not entirely surprised to hear the deputy implicated. Knowing the official sent to help her was also the man causing her such torment should have infuriated her, yet somehow missed the mark. Concern for Tyler mattered more.

"The coward decided he wanted no part of the final outcome. So…" Liza said with a shrug, "that leaves your fate in my hands." Smiling darkly, she aimed the gun at Kylie. "Goodbye, *old friend.*"

Fear shivered through Kylie, terror tempered only by her thoughts of Tyler. She pictured him rising above her as he made love to her, felt the tenderness in his kiss when they'd satisfied the physical need too great and sweet to deny. She could almost feel the warmth of his body curled around hers as they slept; sense the wondrous, enveloping love neither of them had dared to express any other way.

She wished she'd told him she loved him, how much she wanted to share his life. Tears stinging her eyes as she considered how much she'd lost due to her own foolish misgivings, she glanced at the waves surging below. Her heart heavy, Kylie let go of the sapling she'd clung to, spread her fingers to restore the feeling and prepared to jump, more inclined to take her chances in the frigid water than to beg Liza's mercy—mercy she now knew not to expect.

Bracing her hands against the cliff, Kylie took a deep breath and looked up, hoping Liza might be gone, that she wouldn't have to risk her life to save it. Instead, the gun-wielding woman was still there, her head turned as though distracted by something behind her. Kylie heard the dog's eager yelp then, and the low, ferocious growl that followed.

"Chief!" Kylie reached for the slick sapling, hanging on for dear life as she peered up. Thinking the dog must have been alerted by her scream, she hoped the animal would provide the diversion she needed; time for her to think of a way to avoid both the bullet meant for her and the churning water below. Wide-eyed and praying Liza would not harm Tyler's pet, Kylie shouted, "Kiss, Chief. Kiss, boy!"

Kylie watched the dog rear up, plant his huge paws on Liza's chest. Liza screamed, her arms flailing as she struggled to escape what she must have considered certain attack. The gun dropped from her hand, clattering atop the rocks at her feet. Screaming, she pushed at the dog, unaware Chief was simply playing. Liza's foot slid closer to the cliff edge, causing her to teeter wildly as she fought to free herself from the wrestling mutt intending only to lick her.

"Liza!" Kylie shrieked, sure Liza would tumble over the edge and into the lake. "Don't move, Liza! He won't hurt you! Please be still!"

Liza slid closer to the precipice, unable to stop the momentum impelling her. Kylie closed her eyes, unable to bear the thought of Liza dying due to her thoughtless gamble to save her own life.

She heard Liza scream, listened for the splash that would declare her friend's fate. Instead, Kylie heard relieved whimpers, the heart-wrenching sobs of a woman caught in the depths of a despair she hoped she'd never have to bear.

"Kylie?" Tyler's voice boomed loud and clear, the most beautiful sound Kylie could remember ever having heard. "Kylie, are you okay?"

"Tyler? Oh, God! Thank goodness you're here!" Looking up at her love, Kylie choked back the tears clogging her throat and clung to the hope filling her heart. "Is Liza—"

"She's fine, just scared and wet." Tyler spoke quietly to someone, alerting Kylie to the beams of light flashing behind him. He again looked down, concern creasing his brow. "Are you hurt? Can you help us get you up?"

"I'm okay." Better than she'd ever been, in fact…all things considered.

"Hold on, babe. We'll have you safe and warm in no time at all." He smiled, and Kylie knew all would be well.

Twenty-Two

Kylie stirred, shirking free of the slumberous haze keeping her fears at bay. She opened her eyes, blinking as Tyler's worried visage came into view.

"Hello, sleepyhead." Smiling tenderly, he scooted closer, causing the mattress to dip beneath his weight. "How are you feeling?"

"Fine." Kylie sat up, tugging the comforter higher as she braced her back against the headboard. Nestled in her own bed, her sprained wrist bandaged and the telltale orange-brown stain of iodine dotting her many scrapes and scratches, she felt fit and rested. She lowered her eyes, recalling the fuss she'd put up when Tyler insisted she turn in and get some much needed sleep when he brought her home from the emergency room.

Also remembering the bone-crushing hug with which he'd greeted her the instant he and the paramedics had safely pulled her up onto the cliff top, she looked up, into his Cherokee blue eyes brimming with concern and an abiding affection. His relief had been a tangible entity, as real and obvious as the concern that caused him to bark orders the harried medics took in good stride; the bossiness with which he'd demanded the ER staff tend her wounds.

Once back home—her home, where she demanded he take her to recover—and finally satisfied her injuries were minor, he'd tucked her in bed, leaving her to rest. She'd fallen asleep almost immediately, exhausted by her ordeal and exhilarated to know Tyler, too, was safe.

"Breakfast is almost ready." He held her uplifted gaze, his now bright with an emotion Kylie couldn't identify—a mysterious blend of confidence and an

218

endearing touch of expectancy. "Alecia is putting the finishing touches on it now."

"Alecia?" Kylie blinked, shook her head. "When did she get back?"

"A couple of hours ago."

Kylie glanced at the clock, surprised to see she'd slept so late. "Goodness…I can't believe I slept half the day away."

"You needed the rest." Tyler clenched his fists, bunching them as tightly as the muscles along his jaw. "After what you went through, I'm amazed you're awake even now."

"I'm fine…really." Kylie smiled, but couldn't quell the tremor knifing through her as she recalled the horrific events of the night before. Suddenly somber, she asked, "How is Liza? Did they arrest Keets?"

Tyler nodded, unfurled his fingers as though the act also released the tension keeping his shoulders rigid. "They transported Liza to Vinita this morning. She'll undergo a battery of tests and evaluations before her first court appearance."

"And the deputy?"

"He's in the county jail, probably bound for the same mental health facility once we're satisfied no one other than he and Liza were involved."

Kylie nodded, her throat too tight to speak. She wanted to see justice served, but couldn't help pitying Liza—and her former patient. Knowing Liza had manipulated both Keets and the system to achieve her own evil goal did nothing to alter Kylie's feelings. They were sick, and in dire need of treatment.

Kylie suspected she, too, might benefit from counseling—or at least a lengthy vacation.

Alecia appeared in the doorway, smiling sweetly as she balanced the tray of food she carried. Crossing the room, she set the wicker tray over Kylie's lap and snatched up the single red rose lying next to the loaded plate. Kylie looked from the heaping serving of scrambled eggs, crisp bacon and golden brown toast, to the beaming girl.

"Looks like you've been busy." Kylie smiled her appreciation. "Thank you."

"Dad cooked, but I did the rest." Shrugging, Alecia glanced at her silent father, giving him a look Kylie could only describe as impatient. "Well?"

Frowning, Kylie tilted her head, studying the child and then her father. Wondering what the duo had in mind for her, she managed a small, encouraging smile. Surely neither of them would insist she remain in bed, nor force her to endure additional care and coddling she no longer needed. Positive they had something else in store, that Alecia's sudden, mischievous grin and Tyler's equally impulsive shrug meant they'd conspired to entertain her some other way, Kylie straightened.

"What's going on?" she asked, intrigued.

"Tell her, now," Alecia encouraged her father. Rolling her eyes when he said nothing, she handed the long-stemmed rose to Kylie. "We love you."

"You do?" Pleased by the child's earnest declaration, Kylie slanted Tyler a look. "Both of you?"

Still as stone, Tyler held her gaze, his solemn one giving no indication as to how he felt about his daughter's announcement. He reached into his shirt pocket, his slightly unsteady hand and unreadable expression making Kylie increasingly nervous. She couldn't recall ever having been so edgy—not even when she'd clung to the sapling the night before, thinking her next move might be her last.

He extended his hand, palm up to reveal the glittering diamond ring lying there. Kylie blinked back the rush of tears stinging her eyes, raised her misty gaze to his piercing blue one. Her throat ached, as did her heart. She'd planned to tell Tyler how she felt, to find out if he, too, thought their current closeness might heal the wounds inflicted so many years ago. Seeing the intensity darkening his eyes, the somewhat hesitant need also simmering there, made her question his reason for tempting her.

Did she dare respond to the unspoken question raised by that lone, impressive solitaire shining like the fabled star she'd often wished upon? Or should she feign comprehension and force his hand? Make him say what she needed to hear before leaping to the most likely conclusion?

"What does *that* mean?" She indicated the ring with a jerk of her head, and then raised her chin. She deserved an explanation, the words she'd damn well have to hear before releasing the tenuous grip she had on the reservations making her tremble inside. Love and lust were worlds apart, the latter a feeling too fleeting to consider worthwhile without the bond vital to everlasting joy.

"Will you marry us?" Alecia chimed, her enthusiasm causing Kylie another concern. How could she hope to fill Connie's shoes? To mother a child so obviously well adjusted she needed no figurehead to make her life more complete?

"Alecia, would you get Kylie a fresh cup of coffee?" Tyler asked, nodding at the tray. "I'm sure that one's cold by now."

"How long do you need?" Frowning, Alecia picked up the cup and headed for the door. "Ten minutes?"

"Twenty. Better yet, pop in the movie you brought and stay in the den until I come get you."

"That long?" Shaking her head, Alecia paused, her expression rife with frustration. "I'll lock myself in so you won't have to worry about me overhearing something I shouldn't. I'll be invisible...quiet as a mouse..."

"Mice don't grumble."

"Mice don't get banished to the den, either." The girl backed toward the door. "If you don't mind, I think I'll go with Uncle Wyatt."

"Wyatt's here?"

His daughter nodded. "He wanted to make sure Kylie is okay. When I told him you were up here with her, he said we should disappear...and give you time to work up your courage." Turning, Alecia exited the room, her smile indicating she didn't mind being excluded—for the time being.

Chuckling, Tyler waited only until his daughter had entered the hall before lifting the tray from the bed to set it aside. He closed the door and returned to the bed, still smiling as he reached for Kylie's hand. Threading his warm fingers through her cold ones, he raised the ring in his other hand. "Now that we don't have an audience, it's my turn. Will you marry me, Kylie? Will you share my life and have my babies?"

Kylie stared at him, unable to breath and dreading to pose the question she knew she had to ask. "Why? Why now, and not when we'd planned to marry so long ago?"

"I had a feeling you'd want an explanation." Tyler expelled a gust of air, slumped forward.

Still holding her hand, he idly stroked her fingers, causing a ripple of tingles to streak along her entire arm. Kylie held herself rigid, afraid to move for fear he'd stop the delicious touching making her wish he'd hurry so she could take advantage of their brief time alone.

"I wanted to marry you then, Kylie...more than anything, I wanted to make you mine." He stared into her eyes, a storm of emotion visible in his. "Instead, I married the woman carrying my child...the woman who claimed to be pregnant with my child." His jaw hardened, as did his tone. "I didn't find out until weeks after we eloped that Connie wasn't pregnant at all...with my child or any other man's. You were long gone by then—"

"—I had no choice but to leave, Tyler!" Kylie interjected, irritated to think he still didn't understand her motive. She pulled her hand from his, sat up straight. Knowing he'd been duped made her heart ache; thinking he felt she'd taken the easy way out irritated her—tremendously. "I didn't want to hear the gossip or to be the subject of idle speculation and false sympathy."

"I know." He again reached for hand, holding it tight when she would have jerked free. "But that didn't stop me from feeling cheated. I wanted to talk to you, tell you why I married Connie."

"I doubt it would have made a difference." Kylie shrugged, held his steady look though she wanted to avoid those assessing blue eyes. "The damage had been done."

Tyler nodded. "I couldn't agree more. We were all cheated, three—four— lives irrevocably altered due to one woman's petty vengeance…and my own ignorance."

"How so?" Kylie leaned forward, curious as to what he'd done to cause him to criticize himself so harshly.

"Remember the last time we broke up, when I admitted flaunting my dates to make you jealous?" He gave her a half-hearted smile, one so derisive she imagined he must truly have done something terrible. She nodded, a sinking feeling in her chest. He continued, his voice low but firm. "I made an ass of myself that first weekend, drinking so much I had to hitch a ride home from Muskogee. Connie kindly offered to drive me home…but I woke up in her bed…not sure what we'd done before I passed out.

"A few weeks later, she told me she was pregnant. Her father was a strict disciplinarian, and not of a mind to see his first grandchild born out of wedlock."

"So, you married her." Kylie heaved a sigh of relief, understanding why Tyler had felt it his duty to accept an angry father's demand that he make things right. Knowing Tyler hadn't jilted her because of his undying affection for Connie also eased the hurt she'd nursed so long. Had he not acted in a responsible manner, Kylie knew she'd find it difficult, if not impossible, to believe in him now—no matter that he'd proved himself worthy of her trust time and again these past few weeks.

Tyler stood, made his way to the French doors. He drew the drapes aside, obviously weighing his words carefully before turning to face her. "She claimed a miscarriage soon after you'd left town, presenting me a dilemma I hadn't counted on.

"I was caught between the proverbial rock and a hard place, hurt to have lost you and my unborn child in quick succession. In spite of my compassion for Connie, I wanted to divorce her and hunt you down…make you listen.

Luckily for all of us, I realized my ego was bruised, and that I'd likely give you more reason to shun me.

"I also needed someone to blame for the mess I'd gotten myself into. You were the reason I ultimately did nothing. My scapegoat."

"And a handy one," Kylie said tongue-in-cheek, "since I wasn't around to defend myself."

"Exactly." Smiling, Tyler returned to the bed and sat down. "Other factors figured in, too. I'd just started working as a deputy U.S. Marshal, and I didn't want to jeopardize my future. Connie was trying to make a go of it, doing what I thought most new brides did to make a shaky marriage stronger. I felt she deserved my best effort, too." The muscles in his jaw bunched, firming along with the hard look in his eyes. "I had no idea it was all a game to her, that she had no intention of honoring her commitment. By the time I realized she'd never be the happy homemaker she pretended to be, it was too late…for me and for Alecia."

Kylie bristled, thinking he somehow blamed Alecia for his unhappy marriage—much as Carl had wrongly blamed her for her mother's mistakes. It didn't make sense. Even having seen how devoted Tyler was to his daughter, she couldn't stop herself from taking him to task. "How can you say that? She's your daughter, Tyler, an innocent—"

"Alecia is my daughter by choice, Kylie. My name is listed on her birth certificate where her real father's should have been entered." Smiling at her wide-eyed look, he said, "I couldn't love her more if my blood filled her veins as, by rights, it should."

"How do you know she isn't your child? Did you have a paternity test?"

"I didn't have to. Connie confessed her perfidy shortly before she died. Alecia's father—the bastard she married me to spite—wanted nothing to do with her. Faced with imminent death, Connie admitted nothing happened the night I spent in her bed, that she'd duped me. Marriage to me allowed her the freedom to pursue Alecia's father, which she did long enough to become pregnant with his child.

"Connie begged me to care for her baby…She didn't once ask me to forgive her, merely to continue raising the daughter I believed to be mine."

"I'm not sure I would have risked that, no matter how grave the circumstances." Kylie shook her head. "Wasn't she afraid you'd use that information as an excuse to relinquish your parental rights? That you'd feel justified handing Alecia over to her father?"

"She wanted to hurt me, Kylie…to prove she still had the upper hand." He smiled as though what Connie had done made perfect sense, as if she'd done him a grand service. "She failed to realize how much I love Alecia…that, unlike her, I'd never do anything to cause *my* daughter grief."

"I'm so sorry," Kylie choked on a sob, "I had no idea." The misery she'd dealt with seemed trivial compared to the torment Tyler had to have suffered at the hands of his conniving wife; the torture he had to sometimes feel when he looked at his adorable daughter.

Tyler lifted Kylie onto his lap, snuggled her close as she wept—for him and for the child he loved too much to abandon despite her mother's adulterous betrayal. Had Kylie not already been in love with him, his devotion to another man's child would have sent her tumbling, heart over head, in love with the sweet, wonderful man cradling her so tenderly.

"My parents are the only ones aware of the situation," Tyler said softly.

"Do you plan to tell Alecia?" Kylie swiped the moisture from her cheeks, contentment making her limp, secure.

"If she ever asks, yes." Tyler chuckled, causing his chest muscles to ripple where they touched her back. "I hope she never has reason to. I'd hate to disappoint her."

"You'll never disappoint her." Kylie leaned back, aimed a finger at his nose. "I won't let you."

"Does that mean you'll marry me?" he asked, eyes twinkling.

"I'm not sure I should." Kylie bit down on her lower lip, nipping back the smile making it twitch. The consternation creasing his brow amused her, as did his thunderous look that followed.

"You love me…don't you?"

Kylie nodded, but said not a word.

"Then what's the problem?" Scowling, he cupped her chin, raised her head. He kissed her then, a demanding kiss that left her breathless—and more than slightly annoyed. Did he think the heat building inside her because of that slightly chauvinistic kiss would sway her? Did he believe her so shallow she'd allow desire to rule her, make her give him the answer he obviously expected?

"You!" she snapped, only half teasing.

"Me?" Tyler shook his head, frowned. "I want to marry you, Kylie. I love you. I can't imagine living without you…don't want to even think about it."

Her heart pounding, Kylie shrugged, acting as though he hadn't just told her all she needed to know. Thinking he deserved at least a little more taunting before she slipped his engagement ring on her finger, she said, "Besides not being very romantic when you proposed—and trying to brand me with that kiss—you didn't believe me. You even tried to convince me a raccoon kitten was responsible for my fear. You thought I was crying wolf."

Tyler ducked his head, but made no attempt to pretend he didn't know what she was talking about. "Guilty as charged." He peered up at her, so close she could have counted each thick lash fringing his beautiful indigo eyes. Looking too sexy and sincere for her to resist, he again asked, "Will you marry me?"

"Maybe," she conceded, careful to keep her expression neutral. "If you promise to—"

Kylie squealed as Tyler suddenly shifted and toppled her onto the bed, covered her squirming body with his hard, warm one. Her oversized T-shirt was useless, too thin to keep her from feeling the rigid proof of his masculinity straining beneath his fly.

Staring down at her, his blue eyes smoldering, he cupped her cheek, lovingly caressed her tender skin from temple to chin with fingers as hot and knowing as the look holding her own a willing captive.

"I'll do everything possible to make you happy, Kylie. I'll pick up after myself and always call when I'm running late. I'll cook and clean if that's what you want me to do. I'll learn how to be more romantic, bring you wine and roses every day if that'll please you." Grinning mischievously, he flexed his hips. "On the outside chance you haven't noticed, part of me is anxious to put words to action and practice the romance."

"Only one part?" Kylie lowered her lashes, focusing on his mouth. She could feel his breath against her lips, moist and warm. Caught in the web cast by her teasing, she knew the time to yield had arrived. Was long past.

"Marry me, Kylie," he implored, his voice a soft, seductive whisper so arousing she felt scorched by the sound of it, even more needy.

Averting her gaze, she shook her head. "I'm still not sure."

"I love you, Kylie. What more do you want me to say?" Gently bracketing her face, he urged her to look at him, to see the love too pure and real for her to mistake. "Do you love me?"

"Yes," she admitted softly, fervently. "Since I was sixteen. Always."

Tyler tilted his head, gave her a measuring look that told her the jig was up. "Did I mention I'll also extract wicked revenge when I feel you deserve it?"

"I hope that means what I think it does." Kylie wriggled her legs from beneath him, and then wrapped them around his trim hips. Satisfied to see the dark, delicious promise dancing in his eyes, she added, "And that you won't mind a scream or two if I enjoy it."

"You'll definitely enjoy it."

Rolling free long enough to lock the bedroom door and rip off his clothes, Tyler moved toward the bed. Gloriously naked and obviously ready to make good on his velvety pledge, he lay down beside her, trailing his fingers along her torso bared as he lifted the T-shirt over her head.

"I love you, babe...so much."

Punctuating each word with a kiss, Tyler showed her how much, so tenderly and so powerfully Kylie soon did, indeed, scream her pleasure. Groaning hugely as he, too, reached fulfillment, Tyler hugged her close, cuddling her as the sweet aftershocks of satisfaction rippled through her.

"Should I consider that a yes?"

"Definitely."

"One more thing you should probably know," he stated solemnly, causing Kylie to angle her head to meet his tender look. "I'll never complain." Chuckling softly, he added, "so long as you ALWAYS CRY WOLFE."

Printed in the United States
53126LVS00005B/1-81

9 781424 141609